ADVANCE PRAISE FOR

The Final Victory

"What is courage? In this notable debut, Roger Jones explores the strength, resilience, compassion, and willpower of a band of athletes who define courage and triumph over unspeakable odds. These twenty men and women overcome cancer to not merely win a national championship but to survive. I laughed. I cried. I was inspired. *The Final Victory* is an uplifting novel we all need to read."

—**MARY ALICE MONROE**, *NEW YORK TIMES* BESTSELLING AUTHOR.

"A bitter, hardened coach, facing his own illness and inner demons, reluctantly agrees to lead a crew of cancer survivors in their quest for a national championship in a dragon boat race. Ultimately, the race becomes a metaphor not only for the struggle to survive but also a pathway for redemption. Based on a true story, *The Final Victory* is the kind of spiritually uplifting novel that you'll want to share with everyone you know."

—**CASSANDRA KING**, AWARD-WINNING AUTHOR OF
TELL ME A STORY: MY LIFE WITH PAT CONROY

"An inspiring and stirring tale of courage, *The Final Victory* is inspired by the true story of a group of athletes who face life-threatening illnesses and are bonded together by their indomitable will to win. Jones gives us a novel that is equal parts laugh out loud funny, moving, and uplifting. You will love it!"

—**PATTI HENRY**, *NEW YORK TIMES* BESTSELLING AUTHOR OF *BECOMING MRS. LEWIS*

"In this excellent book, Roger Jones plumbs the depths of driven competitors in a powerful, compelling way. What does a father's bitterness do to a talented son when cancer intrudes in ways that would smash most dreams? What does a gutty bunch of survivors do when challenged to defy their terrible pain and fear? In the end, they learn what really matters. Read this wonderful novel and you will as well."

—**BILL CURRY**, AUTHOR OF *TEN MEN YOU MEET IN A HUDDLE*, WINNER OF TWO SUPER BOWLS WITH THE GREEN BAY PACKERS, FORMER HEAD COACH AT GEORGIA TECH AND ALABAMA

"To push oneself to the limit in sport while dealing with a life-debilitating disease defies logic. It's the drive to win against the odds—to conquer the unconquerable—that fuels the members of this incredible dragon boat team. The story of their journey together is truly inspiring!"

—**CATHY GRAHAM**, CO-OWNER, COPPERFISH BOOKS, PUNTA GORDA, FL

"One man tells his story of surviving and living. It is the story of thousands of people. It is an example to us all. As a physician, I thank Roger Jones for sharing awareness of Neuroendocrine cancer. As a human, I thank him for allowing me to experience the power of hope, teamwork and love."

—**ERIC LIU, MD**, INTERNATIONALLY RECOGNIZED SURGEON SPECIALIZING IN NEUROENDOCRINE TUMORS. CO-DIRECTOR, ROCKY MOUNTAIN CANCER CENTERS AND THE NEUROENDOCRINE INSTITUTE

"*The Final Victory* brilliantly demonstrates that women recovering from breast cancer can lead full and active lives—paddle for sure, but also pick up and hug their grandchildren. Dragon boating challenges the limits of human performance, especially for those with more than their share of hurdles to clear. That's the magic that Roger Jones captures, and that's why *The Final Victory* is a great book."

—**DR. DON MCKENZIE**, FOUNDER OF THE ORIGINAL BREAST CANCER DRAGON BOAT TEAM

THE FINAL VICTORY

A Novel
Inspired by True Events

Roger Jones

THE FINAL VICTORY

FIRST EDITION

All events in this book are based upon true events from the author's best recollections of the past and may differ from others' memories of those events. The timing and specific details of some events may have changed and other details may have been added to supplement the storyline. While the events in the book are closely based upon the author's true experiences, many names and other identifying aspects have been changed.

Hardcover: 979-8-9899607-0-5
Ebook: 979-8-9899607-1-2

Published in the United States by Companion Books
www.rogerjonesauthor.com

Distributed by Small Press United
a division of Independent Publisher Group
https://www.ipgbook.com/

Cover designed by David Provolo
Typesetting by Mark Karis

Printed in the United States of America

This novel is dedicated to the many heroes I've paddled with.

To Linda, who defied every physician's diagnosis and earned a seat paddling on the United States National Dragon Boat team in Prague.

To Mark, with stage 4 colon cancer, who paddled through the pain of what he called "Big Scoop" abdominal surgery. Mark compared contracting cancer to winning the lottery.

To Sylvia and all the breast cancer patients/survivors. To all The Pink Ladies! These women give courage a new definition.

And of course, to Bob, whose jaw cancer left him unable to eat and barely able to speak. He gave me the title of this novel when asked if he had the energy to compete in the boat. Bob answered me in a fierce whisper that he must find the strength, as these races would be his "final victory."

The Final Victory is dedicated to your heroes—the people in your life who have faced tragedy or death with great courage and hope. The people who have demonstrated that cancer isn't a way to die but a bold reason to live! The people who have inspired you to live your life with that same courage and hope. My prayer is that these words, as you read them, will prompt you to praise and celebrate these every day, but far from ordinary heroes.

Finally, this novel is dedicated to hope and redemption. The hope that each of us will find mercy, grace, and peace. The redemption in discovering ourselves whole even if our bodies are frail and damaged.

1

Chattanooga, Tennessee

Friday, July 23, 2010
8:30 a.m.

I was sitting in a narrow, wooden forty-eight-foot-long dragon boat surrounded by nineteen other cancer survivors, ready for the race of our lives. As the sole cancer-survivor team in our division, our challenge to win would be a steep uphill battle. And as with my brave teammates, my own body was weak from recent high-dose radiation treatment. We were a group of normal ordinary people attempting to accomplish something extraordinary. We didn't come to win; we came to survive.

I was a successful former high school football coach, current businessman, and the coach of this gutsy team. To my unfathomable surprise, this audacious crew of men and women had become my new family.

The heat index in the balmy city of Chattanooga, Tennessee, was a hundred plus. It hadn't rained for weeks throughout the entire South. As I looked up the boat at my teammates, I witnessed sheer determination. But I was scared. Had I pushed this team too hard? Their bodies were weakened by their malignant tumors and abhorrent treatments. Three full days of racing? Would they become overtaken with extreme exhaustion or, worse, severe dehydration?

A year earlier, we'd lost a teammate to this mad disease—cancer. Our grief was still raw. Had I made a grave error to convince this group they could win the national championship? Some of us sensed the walls of death closing in, and this competition could well be our final effort for a victory among the tribulations of our lives. Our yearlong training had been intense, and we were determined to win. Like the other dragon boat teams, we were trying to find the perfect combination of timing, power, and stamina. But unlike our competition, our training was interspersed with radiation and chemotherapy, so I prayed for strength.

I was fifty-five years old, an ex-college jock with a liver full of tumors. Otherwise, I was in perfect health. I'm sure other cancer patients feel the same. But bitterness ate at my soul. I didn't deserve to have cancer. Why me? Somehow, I'd force this ravaging disease from my body.

I was competitive by nature and training. My personally prescribed therapy was to turn to the calming waters of the Charleston rivers. I felt lucky to wake each morning to a stunning view of the Cooper River and the spectacular cable-stayed bridge with its diamond-shaped towers that, for many Charlestonians, defined our hometown. Maybe it came about with my life-threatening diagnosis, but somehow my tumors made me more aware of the intricacies of my body, and I looked at things in a new way. The river, with its mighty current and ever-changing tides, seemed to connect my teammates like arteries connecting the body's organs and muscles; when I paddled it momentarily freed me and my teammates from our terrible illnesses. Could a river bring healing? I hoped and prayed so.

Dragon boat racing is a two-thousand-year-old sport that originated among the fishing communities in southern-central China along the Yangtze River. The sport boomed as an international sport in the 1980s, with thousands of cancer patients becoming participants during the 1990s, as the sport was recognized for improving healing from the vile cancer treatments through physical exercise and team camaraderie.

Our crew of twenty cancer-ridden paddlers sat knee-to-knee in ten rows in this lengthy, slender canoe, ten paddlers extending their bodies heavily over the boat's starboard side and ten over the port. A drummer sat on a small wooden seat at the bow, banging a cadence to synchronize and motivate the paddlers. A steersperson stood at the stern, using a twenty-foot oar to guide the canoe, finding the straightest possible path along the racecourse.

The weekend's festival was a colorful celebration of life. Thousands of spectators lined the Tennessee River to watch. The boats were made of teak, imported from the Far East, and decorated with a mythical Chinese dragon head and tail. Red-and-gold decorative scales were delicately painted along the hull.

Teams who had arrived from throughout the nation huddled together in strategy. Paddlers hugged in unity. Would their grueling training pay off?

Our team, the Dragon Survivors, was competing for the over-fifty mixed men's and women's national championship. Eight women and twelve men would paddle as one. We'd learned to feel the surge and the glide of the boat. We'd tapped into the canoe's innate rhythm. The winners would earn the privilege of representing the United States at the International Dragon Boat Races in Hong Kong, China.

Twenty anxious paddlers crouched over the canoe's gunwale with the blades of our paddles buried deep in the water. Our emotions dangled in suspense as we anticipated the starter's horn. Three additional boats, in lanes separated by buoys, also intently awaited the signal.

There's probably nothing scarier than sitting at the starting line of a national championship race. A voice shouted, "Ready, ready. We have alignment." The words vibrated like a tsunami across the smooth water. The muscles in my shoulders contracted with tension. The horn finally blew, and twenty paddles forced through the water in perfect unison. Our drummer pounded hard to create the rhythm for our stroke and screamed, "Up, up, up!" Each paddler's blade entered and exited the water like the melody of a great orchestra. The water boiled all around the sides of our highly decorated red-and-gold canoe.

I saw Sean Riley, two seats ahead, a tall, slender man, uncharacteristically grimace with each stroke he made through the murky violet-colored water. The filament within the muscles of his well-developed arms constricted. His stroke was badly out of sync. Sean, one of our team's two captains, never missed a practice, and his stroke was never out of time. Suddenly he pulled his paddle from the water.

What was wrong?

The intensity of my stroke increased as I watched his face scowl in pain. His hand reached to his side. The custom-made belt that secured the pouch containing his colostomy and ileostomy bags had become loose. He held his paddle in one hand and miraculously pushed the bags back inside the pouch with the other hand. More astonishingly, he managed to tighten the belt one-handed underneath his shirt and resumed paddling.

Cancer had stolen my teammates' mastery of their bodies. But the dragon boat had restored our hope as the rulers of our lives. We were learning that perfect harmony can be made out of broken things and broken people. It would be the lesson of our lives.

2

Charleston, South Carolina

Early Spring 2008

My office, located in downtown Charleston at the corner of King and Queen Streets, was my daily refuge, beginning at 5:30 each morning. I'd flip on the lights, make a pot of coffee, and raise my office's window shade exposing the many magnificent glimmering church spires of the Holy City. My morning coffee provided me the opportunity to each day celebrate my wonderful historic port city.

The corner of Charleston's two most historic and romantic streets was beginning to come alive. The brakes of a white-panel truck squealed as it parked along King Street. A husky driver exited and spit brown tobacco juice on the sidewalk as he raised the truck's rear door. The strong aroma of freshly caught fish filled the dense morning air as the burly man delivered his captives, which had been swimming in the ocean only a few hours earlier, to the city's award-winning restaurants. The redolence of ovens were cranking up to prepare the day's savory lunches and dinners.

Thick humidity surrounded the tall church steeples and seemed to carry with it a graceful southern charm that bound the old celebrated and enchanted buildings. The then 340-year-old city, like the grand Southern magnolias, was blossoming for another gracious day. A brave young couple snuck into the dark, shady entrance of the ghostly Unitarian Church's graveyard to view the centuries-old tombstones. The first sliver of sunlight slipped through my office's window causing my wife Amy's painting of Charleston's Battery and its nearby park to glow, signifying the promise of a new day. The morning had begun just like every other satisfying morning for the past ten years. I reviewed my to-do list, checked email, and examined my company's daily financial reports.

I'd dreamed since a young age of owning my own business. Growing up poor in a small South Carolina town dominated with cotton textile mills could permanently brand a young person's psyche. Having to fight for money to buy groceries, not to mention good clothes, could make a person feel small and insignificant. My family, my friends, and I were disparagingly called lintheads. The authentic low-class white people of the South. Being raised poor and angry took a profound toll on most of my friends, as either crime or abject poverty would eventually destroy their lives. But my quest was to prove my worth to the world.

My parents, brother, sister, and I had lived in a five-room house hidden among several hundred identical factory-built homes. The indistinguishable houses surrounded a large three-story redbrick cotton mill, the source of employment and sustenance for our small isolated village. The only buildings that competed with the solid brick windowless and soulless cotton mill were the churches—all Protestant. Baptist, Methodist, and Presbyterian churches dominated our little town. There was one small Catholic church and a tiny Jewish synagogue. Mill villagers didn't necessarily dislike Catholics or Jews, nor did they seem welcome.

All day we kids played ball. Any kind of ball, it didn't matter, except soccer. My dad said soccer was for sissies and Yankees. We'd play football until someone got hurt or broke a leg. We played baseball until some smart aleck hit the ball too far or into a grumpy neighbor's yard. We'd shoot roundball until dark or when our mothers would force us to come home to eat dinner.

I wanted to learn to play the trumpet. My dad fiercely refused. He growled, "A boy who plays a musical instrument will be put into the school's band. You're going to play football just like me." He preached with conviction, "The only future for a young man in this town is through football or baseball." But football was elevated above all other sports. It was the proving ground where boys became men. Friday night high school football games attracted more worshippers than all the churches combined on Sunday morning, including the affluent First Baptist Church.

If you became a hero on the gridiron, were named All-State, or were recruited to play for a Division I university, your future in this town was forever cemented. No matter the course of the rest of your life, your pedestal would stand forever. Gods were created on Friday nights. I wanted to be a god.

Trendy clothes were scarce. A professional haircut even rarer. I wanted to fit in with the boys whose parents lived downtown on Main Street and not the rednecks and lintheads on the mill hill. I wanted to be like the rich kids, to strut and be poised like them—with confidence.

At night I'd stare out the small window of my tiny bedroom. Gazing at the twinkling lights of my mill village friends' trivial homes, I'd wonder what we'd become as grown-ups. The rank smell of the mill's fumes was a heavy cloud floating above our heads. A cloud that would keep us all poor and deprived—for eternity. Our destiny. My bedroom window was my portal to the world. As a young boy, I'd stand before it and dream. At times I was a rock star performing before thousands of screaming fans. Other times, a football hero who'd just returned a kickoff for a hundred yards.

As I stared toward the affluent downtown, I wished I'd been born to a rich man. To never again be laughed at because of the quality of my clothes or the size of my home, to never again be humiliated. My fear and sense of shame would vanish in the clear panes of my magic window. My hope soared. I'd enter that glorious moment when time stood still and all else disappeared. Minutes, hours would pass unnoticed. It was the moment of me and nothing else.

I never understood the magic of that enchanted window, but I felt its power—the power to be more and never again to be ridiculed. Nope, I was going to be somebody. That window gave me the hope and the strength to carry on.

My attention returned to the now-busy Charleston streets. I pivoted from my office window and slowly walked to my ornate cherry desk, sat in my large leather chair, closed my eyes, and breathed in the air of triumph. I'd founded a successful real estate development firm, which owned thousands of apartments. The company's growth had exceeded expectations. Our developments were ahead of schedule, and funds were flowing. I employed a hardworking, committed team, and we loved our jobs. My prosperity was my validation and my passport into the country club society.

The noise in the office increased as my associates arrived to begin the work day. My development assistant, Linda, promptly delivered my firm's monthly financial report, showing year-to-date revenue. The earnings were strong. I leaned back in my chair and placed my hands behind my head. I offered Linda a broad smile. "Not bad for a dumb-jock PE major."

She returned the smile. "Tripp, you've come a long way. And to think you started with one tiny rental property you bought when you were coaching high school sports! Quite an accomplishment."

With immense pride and elation, I said, "As they say, never despise small beginnings."

"You should be very proud."

"I'm proud because I refused to lose. That's why I quit coaching. My players got soft. A bunch of mama's boys. After ten winning seasons, I saw the writing on the wall. A losing season was on the horizon."

Linda nodded solemnly. She knew the real reason I quit coaching, though we'd never discussed it. She'd had a son on the team, after all.

"But not this ole boy. I was in it to win it. So, I resigned, started my company, and never looked back."

Linda started to leave.

"And speaking of satisfaction. Are the slides finalized for my Charleston Chamber of Commerce Businessperson of the Year acceptance speech?"

Linda nervously bit her lip. "They are."

The volume of my voice increased. "Make sure they are in perfect order. I'll not be humiliated in front of all these successful businesspeople."

Her eyes darted away from mine. "Of course, I'll double-check each slide." She looked me in the eyes. "And, oh, I was really proud of our firm's donation to the Susan G. Komen 5K race."

I smiled. "Just felt like something we should do. Glad you're pleased."

Linda grinned and left my office.

The cleaning service had cleaned the previous night so the office smelled of fresh lemons. The cool aroma of my office, the fragrance of the spring jasmines blooming outside, and the clatter of my employees caused a serene peace to arise in my soul.

I wanted it to last forever.

But it didn't.

My phone's intercom buzzed.

"Yes."

Linda's voice quivered with concern. "Dr. Simpson is on the phone. He says it's important."

I picked up the receiver.

The doctor's voice was calm like nothing was wrong. "Mr. Avery, we have the results of the biopsy from your colonoscopy. We found a rare type of cancer in your intestines that has spread to your liver."

My mind swirled. My thoughts were in discord. And Dr. Simpson seemed so calm. He must tell people every day they're about to die. I couldn't have cancer. It was only a routine colonoscopy. I was an uber-successful businessman. I had mountains to conquer.

Dr. Simpson's voice cracked. "The cancer is rare; about one person in a hundred thousand is diagnosed with this type of cancer. These specific kinds of growths are called neuroendocrine tumors, or more commonly labeled as carcinoid cancer. The good news is these tumors typically grow very slowly. We call it the good kind of cancer."

My thoughts were in chaos. My knees weakened with fear. Spread to my liver. Would I die? Was this doctor crazy? I exercised daily! I ate healthy—vegetables, fruits. I didn't smoke and wasn't overweight. I'd lived right, made good decisions—how in the hell could I have cancer?

Bullshit!

Carcinoid cancer? The good kind of cancer?

My voice rattled with anger. "I've never heard of a good kind of cancer. Can this good kind of cancer kill you?"

Dr. Simpson lowered his voice as if to be reassuring. "All cancer is serious. And yes, it can kill you. Have you experienced any flushing or diarrhea?"

My mind flashed to the bar about five years earlier, where, as I sat with my buddies, sipping a beer, my neck, face, and head burned hot and turned beet red. "Sure, my face gets hot and red when I sip wine or swallow some beer. Doesn't that happen to everyone?"

"These tumors secrete abnormally high levels of hormones, especially serotonin, which cause those symptoms, although your odds of survival are good if we treat you immediately. These tumors need to be removed as soon as possible. I've referred your case to a local surgeon, and his office will be in touch later today. I'm confident all will be fine."

All will be fine? "Odds of survival are good?" This doctor had just told me I had cancer. All was not fine.

I had to ask the question. "What's the survival rate?"

Dr. Simpson hesitated. "It's hard to say but many people live a high-quality life for at least five to ten years—some more. Let's get you scheduled for surgery. Then we'll know more."

I'd closed numerous multimillion-dollar deals and didn't break a sweat. But I couldn't stop my hand from shaking as I hung up the phone. Five to ten years. I'd just turned fifty. I'd planned to live a lot longer than five to ten years.

I didn't remember walking past Linda or riding the elevator from my fourth-floor office. I couldn't recall walking onto King Street. I just walked. Everything appeared to be the same as the day before. But nothing was the same.

Berlin's clothing store on the corner of King and Broad Streets hummed with customers. I kept walking. People smiled and laughed as they browsed in the picturesque downtown Charleston stores. I stumbled on Broad Street's ornate sidewalk where a grand oak tree's root had forced a bluestone tile to rise several inches above the rest. I regained my balance. But my mind continued to swirl at a dizzying pace.

Traffic was congested at the intersection of Meeting and Broad Streets, the section of the Holy City the locals call the "Four Corners of Law." A massive federal building stands on one corner, the county courthouse on another, the ornate Charleston city hall on the third corner, and, representing the land's highest order—God's law—St. Michael's, one of the nation's oldest church buildings, at the fourth corner.

I stared at the sky above the white brick church. I seemed to be standing on a windmill, with my body spinning, and stopping only for a second to allow me to view each of the four iconic buildings. I started walking. What law said I had to die at fifty-five? Sixty? What law had I violated? No law. I couldn't die. I wouldn't. Dr. Simpson must be wrong.

I loosened my tie and unbuttoned the collar of my heavily starched white shirt. I smelled the odor of my sweat. I felt droplets of moisture drip off the leather necklace I always wore.

When I stopped walking, I found myself standing next to a thick black steel cannon at the edge of Battery Park. It faced Fort Sumter, which was strategically located in the middle of Charleston Harbor, the site of the beginning of this nation's bloody Civil War. The incoming tide of the Cooper River pulsated toward the large solid concrete battery wall.

I'd hoped to see a colony of ibises, the beautiful white birds with long beaks that turn downward, flocking nearby. Since moving to Charleston, it seemed my sighting of these graceful birds brought good luck and hope. But I saw no birds, only the sun reflecting off the rising water.

I watched the oscillating currents gush where they desired. The river appeared to have its own mind, consuming the earth with each throbbing movement. The river gave life and took life. Like the lifegiving blood that flowed through my body. Except now that blood slowly transported deadly malignant cells. Cells that wanted to kill me. Would cancer consume my body and devour my organs? What irony awaited in the subtle depth of the river's water—and in the flow of my blood. My fate, like the tide, was being enacted by a force beyond my control, on a seemingly unstoppable path.

I stepped onto the high battery wall. I raised my arms to the heavens. The glistening water began to quiet and stand still. It was now slack tide, the moment the tide reverses its direction. My eyes focused on the tranquil water, unable to blink. The tide was turning.

I sat on a bench and pulled my leather necklace from underneath my shirt. At the end of the necklace hung a small chunk of brick wrapped in burlap. As I closed my eyes, I saw my father, a broken man, harshly presenting me this tiny piece of insignificant masonry. I could still hear the anger and shame in his voice as he firmly placed it in my hand. "Son, never forget the anger of your humiliation. Wear your anger like this necklace around your neck. Protect your bitterness, as it will become your wall of protection against your many enemies."

As a young boy, I looked down and away from him, not understanding his words. He slapped me hard across my face. "Look at me, boy," he demanded. "Do you hear me, son? Never let these bastards get to you. Never let go of your anger as it feeds you."

I observed the river's current beginning to flow out toward the sea. The last few minutes seemed like lifetime. A shock wave, an explosion, was building within my chest. My breathing grew shallow. It became difficult.

Was the tide in my life changing?

3

Charleston

On week later

I had been prepped and sat almost naked in a small, cold chair, wearing only a flimsy, pre-worn but clean and backless hospital gown, in a small presurgical room surrounded by white cloth curtains displaying a pinkish floral pattern. For an instant, my brain relaxed, thinking a dire mistake had been made—a sadistic joke—that I really didn't have cancer. But I was ready to go. Let's get this show on the road.

My wife, Amy, sat in a similar chair next to me. She is small in frame, five feet, two inches tall but huge in character. She'd never faltered in her strength since that dreadful "you have cancer" phone call from Dr. Simpson. When I got angry, she'd assured me all would be well. As my frustration grew, she'd encouraged me to continue searching for the right doctor for an answer. When I awoke at night sweating from a dream where I'd died, she'd hold my head close to her breast and calm my fears.

There were days I questioned the existence of God. But I did believe in miracles. Amy and I had met in college, went on one date, and were never apart again. I was confident a greater power knew the wife I needed and led her to me. So, I guess I did believe in God.

She must have sensed my thoughts of her as she placed her hand on my leg. "You look calm."

I was afraid but kept that fear to myself. "I'm calm when you're with me. Thanks for being my wife."

She smiled and kissed me.

I'd combed the internet, trying to discover every bit of available information about this *"good kind of cancer"*—carcinoid. I'd researched neuroendocrine tumors, or NET, as they are also called. I'd learned that folks diagnosed with this rare form of cancer were called zebras as each patient's disease is idiosyncratic. Diagnosis with many patients was difficult, often delayed, as physicians had little experience or training with the disease in medical school. In fact, medical students are taught the expression, "When you hear hoof beats, look for horses, not zebras." NET is rare; so doctors often searched for other, more common diagnoses when presented with a patient expressing NET symptoms.

So now I'd become a damn zebra. And, just as no two zebras have identical stripes, no two NET patients have the same type or location of tumors. Many have their origin in the small intestine, as mine had, while other common areas are the lungs and the pancreas. From these seemingly simple beginnings, they could spread anywhere in the body, but most commonly they loved to make their home in the liver.

Through the opening of the curtains, I saw sick people lying on gurneys and exam tables. I heard hospital workers talking medical-speak, a language I didn't understand. I felt like I was in a foreign country even though the hospital was only a few blocks from my home.

My surgeon pulled back the cloth drape and smiled, seeming surprised to see my expression of calmness. He was a short, well-built man with a neck as thick as an ox's. His voice was a deep bass, and for the fifth time, he explained the procedure and asked if I had any questions. I assured him I was ready.

He told me he would remove my primary tumor, the affected lymph nodes, the tumors in my large intestines and additional ones in my small intestine, along with several feet of my colon. He doubted he could remove the liver tumors as they were too large and there were too many. I just wanted to get these wretched invaders out of my body and start living my life again.

He shared that the death rate from the surgery was extremely low but not zero. Infection and bleeding could be possibilities. I didn't like hearing the words *death rate.* Amy flinched and began to cry. It was her first display of fear; she wanted to be strong. I was in the good hands of a brilliant surgeon in an excellent medical facility. But this procedure would be more dramatic than I expected.

The nurse strapped me on the gurney. I felt like the great river of my life was facing a winding bend, and my life would never be the same. I handed my necklace with the chunk of brick dangling from its end to Amy. The nurse attached an IV bag that began dripping its magic potion into my arm, and a peace transcended my thoughts as she rolled me to the operating room. I drifted into a deep sleep, hearing a male voice counting backward from ten.

My next memory was waking in a stiff bed, covered with only a white sheet and freezing. My abdominal area was pounding with pain. I excruciatingly lifted my hospital gown to inspect the damage. A red, inflamed incision that looked like the tracks of a Union Pacific railroad coursed my gut from two inches below my belly button to the lower tip of my rib cage.

Damn that'd make a great impression when I walked shirtless on the hot sands of Folly Beach. But who cared; I was alive!

During surgery a tube had been rammed through my nose and down my throat and was still there. I gagged and tried to spit it out but couldn't. My throat throbbed with pain. That's when I realized this plastic cylinder ran all the way into my stomach to empty its contents. I could barely breathe. This was an extreme invasion of my body, one I'd not bargained for.

My mind raced with fear. My sense of well-being was gone. I felt like I was in the middle of a nightmare, free-falling from the sky, wildly flinging my arms and legs. The worst-case scenario raced through my mind. Did the surgeon remove all my tumors? Did he cut my liver open? Would I ever breathe normally again? Would I be able to run my company or see my children become successful? Scary thoughts slung through my brain like boomerangs.

When I gathered my senses, I recognized Amy as she patted my forehead with a cool, wet washcloth. I struggled to speak, as the tube inhibited my voice. "Tell me about the liver tumors. Did the surgeon remove them?"

She smiled and continued rubbing my forehead. "They

could not be removed, just too many and too large. But he's confident you'll be able to live a wonderful, normal life."

For some crazy reason I didn't believe her. I don't know why because she never lied. But I didn't. I turned to other family members who were there with us. I asked the same question to my oldest daughter. Same answer. I didn't believe her either.

Crazy.

Maybe I was too scared to believe. I desperately wanted to live a normal life, to walk my daughters down the wedding aisle and to be my son's best man. I wanted to grow old with Amy.

I looked at my mother-in-law. I knew without a doubt—she never lied. George Washington had nothing on this woman. She could not tell a lie. She'd taken notes of the surgeon's comments.

"You tell me and I'll believe it," I said, gagging.

She slowly pulled out her notepad and read: *"Successfully removed the primary tumor, all affected lymph nodes and several feet of the small and large intestine. All tumors were resected except the ones in the liver. They should grow slowly, and Mr. Avery should expect to live a long life."*

My head collapsed onto my pillow. I could hear music streaming through the hospital's hallway. Smooth jazz saxophone, playing "You Are My Lady." The panic rushing through my body subsided. The throbbing pain in my gut eased for a few moments. I managed another deep breath of relief past the devious tube that assaulted my throat, touched my brick necklace, which lay on the table next to my bed, and closed my eyes.

***

My attentive nurse periodically interrupted my sleep the rest of the day to place her ice-cold stethoscope on my stomach and listen for gas—an exciting experience.

Later that evening, I awoke as she was changing the bag on my IV drip.

"And what's your name?" I struggled to asked.

She smiled. Her smile was bright and seemed to capture pure joy. I needed some joy. My hospital room was a better place when she smiled. "Brooke Wyche. Do you feel any pain, Mr. Avery?"

"Only when I cough, sip water, move, or basically lift my eyelids." Yes, I felt pain.

She placed her hand on my forehead. "You had quite an invasive surgery. Just press the morphine pump when your pain is unbearable."

Her words were soft and peaceful. Small lines radiated from the corners of her eyes and edges of her lips. She carried herself with dignity and was quite fit. She must have exercised regularly. I figured she was around fifty.

"I don't think this damn morphine pump works," I growled. "I've been pressing it all afternoon."

She managed a small laugh. "The morphine is metered so you won't overdose. But I promise the pain will ease through the night. Just let us take care of you."

I wanted to believe her encouraging words but wasn't sure I could. I was in the hospital, a despised place and one I never wanted to be. And I didn't like having to depend on anyone, much less a person I'd just met.

On the second day of my delightful hospital visit, my surgeon removed the brutal tube from my throat and showed me scans displaying where he'd removed several feet of my intestines and then reconnected the whole mess. He told me I'd be in the hospital for seven to ten days. He said it'd take that long for my intestines to regain proper function.

I committed myself to staying no more than four days. He told me walking would help my bowels start working again. So, I walked. And I walked. Around the nurses' station every hour. At first, Amy had to assist me by holding my arm. But by the evening I walked by myself, pushing the silvery bag hanging from the IV stand. My nurse, Brooke, with whom I had begun to develop a relationship, laughed at my determination.

My room possessed a westerly view of the Ashley River. The sunset was magnificent. The evening sky was on fire, with bold purple and orange colors reflecting off the clouds. I imagined I could reach out my window and hold the golden hues in my hand. The brilliant scene soothed and relaxed me like one of Amy's encompassing hugs.

As the sun slowly disappeared behind the horizon, Brooke entered my room. She sat down, which I thought was a bit odd since she'd been moving nonstop throughout her shifts. "From reading your file, I understand you're an ex-coach."

I raised my eyebrows. "Yeah."

"And you look to be in good shape."

"I work out."

She slid to the edge of her chair. Her words were soft but direct. "I read in the paper you recently made a generous donation to the Komen run. Thank you for your support."

"You're welcome."

She stared at me—quiet. Something was on her mind.

She finally spoke. "I was recently diagnosed with breast cancer. I'll learn my course of treatment soon. You have a particularly unusual kind of cancer. If you don't mind my saying it, I can tell how worried you are. All day, for some uncanny reason, I've felt compelled to tell you about a group of people who have helped me face my dark days."

"Yeah," I said, realizing I had raised the right side of my lip—my autonomic response when I'm not sure I want to continue a conversation.

But her face possessed a genuine glow of sincerity. "The group is called the Charleston Dragon Boat Club. Most of the paddlers are cancer survivors, just like you and me. Without them, I would have been lost."

"What is a dragon boat?" I asked.

"It's a forty-eight-foot narrow canoe that holds twenty paddlers. It's rather majestic."

"Like rowing?" I asked.

She seemed to relax and smiled. "No, each person holds a paddle, not an oar. It's an ancient Chinese sport that dates back over two thousand years. I've never been athletic and was highly skeptical, but after my first practice, I was hooked. I thought that you, as an ex-coach and a cancer survivor, would relate."

"What hooked you?" I'd always drawn upon an athlete's motivation in my coaching.

"The fact that anyone can do it, even someone like me. All I needed was my drive and desire to be well. And it's a sport of people working together and not one of isolation like running. I believe you'd like it."

The buzzer in her lap vibrated.

I rested my head on my pillow and grimaced with pain as I raised my arms above my head. A signal I routinely used when I was ready to end a conversation. "Well, I need to get out of this place first. I'm just looking forward to a majestic bowel movement."

She laughed. "It'll happen soon enough. We paddle on

Saturday mornings in the Ashley River. Think about giving it a chance. It's changed my life. You may be surprised." She closed the door as she left the room.

I smirked.

I had no intentions of getting into a long, narrow boat with twenty amateurish, unhealthy losers and flipping over in the rushing tide of the Ashley River.

On the third day, Brooke beamed as she firmly pressed her stethoscope against my belly. "I hear rumblings," she said.

"Excellent, that means I can go home."

"Not until you have a bowel movement."

"Great, now my life now revolves around a trip to the bathroom."

"Yes, it does," Brooke said as she patted my arm. "I brought you a book to read about the sport of dragon boating. It was written by our coach, Jamie Barker. My email address is on the back cover. Message me when you get home. I'd love to introduce you to my wonderful teammates."

Although we'd only known each other a few days, Brooke and I had developed a rapport. I wanted to learn more about her disease. I was reluctant to ask questions, but a small voice told me I should.

"Are you doing okay with your recent diagnosis?" I asked.

She gave a long, slow sigh and stood still. Her eyes, crystal blue like the Caribbean Sea, penetrated mine. "I'm scared to death. Of dying, having radical surgery, losing my hair, and especially of being demeaned by looking like a freak. You've probably never experienced those kinds of insecure feelings."

Little did she know that even before my diagnosis, I avoided, like the plague, every situation that could have the smallest potential to place me in a humiliating position.

I felt awkward. But I understood how she felt. I rarely opened my thoughts to anyone but Amy. But for some reason I felt comfortable talking with Brooke. "Could I share my experience?" I asked.

Brooke sat down. "Sure."

"When I was first diagnosed, I constantly worried about dying. I've never been particularly religious, but I began praying. Just give me time, Lord. Please allow me to see my daughters married, play with my grandchildren, that sort of thing. And I thought having cancer was damned unfair. I had friends who'd had affairs, ate like hogs, never exercised . . . and I'd lived right. I mean, come on! Why didn't they get cancer?"

Brooke laughed.

"I immediately went through the stages of grief that Kübler-Ross describes, starting with denial and anger. Recognizing these emotions was key, as I can bite off the heads of a lot of innocents in a heartbeat. I tried to channel my anger, although I wasn't always successful. I began driving aggressively to my office while listening to extremely loud music. Stupid? Yeah. But I had to deal with my aggression and anger before I arrived at my office and eviscerated all of my employees."

Brooke shook her head as if she could relate to every word.

"And then I started bargaining. Okay, God, I'll go to church if you cure me. I'll stop swearing and do good-Karma things. Anything. Just cure me. It didn't work, so for a brief period I went back to stage two—anger. It felt good, and I'm pretty good at it. But after a few days, I finally gained some insight: all I could do was the best I could do. Denial be damned. So, I let the anger go."

Brooke stood and gave me a hug. "Thanks."

Little did she know I'd never opened up like that before to anyone other than Amy and would probably never do so again. And I'd never totally let go.

She firmly instructed me, as she left my room, to immediately inform her if I passed gas or had a bowel movement. I determinedly assured her she'd be the first to know when this great miracle happened.

While dwelling on having a bowel movement and getting the hell out of this hospital, I forced myself to do a little reading. This sport, dragon boating, did look interesting. I read of a legend about an old Chinese patriot and poet who was banished by the Chinese king for having too much power with the people. The poet drowned himself as hundreds of local fishermen raced in their boats in an attempt to save him, to no avail. They beat their drums and splashed their paddles in the water to prevent the fish and water dragons from eating his body.

And this woman wants me to do this sport? But I kept reading and found inspiring comments from seemingly normal people who had participated.

"We all work together as one."

"The perfect race is rewarding."

"It lets you escape."

"Each individual athlete and the team, as a unit, must fuse their physical, mental, and spiritual parts."

And another woman's comment was consistent with Brooke's: *"Dragon boating has totally changed my life."*

Several people called the experience *"a celebration of life."*

Unusual comments from participants of any sport. Maybe when I'm well, I'll check it out, I thought. It might be fun watching these bunches of amateurs splash around in the river.

The morning of day four arrived, and I felt an urge. My stomach growled. I slowly stepped with trepidation into the bathroom. Eureka! A bowel movement. And—it was exciting. In fact, I was so excited, I immediately pulled up my pajama pants and ran out of my room, down the hallway, and to the nurses' station. As I made my grand appearance, I yelled, "I had a bowel movement!"

Three of the four nurses on duty began laughing, but Brooke looked alarmed. In my excitement rushing to their station, I'd ripped out my IV; all she could see was the blood spurting from my arm and onto the hospital's floor. Brooke hurriedly reinserted the damaged IV, cleaned the blood from the floor, and informed the doctor of my moment of triumph.

That day I went home.

4

Charleston

Late Fall 2008

My body had recuperated well from surgery. My abdominal muscles were getting stronger; I could do forty sit-ups without stopping. The aftermath left a nasty scar from below my belly button to my rib cage and still a liver full of tumors. These fiendish hormone-producing tumors in my liver caused my head, neck, and face to flush red-hot. The high levels of serotonin caused night sweats, waking me with perspiration dripping from my hair soaking my pillow. Diarrhea would raise its ugly head without notice.

Cancer had forced me to conclude that my well-planned and -constructed life would never be the same. I'd never been a wimp, yet during these six months after my surgery, my emotions regressed.

I visualized these corrupt cells in my liver scheming to form new tumors and to take my body hostage. I'd lay awake at night wondering if I was soon going to die. It was during the wee hours of the morning, the demon of fear and death visited me, whispering in my mind my life would soon come to screeching halt. Even with Amy lying only a few inches away, I felt totally alone. The anxiety coupled with night sweats made sleeping difficult.

Slowly, as I processed this fear and moved through the stages of grief, my thoughts changed. Like the millstone grinding the rough grain into a smooth flour, my brain began to quiet the demons. I became thankful for the next day. Yes, one day I would die, but I boldly pronounced to myself each morning that that day wasn't going to be my last day on this earth. I'd make every minute count.

Cancer turns the straight and smooth highway of life into a bumpy, curvy mountainous road. The goal to excel becomes the goal to live. But I still wanted to excel. I think that's the reason I considered trying this crazy sport—dragon boating.

The paddlers' comments I'd read in the book stuck in my thoughts. They made me curious to check out the magic they spoke of that made this sport special. The testimonials were enthusiastic. And I could use some enthusiasm.

At 7:30 on a calm fall Saturday morning, I was standing on the docks that connected the Ashley River with the waterfront at Charleston County's Brittlebank Park. I'd emailed Brooke the previous week, and she eagerly agreed to meet me.

She told me to wear runner or biker shorts, a fast-drying shirt, and nonslip shoes—sandals preferably. I wore my black

Tevas and some of my expensive lululemon garb. And, since I was bald and had been for many years, she highly recommended I wear a ball cap and bring some powerful sunscreen.

The morning rays were just beginning to hit the deep-green marsh grass that lined the banks of the wide, winding Ashley River. About twenty or so people had gathered where the dragon boats were tied at the end of the dock.

Suddenly the sedges and rushes that compose the marshland became a canvas of the rising sun's reflections. The bold colors of orange, red, and yellow bled across the still waters. The light was magnified as it reflected from the windows of stately homes that bordered the river. The sun's rays spread across the water's surface, shimmering like tiny diamonds. I began to understand the appeal of a narrow boat sleekly moving and being the only disturbance through the serene water.

Brooke called my name as she walked up the dock in my direction. Not that I was ready to make a verbal admission, but I felt an unusual warm internal sense of safeness and belonging. And to my surprise, nervous butterflies in my gut.

She looked different. As she approached, I noticed she wore a multicolored bandana around her head. When she stepped in front of me, I could see she had no hair—chemo. But then she smiled. It was the same smile that had radiated joy in my hospital room. It was good to see her. She gave me a hug.

She grabbed my arm and pulled me in the direction of the small crowd hanging around a long, narrow wooden canoe. The boat was white with decorative red-and-gold dragon scales painted along the sides. It had seats that crossed its width and a large oar extending from the rear.

Brooke was thinner, and I could tell she'd had a mastectomy.

The chemotherapy must be difficult. She recognized my measuring gaze and smiled. "You like my shiny new scalp? I just had my head-shaving party."

I smiled but my heart hurt.

"Soon after you were discharged from the hospital, I had double-mastectomy surgery. I've been undergoing intense chemotherapy for several months. Actually, today is my first time paddling since the operation. But I remember well the words you spoke from your hospital bed: to let it all go. It feels freeing to be on the water. It's my escape into wholeness."

I couldn't speak. I stared at the absolute sincerity that was painted across her face. I felt humbled and ashamed about my own complaining.

Her smile broadened. "Let me introduce you to my friends."

As we approached the crowd, a tall, muscular woman stepped forward and extended her hand. "I'm Pat Selinsky, and I'll be coaching today."

She held a black carbon fiber paddle in her hand. The paddle was about as high as her armpit, had a T-top handle, and a long oval shaft with a wide blade. On the blade was a decal displaying the words HARDER, FASTER, DEEPER.

Pat wore extremely tight and very short runner's pants and a sleeveless shirt. It was difficult to guess her age. Her arms were toned. But most impressive were her legs. Her thigh muscles ripped down her legs and surrounded her knees. She had well-defined calf muscles. Her hair was blonde, thick, and shoulder length. She was very attractive.

She instructed as she walked toward the boat. "When I get the seating arrangement in the boat finalized, I'll teach you our paddle stroke."

"She's in great shape," I said to Brooke.

Brooke nodded. "Pat's training to try out for the US Senior Women's National Team. She has an excellent chance to qualify and represent the United States in Prague next year."

I raised my eyebrows expressing my newly inspired interest. Maybe these guys weren't a bunch of scraggly losers acting like they're athletes. "Impressive," I said.

As in the hospital room, Brooke's blue eyes again penetrated mine. "That's not what's impressive. Pat was diagnosed seven years ago with advanced ovarian cancer and given two years to live. Her determination for life is what's impressive."

"She sure looks healthy."

A tear formed in the corner of Brooke's eye. Her admiration for Pat was obvious. "She'll tell you quickly, Cancer does not control her life. Her favorite expression is "Cancer is just a condition; that's all it is."

Brooke continued introducing me to the team, but one man stood out. He was an extremely muscular guy of about middle height and weight whom she'd introduced as Thomas Huger. He was handsome and sported stylish gray hair that looked like a wheat field blowing in the wind. His shoulders were wide and stout, and his biceps were as big as most people's thighs. He was hairy and manly. He shook my hand but didn't speak.

His neck was thin and heavily scarred. As Brooke led me to the boat, he offered me a smile of welcome. "What's his story?" I asked Brooke.

"Thomas was an All-American running back at The Citadel." Charlestonians glamourized the graduates of South Carolina's military college. "He was recently inducted into The Citadel's Athletic Hall of Fame. Almost ten years ago, he was diagnosed with throat cancer. He's had numerous neck and mouth surgeries. The surgeons actually used a portion of his leg to rebuild his jaw. He can barely speak and can't eat at all. He's almost sixty but, as you can see, looks thirty. His nickname is The Man Who Never Quits."

"He can't eat?"

Brooke grimaced. I could tell she could feel this man's inner pain. "Underneath his shorts is a feeding tube. He's amazing. Watch him paddle. Every stroke is maximum effort."

"He paddles while wearing a feeding tube?" I asked in awe.

She laughed. "Yes, and is probably our strongest and best paddler."

I was beginning to understand Brooke's passion for this sport and her teammates. I'd known that feeling but not for some time. Being part of a team had been important to me in my younger days. But teams don't always work out. Pride, ego, and selfishness can destroy the tightest of bonds. Believe me, I've witnessed the implosion of several outstanding teams.

Not all the paddlers looked like great athletes. Most appeared in good physical condition but some were a bit overweight—even pudgy. A few appeared to be somewhat clumsy.

Brooke grabbed my arm as the paddlers began to get into the boat. "I wish you could have met Sean Riley today, but he's at the Houston Cancer Center undergoing major surgery for colon cancer. He's the heart of our team."

"I have an appointment next week at the same center to learn about a possible new treatment for my rare liver tumors." The coincidence stunned me.

Brooke's grip on my arm tightened. "You must visit him and his wife, Sarah, when you're there. You must."

I spoke with earnestness. "I will. I promise."

With those words, Pat returned. She stood squarely in front of me and handed me a paddle. She spoke with authority. "Paramount to this sport is teamwork. We fight for the perfect combination of timing, power, and stamina. Most men paddlers think it's all about power, but they soon learn that timing is most important."

I nodded in submission.

She held her paddle in front of her body and extended her arms. One hand held the paddle over the T handle and the other just above the blade. "You see the A-frame I create as I hold my paddle?"

"I do."

"That's the arm extension you need. When you get into the boat—we call it loading the boat—push your hip tight against the gunwale. Hold your paddle as I am and extend your arms outside the boat."

I mimicked her stance with the paddle she'd given me.

"Good." She stepped behind me and twisted my torso. "That's how you get the paddle out in front of you for a stroke. It's called rotation. You want your back toward the shore and your chest facing your seat partner. The goal is to attain sufficient torso rotation so your reach can be maximized, which allows you to use your more powerful back and hip muscles for the stroke."

My body was awkwardly twisted and leaning forward as I held the paddle out in front of me trying to maintain the A-frame.

"Then imagine you're spearing a fish with the blade of your paddle and slam it into the water," she said. "If you're correctly rotated at your waist, you'll properly engage the larger muscles of your back, shoulders, and trunk as you pull the paddle through the water. Do not rely on your smaller arm muscles."

I nodded as I realized this sport was significantly more complicated than I'd thought.

She continued. "When you've pulled the paddle back even with your hip, then visualize you're pulling a sword from its sheath. Rip the paddle from the water, snap it forward, rotate your body, and repeat the stroke." She laughed. "Does all of this make sense?"

I lied and nodded as if I understood everything she'd just said.

"Okay, then," she said. "Let's load the boat. I'm placing you behind Thomas. If you emulate his stroke, you'll be fine."

A man standing in the back of the boat, holding the long oar yelled, "Push way!" The team pushed the boat away from the dock. He then shouted, "Paddles up!" Everyone raised their paddles into the air and twisted their bodies in order to lean over the side of the canoe and creating an A-frame with their paddle. I struggled to rotate my body and get my paddle outside the boat but finally got it into the proper position. His final command: "Take it away!"

Like a fine-tuned machine, twenty individuals, well almost twenty, began to paddle in perfect unison. We moved out of the marina and into the heart of the Ashley River. The water was still and calm. I followed Thomas's motion and was almost in time with the movements of his Superman arms.

As the motion synchronized, my hurried mind began to rest. I'd always lived my life fast. Maybe this sport could be my respite. I heard air blow to my right. As I twisted my head to learn the cause of the noise, I saw a dolphin swimming beside us. His smooth, gray, streamlined body seemed to be guiding us through the strong tidal river.

I turned my attention back to the boat. No one spoke. Perfect stillness and quiet. Even the paddles made little sound as they entered and exited the water. Twenty people became as one in the solace of their thoughts, their hurts and pain but also, their hopes and dreams. We were joined by a carefree dolphin as if he were telling us the water wasn't troubled at all, that all was well.

Maybe I just might like this sport after all.

5

Houston, Texas

Late Fall 2008

The Houston Cancer Center had an excellent reputation in treating all types of cancers, including carcinoid and neuroendocrine tumors. I'd made an appointment with their carcinoid specialist. I packed my fighting spirit, and Amy and I boarded a flight to Texas.

Through my research I'd learned a lot about neuroendocrine tumors. I'd read about a new treatment called Peptide Receptor Radionuclide Therapy or PRRT. The treatment uses targeted radiation to cause damage specifically to NET cancer cells, hopefully destroying the tumors over time. This progressive cancer center had recently received funding to conduct a PRRT clinical trial, and I wanted to learn more.

My laboratory blood tests had confirmed that my tumors were secreting extremely high levels of serotonin, which caused my severe flushing. At times my face and neck would turn beet red, and I'd feel like I'd stuck my head into a hot oven. The elevated serotonin levels also caused asthma-like symptoms, and my breathing had become more difficult. I wanted to find any treatment that could help. Since I'd experienced these symptoms for more than ten years, and my cancer had been missed and misdiagnosed on many occasions, I was concerned I wasn't getting the best and most up-to-date treatment in Charleston. I was searching worldwide for a neuroendocrine cancer specialist.

The medical complex was, in true Texas fashion, huge. Everywhere I looked, I saw cancer patients. An immense vicious war was being fought that I'd never seen—a war of survival. But I was learning the battle wasn't just surviving but living with grace. Their courage took my breath away.

As Amy and I walked through the hospital, we witnessed people at all the different mileposts on their journey: the ones still in shock from their recent diagnosis, others smiling as if they'd just received good news, and people crying who'd gotten bad news. The weary-looking, overburdened heroic and too-often underappreciated caregivers were there. All of us were just sick and tired of being sick and tired. Witnessing so many fighting the same battles gave me strength.

My consultation with the specialist, though, was extremely disappointing. He discouraged me from enrolling in the PRRT trial, stating the treatment should be a final option and was unproven. It appeared he was highly motivated—I'm guessing by money and the backing of a wealthy pharmaceutical company—to instead enroll patients like myself in a clinical trial of a new, recently patented drug. He made several comments about the importance of his publishing the study's data.

My attempt to convince this "specialist" that PRRT had shown positive results in Europe fell on deaf ears—or maybe greedy ears. It seemed to me he was more interested in studying and publishing the results of the new drug than in treating his patients. People seeing their name in print seemed to make them feel superior.

Amy and I left in disgust. I despised being treated like a guinea pig or a second-class citizen, like I had been as a young boy. I learned two important lessons from my visit with this doctor: I needed to be my own health advocate, and I needed to understand my disease and treatment. Even though cancer had attacked my body, *I* was still in control. I would determine my next step.

After a glass of wine at lunch, with Amy patiently listening to my cathartic bitch session, we began our search for Sean Riley and his wife. Although we'd never met, I already held him in great esteem. Sean was a highly successful computer programmer and obviously held a revered place in the hearts of his dragon boat teammates. It seemed every time they mentioned his name, they'd cry.

After much inquiry we learned he was in the building that housed the major surgery center. The walk across the facility's finely landscaped campus was soothing, not like the waiting room we'd soon find.

The cancer center's major surgery center exuded an institutional antiseptic and mordant odor, like people were dying all around. The hallways were decorated with beautiful abstract art that I suppose was designed to lift the spirit and disguise the smell, but it didn't work. I was parched, so I bought a bottle of water from a vending machine. We finally found Sean's wife, Sarah, bowed in prayer in a small plastic chair in the waiting area.

She was a petite, dark-haired woman who looked to be about fifty. She appeared to be perplexed and frightened. Although we'd not met, she knew we were coming. Trembling, Sarah stood and tightly hugged me. Her heart rate must have been at one hundred and fifty or more.

She touched my face. "Brooke told me you were going to find me. Thanks for coming."

"How is Sean doing?" I asked.

She shook her head. "The surgeons just took a break. They'll finish the operation in another four hours."

Amy asked, "How long has he already been in surgery?"

Sarah wiped a tear away. "Six hours, and we're a bit past halfway. Sean calls it the Big Scoop. It's a last resort operation for stage IV colon cancer patients. They've removed his bladder, prostate, and rectum. Now they are working on putting Humpty-Dumpty back together again."

My admiration increased as she was able to maintain her sense of humor during this traumatic surgery.

Amy sighed.

"I know," Sarah said. "It's tough. The urologists are doing a thing called an ileal conduit, which will be the way Sean will pass urine. Plastic surgeons are taking a chunk of his thigh muscles to rebuild his abdominal wall and help fill up the big hole that they've created."

She managed a slight smile. "Sean was bummed his right leg would be weak." She laughed. "He said it ended his dream of being a professional football placekicker."

Her facial muscles stiffened again as she exhaled. "Finally, the surgeon will create the colostomy and ileostomy."

I thought maybe we'd made a mistake visiting her. She looked weak and fragile. We sat in the hard chairs surrounded by stacks of old and boring magazines. I asked, "Are you okay?"

She broke down and began to sob. She could barely speak. "Damn, damn, damn, I hate cancer," she said, slamming her fist against her leg. Sarah lifted her head and looked at Amy and me. She appeared to gain strength. "But Sean and I are third-generation Charlestonians. We're tough, and we stick together."

I nodded. "What happens next?"

"Recovery. A long recovery. Walking again after the difficult plastic surgery on his leg where they removed the muscles will be tough. His leg will be very weak. And he will have to learn how to eat." She moaned and smiled. "But as always, he'll do it all with grace. He's dealt with extreme numbness in his hands and feet from the massive chemotherapy like a champion. He's an absolute warrior. He rarely complained from the intense pain when the surgeons scraped cancer off his sciatic nerve. For him, dealing with an ostomy will be a piece of cake."

Sarah's smile widened. "He's also determined to return to his life and get back in the dragon boat."

Her words inspired me. I gripped her hand with both my hands. "Sean must have more courage than any person I've ever met. I'll consider myself a fortunate man to have the opportunity to paddle in the same boat side by side with your brave husband."

Sarah looked me in the eye. "Have you read Sean's blog?"

"I have not."

She pulled her hand away and sat back. "Without a doubt Sean is the most courageous man I've ever known," she said.

"He compares having cancer to winning the lottery. Can you believe that?"

"That's a pretty tough lottery," Amy said.

I felt the roots of admiration for Sean continue to grow. "No, a pretty tough man." *Extreme grit,* I said to myself.

"He said cancer had opened many doors and created wonderful experiences that he would have never experienced without being sick. His oncologist gave him two years to live after the initial diagnosis. That was eight years ago. He calls every minute 'gravy.' To him, living is all gravy."

I thought about Sean's legs and how weak they'll be after the surgery, and he still desired to paddle. I flashed back to my youth, a memory of a childhood friend who had a terrible accident. A ten-year-old boy, working in a large cornfield alongside his older brother, was picking up cornstalks that'd fallen from the tractor his dad was driving. As his father turned the tractor for another cut through the field, my friend fell. The large cornstalks hid him from his father's careful view.

I was told his screams, as the tractor's wheel crushed both his legs, could be heard all the way to Columbia. But my friend never allowed his heavy, clunky leg braces to break his unbreakable drive to succeed. In the mill village everyone walked to school. He was no exception. I watched his daily pain and his struggle to do something I took for granted. His grace and intense will to live created in me an indomitable passion and appreciation for the spirit within people to survive. Sarah and Sean embodied this spirit.

I stood and walked around the waiting room. I wiped the sweat from my face. I was scared of dying, and Sean had pronounced himself a lottery winner. I guess after fighting cancer for so long, a person learns how to maintain their sanity. Sean and Sarah had found a way to fight this horrible battle and still maintain a semblance of life. I could learn from these people.

I looked at Sarah. "What a hell of an attitude."

Sarah lifted her phone. "Could I read you the latest entry of his blog?"

Amy stood beside me. I nodded. "Yes, I'd like that very much."

Sarah's voice rattled as she read:

If you say, "Okay, this isn't so bad," or even better, "Hey, this is pretty cool," and live in the moment, you can do anything. Getting cancer is better than winning the lottery. If you get cancer, you know who your friends are. If you win the lottery, you are never sure. If you get cancer, you appreciate every day as a gift. If you win the lottery, you blow your time and money. If you get cancer, you take the time to really focus on your life and what it means. If you win the lottery, you can lose yourself. So, if you look at it that way, I'm a very lucky man.

Amy was crying.

I held my bottle of water high above my head. "A toast to the health and speedy recovery of the bravest and wisest man I'll ever meet."

Amy and I walked to where Sarah sat, and the three of us consumed each other in a strong group hug.

Sarah said, "Thank you so much for coming. I can't wait for you to meet Sean back in Charleston."

Amy and I walked outside and were silent for about ten minutes. No words could offer justice for what we'd just witnessed. I finally broke the silence. "I'm beginning to believe these dragon boat paddlers aren't losers after all. They're seekers. Seekers of life."

6

Charleston

Spring 2009

In my quest for success and acceptance I'd developed a deep yearning for significance, not just notoriety but a superiority above others. Truth didn't matter, just the prism.

Back home in Charleston, I became more involved with dragon boating. My body needed the intense physical activity to distract my attention from the tumors that were growing within my liver. Although I remained aloof, I was intrigued with the paddlers' commitment to each other. At times, I felt as if the club's members were more a support group than a team of potential athletes.

I loved the Holy City and its rivers. I especially enjoyed the springtime paddles up the Cooper River and into the Charleston Harbor, the city's important commercial waterway, where huge barges transport goods from all parts of the world through the deep-water channel. Charlestonians arrogantly assert that the Cooper and Ashley Rivers merge to form the Atlantic Ocean.

Paddling around the harbor's infamous Fort Sumter gave me a keen appreciation for the thousands of lives who'd lived and died to create Charleston's rich and complicated heritage. As our boat glid along the city's battery wall and viewing the historic homes and grandiose oak trees draped in Spanish moss was more than cathartic—it was healing. Pent-up anxieties would rush from my body with every spray of water that slammed against our canoe. Spring's new green buds on the massive oak trees and the multicolored azalea blooms provided a short but welcome reprieve for our sick bodies.

But today we weren't in the majestic Charleston rivers. My fellow dragon boat paddlers had taken a temporary respite and traveled inland a few miles with our boats. As we arrived at our destination, I found myself inspecting a small, manmade, skiing lake. A 300-meter course had been marked in the middle of the lake.

Our paddlers had been discussing organizing a team to compete in some of the regional dragon boat races. Specifically, they wanted to compete in a race held in Beaufort, South Carolina. The daylong Beaufort festival featured mostly local corporate teams who came together once a year to raise funds for cancer survivors. But these festivals also attracted a few competitive club teams who practiced year-round. It was against these teams we desired to test our abilities.

Pat had decided we needed to hold a time trial to determine

the club's strongest and fastest paddlers. I'd reluctantly agreed to participate as I assumed I was already the strongest and fastest. Since my surgery, I'd trained hard, running five miles three days a week, and attending CrossFit classes two days a week.

The time trial consisted of a lone paddler in a boat. The objective was to determine how fast one person could move a boat. Our teammates would watch as each paddler demonstrated their power and strength. There were thirty nervous paddlers standing on the bank of this small manmade lake ready to prove their worthiness to be a member of the team.

In addition to this intense peer pressure, time trials required a different type of canoe, a single person outrigger canoe, or an OC-1. An OC-1 is a long, slender carbon-fiber watercraft. It features a lateral support float, called an ama, fastened to the main hull for stability. Outrigger boats were developed thousands of years ago for sea travel between the Southeast Asian islands. Later, they were used as fishing boats. Today they're primarily used for recreation and racing.

I'd never paddled an OC-1, but I figured the technique would be similar to paddling in a dragon boat. Other than the extended ama, the primary difference was the foot pedals that operated a rudder. So, we had to paddle, giving each stroke maximum effort while steering the boat straight along the course.

The women paddlers went first. Allyson, a mild-mannered middle-aged woman and a breast cancer survivor, volunteered to be the first to perform the time trial. She was average height and had short reddish-blond hair with bangs that covered most of her forehead. Allyson's most striking physical feature was a bright smile and white teeth that would make even Tom Cruise jealous. She was our team's encourager. She'd had a double mastectomy, radiation, and reconstructive surgery but never lost one ounce of hope. She was one of the club's original members and hated confrontation.

Allyson had founded the Second Base Club, a support group for breast cancer patients, survivors, and their families. The club's slogan was "Breast cancer doesn't discriminate against any woman, nor do we." The support group provided much-needed understanding, advice, and encouragement. She was a perfect teammate and was willing to do whatever was necessary. It was fitting she volunteered to be first to put pride on the line.

The starting line was marked by a white-and-orange stake driven into the ground on the bank. She paddled the OC-1 to the starting line. Pat blew the whistle, and Allyson started paddling. My teammates, who'd lined the lake's bank, yelled words of encouragement toward Allyson. "Paddle harder, faster, deeper!"

Allyson's husband Kent stood a few feet into the water, cheering for his wife's every stroke. His loud reassuring words seemed to give her strength.

My heart rate increased as I witnessed Allyson's exhaustion as she reached the course's halfway point. She was a good paddler, and she was struggling. Paddling a canoe solo might be significantly different than with nineteen other paddlers in the boat. This exercise could be more challenging than I first imagined.

I walked toward an oak tree and sat down on a pile of pine straw. I visualized paddling down the course. I slowly pictured each stroke in my head. I envisioned my muscles strong and full of endurance. I refused to be weak. I was an athlete, presumably the best athlete on the team. I was a winner. Being anything but the best and fastest was not an option.

Allyson's time was good—two minutes and forty seconds.

Brooke was the next paddler. Her stroke was stronger and smoother, and she finished with what seemed to be strong, a time of two minutes and thirty-eight seconds. Two more female paddlers tested the course but didn't beat Brooke's times.

As I watched another paddler begin her time trial, I heard my name called and turned around. "I understand you visited me in my Texas hospital." I'd only seen pictures of Sean, but he looked great. He was standing in front a row of black carbon-fiber paddles strung from a rope that was tied between two tall pine trees. He looked healthy. Seeing him overwhelmed me with a rare sense of humility. "I'm ready to get back into the boat."

"Glad to see you up and taking nourishment," I said as a feeble attempt to be amusing.

He laughed. "Eating food isn't the problem. Getting rid of it—now that's a different story. He pointed toward his sides with each hand. "Meet Stan the Stoma and Pete the Pee-ostomy, my two newly installed colostomy bags."

I laughed but was extraordinarily impressed by his ability to joke about his lamentable fate. After an experience like his, most people would find themselves in a deep depression. They'd go to great lengths to create excuses why they couldn't participate rather than making bold resolute decisions to move forward and live life to its fullest.

He said in a firm voice, "Really, I'm determined to get back into that boat."

I fixed my gaze upon him with awe. "I'll consider it a privilege to paddle with you."

He placed his hand on my shoulder. "After fourteen rounds of chemo and a surgery that literally ripped out my guts, you should realize that I'll never give up."

I took a deep breath and nodded. I could think of no words to adequately express my overwhelming admiration.

He slapped my back and smiled big. "We're going to do some great things together, my friend." He then looked up the lake, and Sean and I stood shoulder to shoulder, watching five more female paddlers endure the course. None bettered Brooke's time.

Pat was the last female paddler. Everyone in the club was aware she was trying out for the United States women's team that would compete in the world championships to be held Prague. But we were also aware she'd just completed her fourth round of chemotherapy. Her body had to be exhausted. Her muscles were compromised and weak.

I intensely watched her start, which was swift and smooth. She'd diligently worked to develop the almost-perfect stroke, with full rotation of her torso. The paddle's blade completely buried in the water before she pulled back, then a quick recovery, and another rapid torso rotation. She gained strength with each stroke as she progressed down the course. Everyone on the bank screamed encouragement.

Her head collapsed into her lap with exhaustion as she crossed the finish line. She gasped for air to fill her lungs. Her arms and legs looked like wet spaghetti hanging from a pot of boiling water. She slowly regained her strength, raised her head, and looked in our direction. Her time was announced—two minutes and twenty-seven seconds. We erupted in applause. Several slammed their paddles on the surface of the water in celebration.

Fourteen men were participating in the time trials. I told Pat I'd go last as I wanted to know the time I'd need to beat. But Pat insisted Thomas be the final paddler. I reluctantly agreed.

The first male time was two minutes and twenty-eight seconds. After eleven more male paddlers, the best time of the day was two minutes and twenty-two seconds. It was now my turn.

I slowly paddled to the start line. I stabilized my boat and rotated my body so my back squarely faced the lake's shore. With my torso fully twisted, I extended my body over the canoe's side and completely buried the blade of my paddle in the water. My arms were fully extended, creating the A-frame Pat had taught me. My legs were coiled, ready to erupt like an exploding canon to begin my stroke. I believed I had been working out harder and longer than anyone on the team. I breathed deep and long and filled my lungs with air.

The calf and thigh muscles of both my legs ripped backward as the whistle blew. My waist uncoiled, and my back and abdominal muscles pulled the paddle toward my hip. I snapped the blade from the water as it reached my hip, forcing it forward again and contorting my torso into position to begin another stroke. I felt my brick necklace, which was secured safely in my pants pocket, jab into my thigh.

I focused on pacing and my stroke rate. Three hundred meters is a long way in a canoe with a single paddler. I wanted every stroke to be perfect and consistent. I felt strong as I reached the halfway marker and began to bury my paddle's blade deeper into the water and increase my stroke rate. I hoped my conditioning would pay off. I was determined to clock the fastest time.

I pushed my body to perform. Nausea suddenly tightened in my stomach. I felt the urge to vomit. My thigh muscles burned in pain. My hip muscles cramped. As I became alarmed that I'd not finish the course and clock the fastest time, I felt endorphins release inside my brain. My concern disappeared; I was able to ignore my discomfort, and my stroke intensified. I was fifty meters from the finish line.

My heart pounded hard. My vision was fuzzy. I struggled to force oxygen deep into my lungs. I knew I had to finish strong and couldn't slow down. As I crossed the finish line, my heart raced, and the arteries in my neck throbbed. I heard the time of two minutes and nineteen seconds announced. A strong time. The best of the day, but was it good enough to beat Thomas? When I dragged my wearied body from my boat, I saw Thomas paddling to the starting line.

I lay prostrate on the ground under a large oak tree when I heard the whistle blow. I could barely sit up to watch Thomas, yet I couldn't take my eyes off him. His tight shirt exposed the well-formed lines of his back muscles with each eloquent stroke. The intensity of his focus was chilling. He actually gained speed as he approached the finish line. A few seconds later and with much anticipation, I heard his time announced—two minutes and twenty seconds.

I collapsed against the oak tree. I was the best.

***

The time trials were encouraging. Our team possessed a number of high-quality and strong paddlers. Competing in a few regional races would be a good idea. The club members' mood was festive. Paddlers were bonding—becoming a team. But I kept reminding myself that, although part of the team, I was only there to stay in shape and keep my mind off my illness. I knew this team wasn't at the level of competition I was accustomed to, nor did I plan to be totally committed to a team again.

Several club members had brought grills, hamburgers, and

hot dogs for a picnic. I'd brought shrimp to boil. I drank a cold beer while the shrimp cooked. Not many things compared with the taste of a cold beer after a demanding workout. Popping the top of a malty IPA relaxed me like little other. Having the best time of the day settled my anxiety and made me proud. I hated to lose with a passion.

After peeling some shrimp, I found a cool, shady area under the large oak tree I'd used all day as my refuge. I placed my chair and relaxed, enjoying my beer. I was peaceful as I watched the others eat hot dogs, drink beer, celebrate, and laugh. They hugged and teased each other. I laughed as they good-heartedly ridiculed each other's hilarious physical collapse at the racecourse's finish line. I hoped no one had actually noticed my own body's humiliating crumbling in the boat at the finish.

A tall, attractive, white-haired woman who looked to be in her mid-fifties set a chair beside mine. She extended her hand. "You know they call him the man that would never quit."

I must have looked confused as she leaned back. "I'm Bonnie Huger, Thomas's wife. He likes you a lot."

"He's a real inspiration. I can't imagine what he's had to endure."

She leaned forward. "Paddling with you and his friends in the dragon boat is very important to him. And I've witnessed a renewed hope and energy since you've joined the team. He says you're a great addition."

I raised my eyebrows. "Thanks, that means a lot. How is Thomas doing with the cancer?"

She swallowed hard. "It's come back, you know. I work in administration at MUSC and I've seen the scans. It's beginning to spread throughout his body. But you'd never know it."

Her eyes looked sad and tired. I asked, "And how are you doing?"

She slumped in her chair. "The greatest understatement of all time is when people say cancer changes your life. Thomas's diagnosis hit us both hard. I cried every day for a month. Truthfully, I still cry a lot. I prayed and hoped we'd live a normal, long life together, but now a big part of me realizes I'm sure I'll lose him."

My hands formed a tighter grip on the arms of my chair. "Does the doctor say how long he has to live?"

She ignored my question and gazed out at the water. "He was so successful. A highly respected contractor. He made his way from Pennsylvania to The Citadel, walked onto the football team, and became an All-American."

"He is a strong-minded man," I said.

A tear rolled down her face. "I just can't deal with the injustice of it all. At the time Thomas was diagnosed, an acquaintance of mine was having an affair with a coworker and callously left her husband. I didn't wish her ill, but still it made me angry. Thomas and I were the ones who'd worked hard to have a happy marriage. We were the ones doing the right things, and *my* husband was dying. I mean, come on! Why didn't she get cancer?"

My lower lip quivered in sadness. "I understand. It's impossible to ever know the answer to that inscrutable question—why me?"

She nodded in agreement and placed her hand on my bicep. It was obvious she meant her next words seriously. "Thomas is like an ox. He's so strong." She stopped talking as her eyes darted away. "The night we learned he had cancer; we attended a Spoleto event with another couple. The wife had been fighting cancer for years. She was feisty and funny. Her positive attitude greatly improved my spirits. I learned there was life after a cancer diagnosis. Life doesn't have to be all about cancer, at least not all the time. It was a valuable lesson."

I closed my eyes and slowly nodded. Maybe a higher power had sent her to talk to me. I placed my hand on hers. "A lesson I must learn."

She finally smiled. "Cancer can isolate a person, but Thomas and I have learned we need to be around other survivors. That's the reason Thomas began paddling. He has meltdowns, but he doesn't want anyone to know how bad he's feeling—especially his special team of dragon boat paddlers. Of course, being the closest to him, I realize how sick he is. But even still, rare is the day he doesn't give me a sincere smile."

I was too humbled to speak. Any words got stuck in my throat. I sat quietly, admiring this man of steel.

"All of you have your own horrible struggles, but when you're together as a group, everything seems normal again to Thomas. You know—like before cancer."

I nodded. I understood clearly.

Her smile broadened. Her love for her husband radiated on her face. "The reason I get up every day is because I make a conscious decision not to dwell in either the past or the future. I try to balance my anger and negativity with the hope all will be well, even if it's just for that moment of that day. If I can find that balance, I can make it through the day."

"Thomas is a blessed man to have you as his wife."

"But at times rather than being his wife I feel like his mother. Like most mothers, I nag too much. You know, take your medicine, don't work too hard, you need to go to bed now. When he's sick from the radiation, I take control of everything. I don't want him to worry about anything. Maybe I do this to control my own sense of panic. I'll admit, being the primary caregiver of a person with a chronic illness is not a walk in the park."

Shame overpowered me. I wish I'd possessed just ten percent of this woman's and Thomas's courage.

Bonnie stood. "That's why you need to help this team become a winner. Thomas is counting on you. You brought him hope, something to fight for. He needs you. I need you."

As she stopped speaking, Pat appeared. I stood and gave Bonnie a hug. We hugged for several minutes. She nodded, smiled, and said as she began to walk away, "Please do what you've been called to do."

I didn't want to acknowledge her charge to me, and I refused to take on the weight of the world for everyone else. I had my own battle to win.

Pat sat down in the chair Bonnie vacated. I could tell she wanted to talk, but I was emotionally drained from my conversation with Bonnie. She ignored my apparent exhaustion. "Every three weeks since January I've had to be admitted overnight in the hospital for desensitization and an infusion of chemotherapy. I have two treatments left, and then I start training for the world championship. I need to ask a favor."

After hearing about her bravery, how could I deny her anything? "Sure. Whatever I can do."

"Since I'll be incapacitated with treatments and out of town with the training, I need you to coach the team at the Beaufort races."

I froze. My eyes didn't show it. My face disguised it. But I was afraid—scared as hell to coach again. I said emphatically, "I don't coach anymore."

She pursed her lips. "I really need you to do this. The team needs you to do it."

My blood pressure shot up. "I said *no.* I don't coach anymore."

I couldn't—wouldn't take the risk of coaching this team. Another horrible tragedy occurring under my command would destroy me. The threat of doing harm to one these people was a gamble I'd never chance.

"The team—"

I responded with the anger my father had so adequately taught me. "What the hell about *no* don't you understand?"

Pat's face flushed red. Her jaw muscles clenched. "The team thinks you're this wonderful successful businessman and a great addition to this team. Personally, I just think you're an ass." She stood and walked away.

I knew she was right. I had too much bottled up inside of me. Yes, I was being an ass; she did not deserve my anger. I was relieved when she was gone. I had no intention of ever again being a coach. Especially of a boat full of sick amateurs. Just because the time trials had gone well today didn't mean that we'd be able to hold our own against boats full of healthy, well-trained athletic paddlers.

Maybe joining this team had been a mistake.

7

Charleston

Spring 2009
One week later

As a young boy I watched my mother water and prune the flowers in the front yard of our small house. Through her care of these fragile blossoms, I grew to love flowers. Their sweet scent seemed to act as a switch in my brain that made me relax. Their beauty made me appreciate the small things in life. Their bright colors spoke of innocence—a place to rest.

Amy was my place of solace. She grounded my unreasonable ambition. She brought balance and rest where chaos existed. She was an accomplished artist within the highly talented Charleston art scene. On Wednesdays, she took art classes. So on Wednesdays I not only prepared dinner but bought her fresh-cut flowers. It was my way of expressing my gratitude for which I have no words.

Our bonding through my gift of flowers was why we both love the magnificent gardens of the historic Charleston plantations. Magnolia Plantation and Gardens was our favorite. Springtime at Magnolia reigns with no comparison. The gardens were strategically planned to be informal, designed as a romantic garden and not of the strict formal English style, with acres of vibrant azaleas and rhododendrons. Hundreds of diverse colors and sizes. Deep purple tones and soft lilac colors. The red petals sparkling from the sun's reflection. The pure white blooms appearing to illuminate the entire gardens. As I walked the multicolored paths, the countless sweet fragrances bombarded my senses from all directions.

The bouquet of scents reminded me of an orchestra expertly blending its well-tuned instruments into one perfect sound. The camellias and petunias were like an ensemble of ripe fruit resting in the warm sun. People say beauty has its limits, but I'm not so sure.

Amy and I became volunteers committed to maintaining the beauty of the gardens at Magnolia. Digging in the soil at America's largest-scale romantic garden made me feel as if I was connecting with God's beauty. Losing myself as I worked in the centuries-old cultivated dirt provided a welcome pause to life's stress. I enjoyed learning how to make a plant survive and flourish.

But today would not be one of those pleasant or relaxing volunteer work days. It'd been a week since Pat had approached me to coach the team in Beaufort, and Amy wasn't happy with my bearish and selfish decision. Her lips were pressed tight as she worked in an unusual silence. She avoided eye contact. She wanted me to let go of my past and move forward. I disagreed.

The tension in Amy's body appeared to cause the tall, course cordgrass to lie flat as we walked onto the 180-year-old white wooden Long Bridge. I stopped and stared at the bridge's perfect reflection in the still, black swamp and ignored her obvious frustration.

Amy snubbed my avoidance. "You need to reconsider coaching your dragon boat team in Beaufort. Stop condemning yourself, be willing to make yourself vulnerable, and move on."

I refused to look at her. Experience had taught me her eyes would break me faster than her words. "I told you I'll never coach again. And besides, these people aren't competitors."

She raised her voice. "You're being foolish. What happened wasn't your fault. It was extraordinarily hot. You did nothing different at that football practice than a thousand practices before. And you're also being arrogant."

I rejected her words. I peered from beneath the crown of my hat to see if our fellow volunteers were listening to our conversation. We continued walking through the camellia trail, and I caught the pleasant aroma of the Ashley River waterfowl refuge area. The huge multicolored azalea plants had begun to bloom and created renewed life along the dark waters. Hopefully the amiable scent would distract Amy, and the gardens would again become my refuge. I wanted this conversation to end so I could enjoy the peace of the new blooms and the hush of the fresh spring wind. But as I glanced at Amy and saw her pointed scowl, I knew I needed to respond.

"Amy, he died on my watch. I was the head coach. I was in charge." *You didn't experience the horror of holding him in your arms and watching a boy die*, I thought.

Amy stopped walking. She spoke softly. "I understand your pain."

I snapped as I stopped walking and turned to her. "I'm not sure you do or can. Have you ever held another parent's dying child in your arms? I have no intentions of reliving that moment or coaching a bunch of amateur folks whose bodies are eaten up with cancer and who could die at any moment."

She looked away and exhaled. "Don't be cruel, Tripp."

I bowed my head. "Sorry, but it's true."

We started walking again and were silent for a few moments. As we approached the Cypress Pond Garden, she said, "Those young boys on your team loved you."

I grimaced as I witnessed a few heads turn in our direction.

She spoke with authority. "How many of your players visited you in the hospital when you were sick?"

I stared at the azalea bushes. "All of them."

"And how many of your players attended your award ceremony when you were selected South Carolina coach of the year?"

I refused to look at her. "All of them."

Her voice expressed frustration. "And how many of your players gave you a standing ovation when you approached the podium to give your speech?"

I finally looked at her as we both stopped walking. I gritted my teeth. "All of them."

She opened her arms and held her palms up toward me. "Your players loved you, and you loved them."

My hands shook. "But I failed them. I pushed them too hard. That kid would be alive today if it wasn't for my constant driving."

Amy brushed her body against mine. It seemed, at least for a moment, as if the earth had stopped spinning. It was as if the other workers in the gardens had disappeared, and it was just the two of us standing alone within this imposing sea of flowers. She gently grabbed my hand. I could feel her compassion.

"Sweetheart, no one knew about his congenital heart abnormality. It was a freak accident—it wasn't your fault. Please, for me—coach this team. You need to begin healing. They may not be real athletes, but they need you. Tripp, it's time."

She started walking, pulling me along. We strolled silently through the camellia-lined pathway. We reached the small plot of soil we had been delegated to plant with petunias. We knelt, put on gloves, and began planting the flowers the staff had left earlier that day.

For ten minutes, we dug in the rich black soil and gently placed the plants in the ground. I'd hoped to forget the conversation we'd just had, but Amy's words resounded in my mind. My heart pounded as I thought about her request. What if I screwed up again? What if I pushed the team too hard and hurt someone or—worse—they died? I would never forgive myself. I couldn't take this risk. It would be too painful to relive my failure. And would they be good enough to not just compete, but to win? Losing would not be an option for me. The prospect of coaching again scared the hell out of me. The stress of recalling my past and fearing a repeat caused my tumors to flood my body with serotonin, and my face and head flushed with uncomfortable heat.

Perhaps sensing my panic, Amy broke the silence. "You remember the poem you wrote me as a gift for our first wedding anniversary?"

I hesitated. I nodded.

"What was the first line? Say it. Quote it to me now," she demanded.

"Damn, Amy, I'm not going to quote a poem in front of all these people."

She stood and placed her hands on her hips. "You are not speaking to all of these people. You are speaking to me."

I hesitated. Shit. I stood and looked at her. Her staunch stance and iron-like stare told me she was not backing down. I gave in and spoke clearly, *"Your generous mercy gave me a hope for the future."*

She smiled. "Now have mercy on yourself. Forgive yourself. Humble yourself. Coach this team."

I attempted to stop my hands from shaking. "Amy, I can't."

Amy removed her gloves and delicately lifted her hand to my face. "Don't look at these people as if they're sick and lesser than you and you're reaching down to lift them up to your level. See yourself as one of them, sitting together, holding *one another* up. You are all the same. You are not better, nor worse. Care for them; don't judge them. And stop judging yourself."

I shook my head. "This is a bridge I can't cross."

"Tripp, we have been married over thirty years, and together we raised two wonderful daughters. I've watched you, with great admiration, be gentle and treat them like little queens. But I've also seen you be the biggest jerk in the world. It's like there's a constant war going on inside your head."

Amy's words rang true. The relentless mental gymnastics within my brain to be compassionate, rather than harsh or tender instead of tough, made me insane. Since my youth I'd been a tormented man, pulled in opposing directions. But how could I ever let go of my anger and bitterness? Do I want to let go? These emotions had protected and served me well.

I wondered if a person could truly overcome their deep-seated emotional wounds and defeat the beastly internal scars of their youth? I asked myself—what kind of world we live in if each of us could let go of these haunting past traumas? An intriguing thought. But I wasn't sure I could. Or would.

Amy continued caressing my face. "Trust yourself. If you agree to do this, the strength will come. You may not know from where or whom, but it will come. Please coach this one race for me."

The young boy's face flashed in my brain. My neck and head felt like burning coals. Heaviness filled my stomach. Amy's sincere plea was a knockout punch I couldn't ignore, and Amy's intuition was rarely wrong. I looked at her. "One race. No more."

Her smile grew as she kissed me, but I wasn't sure this decision was a good one at all. My stomach knotted in anguish.

8

Beaufort, SC

Summer 2009

Our dragon boat team left Charleston before sunrise to travel the sixty miles south to Beaufort. After I'd agreed to coach, Pat had thanked me. The nineteen paddlers who'd been chosen to compete had been training with me for three months, and today was the day. I was thrilled Amy decided to attend as a spectator for the festival's activities, and I was especially glad to have her nearby in case panic consumed me once again. Though I'd accepted the decision to coach for this one race only, the underlying terror from the past remained.

As our caravan of cars made the sharp curve onto Bay Street heading to the Chambers Waterfront Park, the sunlight pierced the morning, blinding us. The collection of the sun's colors on the storefront windows reflected a kaleidoscope of lively pinks, effervescent oranges, and grand purples onto the sidewalks. As we parked, the sun's bright scarlet light streaked across the Beaufort River like a laser piercing the shiny water. We paused, shocked and humbled by its glory, then gathered our gear and walked to the water.

The loud pounding of Chinese drums rang in our ears, and we saw women dressed in radiant dragon costumes dancing by the riverfront. Adrenaline coursed through my body. White tents were scattered about the grounds. Paddlers were assembling around their team's tents. They stretched muscles, organized tables of food, and hung elaborate signs with their team's name on the front of their tents. The park area was festive. I could smell the scent of competition.

I slowly walked to the riverfront watching the festival organizers set up the marshaling tent. I crossed the manicured lawn and a white stone walkway to the river front. I stood at a hip-high, sun-bleached concrete column and watched the volunteers ready the boats for the day's racing. A comforting breeze swept across my face. And then I witnessed a marvelous sight. A large colony, maybe a hundred, of ibises were feeding effortlessly in marshes by the water. My heart calmed. A message, as Amy had promised, of faith and hope. I thought our team would need both.

The Beaufort festival was relatively small with only thirty teams competing, and of those, only four club teams that practiced year-round: teams from Charlotte, North Carolina; Jacksonville, Florida; Atlanta, Georgia; and our Charleston team. The Atlanta team was young and considered the favorite to win gold.

The other teams were formed from local businesses, community groups, and friends. They'd gathered a few weeks prior to the festival to practice. Their timing was horrible, and they looked like an army of caterpillars with arms flailing in all directions. But their full-fledged zest to have fun and celebrate life was contagious. I'd later learn these enthusiastic paddlers would raise over thirty thousand dollars that day to assist cancer survivors and their families who couldn't afford healthcare.

Brooke approached me. "This race is Allyson's first competitive event of any kind, and she's scared to death. I think she's about to throw up. Would you talk to her and settle her nerves?"

I grimaced. "That's not what I agreed to do. I'm here to coach teamwork, race strategy, and how to win. I have no desire to get involved with any individual or personal issues. I suggest you talk with her."

Brooke scoffed, flicked her fingers off her chin toward me, and walked away.

I saw Amy frown and lower her head as she overheard the conversation.

We'd practiced hard for three months preparing for this race. Our start was solid, timing was adequate, and paddling technique had significantly improved. And as a coach, I'd been exceedingly careful not to push the team too hard. I was proud of myself. We scattered around our tent area and began to stretch our muscles and mentally prepare for the first race.

I fought to not allow myself to engage with the team's emotional connection and comradery. But the passion that envelopes a paddler toward their teammates is difficult to resist. It begins with enduring 6:00 a.m. practices when we're barely awake. It was built upon the evening practices when we're tired from a hard day's work and our bodies weak from chemotherapy or radiation. It was clear and evident paddling in these difficult conditions made these races hold significant purpose with my teammates.

I was hopeful this motley crew would turn out to be a bona fide team. I'd learned a lot about the sport of dragon boating during the past six months. I'd begun to understand these modern dragon boat races and festivals were emblematic of the cycles of life, raising hopes for things not seen and promises of life and living.

The festivals are based on a traditional reenactment of the race to save Qu Yuan, the much-admired and loved Chinese patriot and poet who was exiled by the jealous Chinese king. He drowned himself in the Miluo River in an effort to bring healing and prosperity to the people of his country. In doing so, he became regarded as a powerful deity. Over the centuries, village fishing boats went out into the river each year on the anniversary of his death in a symbolic search for his body. The fishermen ultimately began to take part in races that over a long period of time evolved into dragon boat racing's present form.

As I approached the docks where the paddlers loaded the boats, I witnessed numerous multicolored long canoes decorated with fierce dragon heads, scaly bodies, and elaborate details. It would be our team of twenty paddlers powering this canoe with all our might for 250 meters against fierce competition. I wanted to win. I was beginning to understand why dragon boat racing is one of the fastest-growing water sports in the world. Anyone can do it—even a group of cancer patients or a community group that only practices for three weeks. But the true distinctiveness was the lifelong friendships and support that developed.

As our first race drew closer, I pulled the team together for a famous Tripp Avery motivational speech. Although I had been reserved in my coaching, I knew the value of the inspirational talk before the clash of battle and was a master at carrying a team into competition. It fed the competitive hunger in my soul. I sensed today was going to be one mad, wet adrenaline rush! We stood in a circle, paddles in hand, and I lowered the octave of my voice to express a calm seriousness. "Relax and focus. In the same manner we took one practice at a time to prepare for this race, we'll win by focusing on one paddle stroke at a time. Bury your blades at the start. Look straight ahead. Concentrate on upper body rotation, forceful leg drive, and a hard pull through the water."

The team's focus pleased me. They hung on my every word.

I raised the volume of my voice. "Keep your heads in the boat. If you look at the other team, you're looking at the winner of the race. Think of nothing but performing one perfect stroke after another."

I rubbed the sweat off my brow. "Remember you compete using your soul as well as your body. Relax your body. Don't tense up and calm your mind."

Of course, staying relaxed is probably the most difficult part of the stroke. Especially when you feel like a sardine wedged into a narrow dragon boat with nineteen other paddlers.

I took a deep breath. A surprising calm transcended my anxiety. The next words I hadn't planned. "And have no doubt of how proud I am of you and how privileged I am to be your teammate and your coach. Let's gather close and high-five."

We formed a tight circle, extended our paddles so the tips of our blades touched, and then we screamed as loud as we could, "Dragon Survivors!"

The voice over the loudspeaker called for the teams in our first race to marshal and prepare to load the boats. It would be our first of the day's three races. As a team, we were led by one of the event's marshalers to the dock and carefully entered the canoe in our assigned seats: The stroke paddlers were in the two front seats; the big men were in the middle of the boat, called the engine room; and our smaller paddlers with perfect timing in the back. After a few minutes, all twenty paddlers including me sat quietly on the wooden benches in the colorful boat.

Each team provided their own drummer, but the festival organizers provided the steersperson. Our drummer, a friend of Pat's, was a small woman with a fierce voice. The less weight the better. She sat facing us on a wooden seat in the front of the lengthy skinny canoe. The steersperson stood in the back, holding a long wooden steering oar. I breathed deeply to calm my nerves.

The steersperson yelled, "Push off." With that command, we pushed the canoe away from the dock with our paddles. "Paddles up. Take it away." We paddled slowly in perfect timing toward the starting line.

At the starting line, the race official expertly ordered the four boats racing to line up. We were racing against three corporate teams, so our odds of winning were high. We'd practiced the starter's commands many times. "Ready, ready. We have alignment!"

Our canoe came to a stop at the starting line. Our upper bodies were extremely rotated forcing our backs to face the river's bank and our chests toward the paddler sitting next to us. Our paddle blades buried in the water. The starter's commands blared, and there was a loud blast of the starting pistol. As one, our team groaned and pulled our paddles through the water for our initial stroke. We were off to a good start. As we reached the halfway mark. I couldn't see another boat in my peripheral vision, which meant we were far in the lead. As we crossed the finish line, we celebrated our team's first race and our first victory.

We paddled back to the dock, exited the canoe, and walked back to our tent. I don't remember a step. It was like I floated back, experiencing complete satisfaction with the win. I knew there was much more difficult competition ahead. But for now, I was going to savor this victory.

Sitting underneath our tent trying to recover physically and prepare for the next race, I studied the Beaufort waterfront, with its beautiful brick walkways and wooden gazebos. Enticing restaurants lined the walkways with inviting outdoor eating areas. One of the better restaurants was called Saltus. Legend has it that a gracious, wise older Romanian gentleman who immigrated many years ago and a sagacious local Black man hold court every evening at the bar to share their combined wisdom with anyone who'll listen. I thought I might one day visit their courtroom and learn a few of life's valuable lessons.

The announcer finally called our second race. As we entered the marshaling area, I saw the times posted for all the first races. Currently, we had the second fastest time of the day. The Atlanta team had bested us.

This second race was important as the four teams with the best combined times of the first two races would compete in the final race of the day for the festival's championship. In addition to our team, this heat consisted of two corporate teams and the Jacksonville club team. They'd be gunning for us. We needed to paddle harder.

The sound of the pistol cracked. We had another good start. But the Jacksonville boat began dead even with our canoe. My heart pumped. I forced the blade of my paddle deeper into the river. I pulled the paddle back through the water with greater intensity. I increased the force of my core muscles and pushed harder with my legs. At the midway buoy, we were neck and neck with the Jacksonville team.

Our steersperson screamed, "Finish!" Our boat surged forward and took a small lead. With each stroke we gained an inch. When we crossed the finish line, we were a few feet ahead of the Jacksonville team. I was too exhausted to celebrate.

We'd qualified, along with the other three club teams, to compete in the final race for the festival's gold medal. As we rested, we were quiet. I closed my eyes and visualized each stroke of the final race. I wanted to win.

So far, I was pleased with my coaching. I hadn't pushed the team too hard, but I could sense the old coaching demon coming back to life. I needed to resist. This sport was recreational and not professional. But damnit, I did want to win. I didn't coach losers.

Our third and final race was announced. As we paddled to the starting line, I yelled, "Stop the boat." Everyone stuck their paddles deep into the water to check the boat. "I want to practice the finish. Let's paddle ten strokes, I'll yell 'finish' and I want ten more hard, deep, focused strokes. Give me more rotation, and I want you to drive your blades deeper than ever into the water. And I better see this boat surge forward."

The steersperson yelled, "Paddles up. Go!"

We paddled ten strokes and I yelled, "Finish!"

It was a beautiful sight. Heads looking straight ahead.

Paddlers twisting their bodies in an abnormal motion to achieve maximum torso rotation. Paddle blades jabbed deep into the water as if they were trying to kill that great white shark. The boat rushed forward with a powerful jolt.

I yelled, "Let it run." The canoe stopped with everyone high-fiving. The team was laughing and emboldened with confidence. We were ready to compete.

We paddled to the starting line. The starter lined up the four boats. The pistol blasted. We experienced our third good start of the day. As we passed the fifty-meters buoy, we were in second place, barely behind the Atlanta team. Fans as well as the paddlers from the other boats stood on the river's battery wall and screamed. I heard the announcer's voice blast through the speakers calling the race. At the halfway marker, we were half of a boat length behind.

Our team had settled into a strong rhythm. Our boat surged with each stroke. An increased determination enveloped our team. It flowed through the boat like a still river. I heard no noise except the rustling of water from my teammate's paddles pressing through the river. We gained on the Atlanta team.

The steersperson yelled, "Finish!" Our canoe seemed to float on the water's surface racing toward the finish line. The Atlanta team's steersperson's voice intensified and became louder as he screamed at his team to paddle harder.

We surged at the finish line, but it wasn't enough. We finished a strong second to a much younger and healthier Atlanta team. But I was proud of myself and my coaching. I could not have been prouder of my nineteen physically compromised but determined teammates.

After this final race, the crowd dispersed, everyone rejoicing in life and reveling in friendship. I walked along the waterway's brick path. Storm clouds were building at sea and heading our way. Whitecaps began to emerge on top of the river. Gusts of wind scattered trash left behind by the paddlers and fans. When I stopped walking, I turned and studied my teammates. Sean, who hadn't healed enough to paddle, was slapping everyone on the back. The team had wide smiles and gave each other big high-fives. I paused and whispered a prayer of thanks.

9

Charleston

Summer 2009

The successful Beaufort performance was encouraging. But the team's next decisions and actions were critical. I approached the team's next practice with excitement and dread. I wanted to celebrate with these courageous folks, but I was apprehensive about being viewed as their coach.

The team was at a crossroads. Would they commit themselves to even more disciplined practice and to winning? Or, would they become satisfied with the previous accomplishment and settle into complacency? And, if they were to become a truly competitive team, they'd need a coach—a leader. That crucial person wasn't going to be me. I hadn't decided yet if I'd remain as a paddler either.

I'd been exceedingly clear with everyone the Beaufort race would be my first and last time coaching. I remained only to be a paddler and a strong competitor.

As I approached the dock for the first practice after the Beaufort races, most of the others had already assembled at the boats. They splashed water on each other and had wide smiles. The team had put their heart and soul into the Beaufort races. They'd worked hard. They deserved to be proud and celebrate their success. Their broad, welcoming smiles gave me a strong sense of satisfaction.

Brooke rushed toward me, wrapping her arms around my chest. "What a great event. I'm so proud of our team." She smiled, "Simply blissful."

I frowned. Sporting activities are mechanical and objective. You do the work, you win. You have the discipline—it pays off. It's definitely not blissful. As she released me from her gracious hug, Sean and Pat approached. I looked at Sean and asked, "You doing okay?"

Sean's energy and determination were hard to hide. "Stronger than an acre of garlic."

I laughed. He looked good. I could hardly believe he'd had major surgery less than a year ago. He was slim and fit. I envisioned him having no intestines, with muscles cut from his legs supporting his internal organs. And here he was standing before me. Damn, I needed his courage.

He slapped my shoulder. "I'm ready to practice, coach. We have more races to win."

I felt the alarm rise in my bones. I ignored the coach's comment. "You sure you can paddle? How about your colostomy bags?"

He rolled his eyes and chuckled. "Never count me out, buddy. I had a seamstress make a special belt, like a girdle, that secures them in place. Hell, yeah, I can paddle. Let's load the boat."

I looked at his midsection. His shirt fit perfectly. He looked no different than any of us. I peered into his eyes and shook my head in disbelief. As he proudly pounded his chest, Pat stepped close. "I hear you did a great job coaching in Beaufort."

I offered a half smile. "I did okay."

"The team loved you. Everyone's feedback has been positive," she said.

Sean stepped closer and stood beside Pat, his eyes shifty. "Pat and I have been scheming. We think this team has a shot to win the Grand Masters Mixed category at the national competition next summer. And—we want you to be our coach."

I stepped back and raised my voice. "I made it clear I'd coach in Beaufort but no more. What the hell is the national competition?"

Pat said, "The national races are sponsored by the International Dragon Boat Federation. It'll be held in Chattanooga, Tennessee, next July. We want to compete in the Grand Masters Mixed division, which is twelve men and eight women all over the age of fifty."

"Like I said, I'll paddle, but I'm not coaching."

Pat said, "Sean and I believe if we work hard enough, we have a good chance to compete for gold. And if we win, we earn the opportunity to represent the United States at the international races in Hong Kong the following year. It would be a great honor and an amazing experience for a team like us."

I raised my voice. "That's my point—'a team like us.' We're sick, weak. How could we compete against a healthy team?"

Pat's lip quivered. "Because we have heart. We will be sustained by our hope. No one lives forever. But together we can be unshakable regardless of our circumstances. You coaching gives us a chance."

I pointed my finger at Pat and felt a vein throb on my neck. "I was very clear when I told you I would not coach the team after Beaufort. I am not interested."

Sean stepped closer and pointed his finger at me. "It would give us all something to fight for, and you'd be a great coach. Don't be a complete piece of crap."

During my short time as a cancer survivor, I'd experienced people with cancer say what's on their mind. Maybe their filter had been removed with the surgery or dulled by radiation. Or maybe, they figured time was limited and precious and they needed to get on with life. Regardless, piece of crap or not, I wasn't going to be the team's coach.

"Call me an ass. Call me whatever the hell you like. I'm not coaching."

"Okay, asshole," Sean said as he walked away.

Pat was more diplomatic. "Please agree to think about it. Tripp, we need your expertise and your experience. You could help us win."

These people wouldn't quit. No wonder they're called survivors. "Sorry I've confused you. Instead of no, let me say *hell no*."

Pat waved her hand in an angry, dismissive manner. "Let's load the damn boat," she said as she walked away.

Good, I thought. Now I can do what I came to do. Paddle, mind my own business, and get some exercise. What's the hell is wrong with that?

As we paddled away from the dock my anger increased. Why

should I be made to feel like the jerk? I did what I agreed to do. I honored my commitment. And did a hell of a job. No, they're the jerks, not me. Hell, I'm the one that deserves to be upset.

With each stroke, I paddled harder and stronger. I grunted as I pulled the blade of my paddle through the water. I forced my leg muscles to push hard against the bottom of the boat. I twisted and thrust my core muscles harder than ever before. I felt the vibration in my teeth with every stroke.

I repeated to myself: I'm not the jerk here.

As we finished practice and unloaded the boat at the docks, I grabbed my gear, spoke to no one, and left. I was angry—no, pissed. Angry with the team, incensed with Sean and Pat for asking me to coach. How dare they make me feel like the bad guy. Make me look like an ass to my teammates. Now everyone hated me. It was humiliating. Fuck them.

But I was mostly angry with Amy. She was the one who convinced me to coach in Beaufort. I knew it was a mistake. And I was right!

10

Charleston

Summer 2009

My body jerked upward in my bed with a searing pain. I grabbed my gut as I glanced at the clock on the nightstand beside my bed. It read two o'clock. What the hell? I tried to take a deep breath but couldn't. Pain bolted through my abdomen. I tried to yell and wake Amy but only a half-muffled cry emerged.

I grunted as my hand shook Amy's shoulder. I thought my liver was exploding inside my body. Waves of pain jostled through my gut and into my back and shoulders. Amy wrapped her arms around me. Her eyes were full of fear.

"What's wrong, honey?"

Ten seconds passed before I answered, as I couldn't breathe.

The words finally squeaked through my lips. "It's my insides. I'm hurting inside."

"Can you stand?"

I slipped from my bed and stood. The pain was harsh and defiant. I bent over and grimaced.

"I'm taking you to the ER." Amy grabbed my pants and slowly helped me slide in a leg, then another. I couldn't straighten up long enough to put on a shirt so she slid a sweater over my head.

She parked the car in front of the Medical University of South Carolina emergency room, and two men helped me from the car and onto a gurney. The pain rippled from my midsection and through my body. A nurse slid a needle into my left arm and attached an intravenous line. She stuck a needle into the IV, infusing Dilaudid into me, and within seconds my head became warm. A soothing wave of euphoria enveloped my brain. The pain stopped.

The ER physician took me to the radiology imaging department for an MRI. Although the room was cold, my trembling fingers rubbed sweat from my face. I looked around the room, but my eyes couldn't focus.

The technician instructed me to remove my belt, rings, and any metal objects in my pockets. He asked me if I had any hidden body piercings or tattoos. The effects of the Dilaudid made me laugh and tell him I had my wedding ring pierced through my belly button and an image of my wife tattooed on my left scrotum. He didn't appear to appreciate my humor.

He told me to lie on a table and asked me what kind of music I liked. I told him the seventies. He gave me ear phones to wear. I heard Karen Carpenter begin to sing, "We've Only

Just Begun," as the table began to slide my body into the oblong tunnel-like machine. The heinous contraption vibrated and banged as the humorless technician instructed me when to hold my breath and not move.

After about twenty minutes, he said he was dispensing a contrast liquid through the IV in my arm. I felt the fluid flow through my veins. It seemed to stop in my crotch area. I felt the urge to pee. I swished my tongue inside my mouth as it tasted like I'd just eaten a twelve-ounce steak made of tin foil. I could sense the magnetic protons flowing through my liver.

About thirty minutes after I returned to my small cubbyhole of a room in the ER, the doctor entered. He told me my tumors had begun to grow aggressively, and he'd scheduled an appointment with my oncologist for the following day.

***

Amy and I sat in a small examining room at my oncologist's office. He'd been treating me for several years, and since carcinoid tumors typically grow slowly, he'd adopted the watch-and-see approach. Before today, my tumors hadn't grown and I'd felt lucky. But I should have known better.

He entered the room with a smile. Well, maybe the results of the MRI scan weren't all that bad. He was highly trained—a Johns Hopkins grad, well-dressed, and articulate. Everything you'd want in the doctor who was responsible for your life.

Or—maybe not.

"Your tumors have significantly grown," he said.

I bit my lip as I asked, "Can I see?"

He pulled up the scans on the computer screen and pointed to a tumor located in the top-right quadrant of my liver. "It's doubled in size—it measures over seven centimeters, or about the size of a small grapefruit."

Amy started to cry.

He pointed to other large tumors in different sections of my liver. "There's fourteen large tumors and many smaller ones. The tumors are in all eight quadrants of your liver."

I held my breath before I spoke. I handed him a white three-ring binder. "I've been doing some research and have compiled information regarding several possible treatment options. Detailed information of each treatment is in the binder. What do you think?"

Amy stopped crying and leaned forward to listen as he thumbed through the pages in my binder. He narrowed his eyes in skepticism and handed the binder back to me. "I'd suggest you go live the rest of your life as best you can."

"What the hell does that mean?" I asked.

He slid his chair closer to me. "Mr. Avery, you have too many tumors in your liver. No one will treat you. There comes a time when you must choose quality of life over quantity of life."

Amy began to cry again. He handed her a tissue.

Bullshit!

I clenched my jaw and pointed at my binder. "None of these treatments are options?"

"I'm afraid not. You simply have too many tumors in your liver to treat."

My hand holding the binder began to tremble. My eyes rapidly blinked. I could smell the sweat easing through my skin. I wanted to grab him by the collar of his starched white jacket and beat the crap out of his condescending, sneering face.

But instead, I stood, gently grabbed Amy's hand, and led

her from his office. We sat in the car, silent, not looking at each other, for what seemed like an eternity. I finally spoke. "We're going to find the man or the woman that can help me. The specialist that understands this disease and how to treat it. They're out there. Fuck that doctor. I'm not giving up."

We looked intently at each other. "Listen carefully to me," I said. "If I'm breathing, I'm fighting."

I could see the determination and hope return in her eyes. She squeezed my hand to communicate her agreement. I pulled my chunk of brick from my pocket and rubbed it. I said in a low, confident voice, "You and me, Amy, we're going to grow old together."

***

The next day, when the sun on the Ashley River hadn't yet risen, I sat in my single outrigger canoe and floated as the current took me. I couldn't see the river's bank, but I could smell the pluff mud that filled the marshes and estuaries. I peered at the moon. It was almost full. I remembered the first time my mother pointed out the beam of silky light from the full moon illuminating the backyard of our small, dingy mill house.

She told me the moon pulled the waters of the earth toward it every day. She taught me water was the source of life. As long as I had water, I could live. As long as I could see the moon, there was hope.

I needed hope this morning.

I'd become a cold man. Stubborn and obstinate. Could I now become a different man? It was like the river that ran through my soul had dried up. Muddy and murky. It smelled. A dolphin blew water into the air as he swam by my boat. The euphoria I experienced a year ago when I saw a dolphin swimming gracefully in the river didn't happen.

I knew the chambers of my heart. I wanted to do the right thing. But I was afraid.

I could see the young boy's face as I held his dying body. The face of a determined but small and fragile sixteen-year-old boy. His eyes stared at mine. Acne had scarred one cheek, but he was handsome. His brown hair was wet from running during the afternoon's football practice. He struggled to breathe.

As a successful high school football coach, I pushed my players hard. I knew what it took to win, and I always won. My teams had won state championships, and I was committed to defending that title. The South Carolina August heat turned a football uniform into an enclosed heated oven. It could be unbearable.

I had two weeks before school began to chisel away the summer fat and laziness from their bodies. Three practices a day. In the morning, we practiced offensive plays and blocking techniques. The early afternoon practice, we drilled defensive skills and schemes. Late afternoon practices were reserved for perfecting our kicking game and for physical conditioning. As Vince Lombardi said, "Fatigue makes cowards of us all."

That day's practice had been grueling and the heat exhausting. We finished practicing punts and started running wind sprints. The kid just collapsed. Without notice. The little guy was all heart, even if he had little skill. He gave one hundred percent effort on every play.

The EMS personnel pulled the young boy's body from my grasp. His head swung back as he peered at me. The usual shine in his eyes was gone. I knew his primary desire was to make me—his coach—proud. The vision of his eyes peering at me will never fade from my memory. My hope of making my mark as a successful coach or, more importantly, a good man was forever dashed that hot, sweaty afternoon.

The walk from the field to my office was like a dead man's walk to the gas chambers. I felt like I'd vomit. I bent over as if my guts would erupt from my mouth. Nothing came out. Only the despair that rushed into my body. One of my assistant coaches wrapped his arm around me and helped me into my office.

The young boy died the next day. My ambition and persistent hard-driving coaching killed him.

One week later, I quit as a coach. I continued to build my wall of anger and bitterness to protect myself.

Now I have an aggressive cancer. My world had turned on a dime. Would I die without redemption? I longed for forgiveness. Would God give me another chance? An opportunity to atone for my sin and restore my soul?

As I slowly drifted in the twilight, I reflected upon the strangest of scenarios—a group of people whose bodies are being eaten alive with cancer wanting me to coach them to win a national dragon boat championship. God does work in mysterious ways.

Could it be my path to redemption?

The sun rose and I sat motionless in my canoe. I saw nothing. I smelled nothing. I only sensed the hand of God guiding my life. The heat from the sun soothed my damaged spirit.

I'd take these frail bodies, who otherwise had no chance in hell of winning the national championship, and who might or might not survive the journey of physical discipline, and mold them into a group of winners. And maybe my soul would find peace.

I'd be their coach.

My deliverance came to me in the most unexpected manner. It arrived in the murky waters of the Ashley River in the blade of a carbon fiber dragon boat paddle. But mostly, in the faces of determination in each of my sick friends.

Maybe I'd found the deliverance for the agony within my soul.

11

Charleston

Summer 2009

The large wooden outdoor table in my backyard, together with Amy's steamed crab legs, created the perfect setting for my meeting with Sean, Pat, and Thomas. I'd informed them of my willingness to coach the team at the national dragon boat competition and invited them over to talk through the next steps and, though they didn't yet know it, to establish a few ground rules.

Learning to crack open a crab leg so the delicate reddish-white meat remains intact is a generational skill taught to young Charlestonians. Pulling a three-inch-long piece of succulent meat from the hard-shelled leg without it falling apart requires skill—a skill that, once mastered, would earn a person passage into the historic snobbish Charleston society.

Amy set a large metal pot of steaming hot crab legs in the middle of the table as the four of us sat down. We immediately grabbed a cluster except for Thomas, who couldn't eat. I pulled a long leg from the body, cracked it open, and graciously slid out a long, tender piece of crab meat. I dipped it into a cup of hot butter and ate as butter dripped from my chin.

I cleaned my mouth with a cloth napkin and spoke. "I've decided to coach your dragon boat team at the nationals in Chattanooga. But I have a few rules that everyone must agree to follow."

Pat asked with reservation, "And what would these rules be?"

As everyone stopped eating and stared intently at me, I spoke with conviction. "I have three rules."

I hesitated, to ensure everyone was listening carefully.

"Rule number one: I will not be a counselor or a team therapist. I'll not get involved with anyone's personal issues. I'll teach the team how to win. I'll coach paddling techniques, race strategy, and the winning attitude."

Everyone nodded, as they resumed cracking open crab legs.

"Rule number two: I'll accept no excuses. All of us have cancer or have survived cancer. Some of us are still undergoing aggressive treatment, but we know this fact going in. Cancer cannot be used as an excuse for not winning or working hard."

"I think that's extreme," Sean said. "They'll be times when some of us will have problems attending practice. If we've had a high-dose radiation or an intense chemo treatment, we'll be sick. You can't expect us to attend practice when we're sick."

I peered into Sean's eyes. "We'll practice every Tuesday morning at six o'clock, Thursday afternoon at six o'clock, and

Saturday morning at eight o'clock. I'll accept no missed practices and especially no excuses for not giving the team your best effort. If I coach, I'm coaching to win. We'll be competing against teams of healthy people, so we have to train like them too. I'm not interested in a moral victory that a team of sick people did pretty well but won nothing. If you're looking for the mercy or pity from the other teams—I'm out. Understood?"

Pat pointed her finger at me. "I'm not going to agree to allow you to place anyone's life in danger. Do you understand?"

Everyone stopped eating and awaited my response.

My jaw muscles tightened. I flashed back to fifteen years ago. No one but Amy knew the true reason I'd resisted coaching this team, how my past haunted me. Pat's comment was merely intended to protect her teammates, nothing more. I'd need to be careful not to drive this team too hard. A twitch in my gut screamed *don't coach this team. Don't take this risk.* I thought about leaving the table and walking away from it all.

But then I surprised myself by realizing how badly I wanted—no, needed—to coach them to a victory.

I continued: "I'm not an idiot. I acknowledge all of our lives are in jeopardy. I won't put anyone's life in additional danger. But I'll not accept a half-ass excuse from anyone for not giving it their all for this team to win." I stared at Pat in challenge, waiting for her response.

She pressed her lips together with a slight frown but nodded her agreement.

Amy touched my arm and quietly said, "You'll be just fine."

"Your third rule?" Thomas asked with a faint whisper.

"As the coach, I'll have the final say. I'll not accept anyone questioning my decisions."

"Pat and I are team captains. Are you saying—we'll have no input?" Sean asked.

I leaned forward, "I'll give fair consideration to your thoughts and suggestions, but there can be only one head coach. The final decision will be mine, and it'll not be questioned."

Everyone sat quietly. The crab legs cooled.

"Do you agree to my rules?" I asked.

"I agree," Thomas said. "As an ex-athlete, I understand there can only be one head coach."

Sean nodded. "I agree."

I looked at Pat. She leaned back and crossed her arms over her chest. She peered at me as if her words were coming from the pits of hell. "I agree, but don't you fuck up and hurt someone."

Amy reheated the crab legs as we made small talk, and as soon as she returned with the pot of hot crab legs, everyone began to eat again. I mulled over Pat's comment, and it terrified me.

Amy recognized my anxiety and wrapped her arms around my shoulders as if to communicate that everything would be okay. Her touch calmed me.

But I continued to ask myself that horrifying question: *Would I fuck up again and hurt someone?*

12

Charleston

Summer 2009

Brittlebank Park at five-thirty in the morning was silent, and the only light came from the stars. The curved trunks of the centuries-old grand oak trees provided a resplendent cover, some with a girth of twenty feet or more. Reflections from the trees' branches pirouetted in the moonlight over the still waters of the Ashley River like dancers behind a silk screen. These oak trees were symbols of strength and held many stories of Charleston's history in their leathery bark. Could my dragon boat team create a majestic story for these grand trees to tell future generations?

I stood by the bank, rehearsing my first motivational speech, which would demand total commitment from this team.

Without warning, my heart raced. I grabbed a towel from my paddle bag and whipped the sweat from my face. I struggled to breathe. Why in the hell had I agreed to do this? To again—be a coach?

Was it because I had metastatic cancer and might die? Or was it because Amy had pushed so hard? Or because I loved the challenge of turning underdogs into victors? I reminded myself that my lifelong selfish agenda needed to change—today. I couldn't wait until tomorrow. How many tomorrows did I have left? For once—I needed to do something good for others and not myself.

I secured my brick necklace under my shirt. It had become a symbol of my motivation, pushing me to achieve—to prove my worth. The necklace was my brick of bitterness, the bitterness that protected me. I needed it to survive.

I grabbed my paddle bag and water bottle, and slowly walked toward the marina where our boats were docked. The team was present. Sean and Thomas were lying on the dock stretching their leg muscles. Brooke waved. Pat looked away.

"Welcome, Coach," Brooke said, smiling.

We hugged. "How are you doing?" I asked.

"Wonderful," she said with a wider smile. "I'm having a chemo-vacation, and I'm taking advantage of every second. I feel great today, and that's all that matters."

I stood in the middle of the dock. "Would everyone please gather around?"

They sat on the wooden planks in a semicircle in front of me. I looked beyond them and over the water toward the horizon. The rising sun was increasing in size and brightness. I heard the brown pelicans splashing water as they dove headfirst into the river, snatching a herring for breakfast. The golden ray's warmth caused goose bumps to rise on my arms. The sun typically brought me peace and solitude—but not this morning.

I began my speech. "You've asked me to be your coach. To help you win the Grand Masters Mixed national championship next summer in Chattanooga. Do not be confused. If we go, we go to win. But the winning starts now—this morning. We're a team, one unit, and we will practice as a team."

I hesitated to emphasize the harsh message of my next point. "You need to ask yourself: Will you be satisfied with being just a good team, or will you force yourself, through the pain of difficult practices and the agony of our disease and treatments, to be a great team?"

I took another breath. Everyone's eyes bored through me as they analyzed each word.

"Let me leave no doubt. We've all been dealt a raw hand. But I will accept no excuses. Cancer isn't an excuse. Pain is no excuse. Treatment, chemo, radiation is no excuse. Each of you were fully aware you had cancer when you asked me to be your coach."

No one spoke or moved. Not an eye blinked.

"This is not about me. It's not about you or even the team. It's about winning the gold. If you're not willing to commit one hundred percent to this goal, you are free to leave. Don't waste my time or yours. I will not allow you to humiliate me or your teammates in front of thousands of spectators."

Thomas stood. He could barely speak. His muted and whispered words were difficult to hear. Everyone was silent. You could have heard a pelican's feather drop onto the dock. "I'm all in, coach. I have cancer, but it will not rule my day. This day belongs to me, and I belong to this team. Cancer may steal my life, but I'm ready. This may be . . . my life's final victory."

His subdued and sincere words about dying jarred me. My vision blurred as I thought about holding the dying young man in my arms fifteen years ago. A tightness roiled my stomach. My face and neck flushed from the serotonin charge my liver leveled at me. But I didn't know any other way to coach except to coach to win.

What if I failed these people? Caused them harm?

Pat stood and confidently said, "We're a team of twenty individuals becoming one. I'll never quit. I'll never give up. Like Thomas, I'm all in."

Witnessing the commitment on the face of each paddler, I felt the heat of fear within my body loosen its grip. I needed to accept the leadership of these courageous people. My voice steadied and became confident.

"Let's load the boat."

After each paddler sat still, erect, and confident in their assigned seat and for the first time as the permanent coach of the team called the Dragon Survivors, I announced, "Paddles up! Take it away!"

***

Practice was going well. The team's timing during the warm-up was close to perfect. We'd just completed twenty minutes of endurance paddling and began to practice the race start. The start was called the "6/16." It began with six long, hard, slow but powerful strokes to propel the deadweight of the stationary dragon boat forward. The stroke rate was significantly accelerated for the next sixteen strokes. The goal was to plane the boat and reach top speed by the sixteenth stroke.

We rotated our torsos over the canoe's gunwale, buried our

paddles deep into the water, and prepared ourselves to begin the first start practice. I yelled the start command. Several paddlers were out of timing for a few strokes, but all in all, it was good. We checked the boat to come to a dead stop; I gave the commands. The first six strokes were perfect, but then suddenly the boat went afoul. Paddles clanging against paddles.

Thomas had stopped paddling and abruptly leaned back. He yelled and grabbed his waist with one hand. The teammate behind him fell forward, and his paddle rammed against Thomas's back. Thomas slammed his fist against the side of the boat. It sounded like thunder. Pain and anger ripped across his face.

The team stopped paddling as Thomas pounded his paddle against the river, splashing water throughout the boat. He beat his clenched fist against his leg. I jumped three rows of seats and wrapped my arms around him. He was trying to scream, but very little sound emerged from his surgery-reconfigured, deformed throat. I could scarcely hear his words, "Why me? Why me?" He violently shook and hit me in my gut. I felt the power of his strength with each punch.

I held his shoulders tight against my body. With all my might I tried to calm him. He collapsed into my lap. As he cried, I saw a small clear tube that was typically hidden beneath his shorts shaking across his legs. A viscous fluid dripped onto the bottom of the boat. His feeding tube had become unattached from his body.

His muted words continued. "Why me? Why me?"

I held him as close to me as I possibly could.

That was the question we all had asked ourselves.

"Why me?"

13

Charleston

Early Fall 2009

The buffeting ocean breezes in the Charleston Harbor were beginning to change directions. The gusts were building out of the East and slapped against the tugboats that rested in their berths at Ports Authority's large terminal dock. The river's channel, which forged between Fort Moultrie on Sullivan's Island and Fort Sumter in the harbor was filled with huge ships and monstrous barges, transporting goods and supplies from the world to be unloaded and dispersed to the citizens of our country. The trade winds in the North Atlantic Basin were blowing in the change of the season and, with it, the prosperity that fueled much of the Carolinas.

Also changing, our dragon boat team was transforming from twenty independent paddlers into a synchronized effort, working as one to achieve that perfect stroke. It had become a joy to watch and participate. The team seemed healthy, including Thomas. Twenty people's paddles were orchestrating like the brush on an artist's canvas, completely in sync. We were becoming focused on one thing: winning the gold medal at the nationals.

And in the same manner, I'd made significant progress finding a potential treatment that could shrink or possibly destroy my tumors. Over the summer, Amy and I had consulted with numerous physicians and hospitals, including a week-long liver-transplant evaluation at the University of Nebraska Medical Center in Omaha.

After much conversation, reading, and my being poked and prodded, we decided that Peptide Receptor Radionuclide Therapy or PRRT, which was only available in Europe, was my wisest option. A hospital in eastern Germany, where a physician had been instrumental in developing the technology, appeared to be my best choice. I'd sent the doctor my MRI scans in hopes I'd be a candidate for the therapy.

My optimism in our team's progress and the promising prognosis of my cancer offered hope. The abyss of despair my pessimistic and depressing oncologist had inflicted upon me was slowly escaping my thoughts. I now gratefully anticipated the delights that arose with each day. Especially this day.

Thomas had gotten all twenty Dragon Survivor teammates sideline passes for The Citadel football team's season-opening home game. The Bulldogs were playing their in-state rival, Furman University from Greenville, South Carolina. The prospect of watching an excellent college football game only a few miles from my house was enthralling. I was also captivated with Furman University; although a strict religious Baptist institution, all their fans wore shirts and sweaters emblazoned with the initials *FU*.

I loved football, and to have sideline passes was a real treat. I began playing football when I was eight. I tried out for the mill village team where I lived. These linthead football teams were notorious for sporting fast and strong players who relished playing rough and dirty. One family, the Connors, dominated my team back then. The oldest brother, Donald, was a former star high school running back who had risen to be head coach. The middle brother, Ray, had replaced his older brother as the current ace high school running back. But word around the town was that the youngest brother, David, was the true rising star, possessing sensational talent.

I was small and skinny but quick. My uniform was too big and fit loosely. I had to pull my padded pants high up on my stomach and triple-roll the waistband downward so they'd not suddenly drop to my knees. The helmet they'd given me was so large, it could swirl around my entire head without stopping. I felt like the demon-possessed girl in the movie *The Exorcist*. I stuffed extra socks in the sides of the helmet so it would stay in place and protect my head. And also so I could see. I walked onto the practice field all suited up and ready to be the next Johnny Unitas or Dick Butkus.

The coach seemed reluctant to play me, as I think he thought I was too small and would get killed. He knew my dad was a real hothead and would be in his face if I got injured. So, he positioned me in the defensive backfield as far away as possible from the action. But I had no intention of not participating in the battle that was to come.

The offense huddled and the coach called a play. The quarterback took the snap from the center and handed the ball to Ray, the middle Connor brother. He broke through the defensive line like he was walking through butter and was headed my way. I rushed toward him, instinctively squared my hips, wrapped my arms around his legs, and brought him, falling on top of me, to the ground. The coach appeared stunned and squinted his eyes to see who'd just tackled his star running back.

The next play was the identical off-tackle run. The same stellar Connor running back again rushed past the defensive line and headed my way. Just before we were about to make contact, he firmly planted his right foot into the ground and pivoted to the left trying to fake me out, but I moved with him like I was his shadow and repeated my tackle.

The star running back grunted with frustration as he lifted his body from the ground. Donald, the coach, walked to me and asked, as if he didn't know who I was, "What's your name, son?"

"Tripp Avery," I answered.

He patted my helmet. "Keep up the good work."

I continued to tackle well that day and for many years to come. Unlike most of my friends, football was easy for me to play. I was never afraid of hitting hard or getting hurt. I had a natural ability to see and understand the plays as they developed. I eventually played in college and went on to coach high school football. I still loved being around the coaches and players, and Thomas's tickets to The Citadel sideline were a special treat.

As a military college, The Citadel had many long-standing traditions. One especially distinctive ritual was the marching of the entire cadet student body from their barracks and into the stadium prior to the game.

With fervor, Thomas led us to the corner of Hagood Avenue and Congress Street to watch the ceremony. He fervently waved his arms forward to herd us, his teammates, to the exact place he wanted us to stand so we'd have a prime view of the parading cadets. He grabbed Pat's hand as if he was about to separate her shoulder and pulled her along behind him. She could barely keep up with his pace. His body seemed to swell in delight as we gathered around him.

Brooke grabbed my hand and squeezed as we heard the melodic chanter of the college's Regimental Pipe Band's bagpipes. The instruments created both a shrill and a soothing sound. The band wore blue-and-white tartans as they were led by a strutting, kilted drum major. He wore a colorful Highlands feather bonnet and high-stepped like he was superior to the entire viewing crowd.

Maybe he was.

The cadets walked over the baby-blue Citadel bulldog paws that were painted on the black asphalt of Hagood Avenue. The dulcet bagpipes were followed by the rat-a-tat, rat-a-tat, ratta-tatta-tat-tat procession of drums and the rest of The Citadel's marching band.

Our entire dragon boat team stood silent and watched the enchanting parade. Especially Thomas, who was now flanked by both Pat and Allyson, with their arms securely wrapped around his waist. We wore huge smiles and gave each other mighty hugs as we swayed with the music.

The loud sound of coordinated, highly polished shoes marching on the hard, black road grabbed my attention. Behind the band was the procession of the entire Citadel student body, organized by battalions and dressed in full uniform. Their legs, covered with white linen trousers, moved in perfect harmony. Their brass buttons were highly polished, and the officers' dark-blue cloth coats with shoulder straps of black velvet were neatly pressed, exposing not one wrinkle. The pageantry was led by a vaunting student captain whose shoulder strap sported three additional embroidered gold Palmetto trees, the South Carolina state tree. Hundreds of alumni lined the streets and saluted as the cadets passed.

The cadets marched into Johnson Haygood Stadium and onto the football field as the national anthem began to play. We followed them onto the field. The stadium of twenty thousand fans stood in reverence. I sang the words of our nation's great song with devotion, gratitude, and pride. The scene was holy.

Not that anyone noticed, but as the music stopped playing, I respectfully bowed to the crowd of worthy patriots to express my heartfelt appreciation and admiration. The endorphins of thankfulness spread through my body. It was great to be alive and in this grand stadium with my dear friends.

As the game began, I stood next to Thomas on The Citadel's sideline. His expression was stoic. It was obvious he missed his younger glory days of being a college football star. The screaming fans sat down on the metal bleachers. All but one group of young baby-faced cadets. I punched Thomas's shoulder. "Why are those students still standing?"

He chuckled. His words struggled and were muted. "Freshmen. Nobs. Must stand until we score."

I laughed. I love these military rituals—the rites and traditions that created lifelong bonds between these proud men and women. There's an understanding around Charleston that if you're wearing The Citadel ring, you've got automatic entry into many clubs, events, and other activities. The cadets maintained close unions, with tentacles that stretched far into the world.

The Citadel led at halftime. As the band played, Thomas waved for us to follow him into the inner belly of the stadium. We walked through a gate and underneath a sign that read LETTERMEN ONLY. This was going to be fun. We'd walked for about five minutes when Pat finally asked, "Where the hell you taking us?"

Thomas kept walking, never turning to look at us as he waved his hand instructing us to follow. We ultimately stopped in front of a nondescript gray metal door. Thomas thumped on the door in a manner as if his little knocks were sending a code to someone on the other side. After a few seconds, the door swung open. A large burly man wearing a Citadel hat and a broad smile stood in the opening. He reached out his arms, grabbed Thomas, pulled him forward, and gave him a big bear hug.

As they hugged, the large man screamed as if he was speaking to a crowd of a hundred people. "Where the hell you been, you old Cadick?"

Thomas frowned; obviously it was a nickname he didn't approve of. The man weighed about two fifty and had arms like an elephant. I figured an ex-offensive lineman. He stared at Thomas's large entourage and jovially asked, "You got friends now?"

The words struggled from Thomas's throat. "Some of my best friends." Thomas pressed the index finger of his right hand into the man's chest and looked at us. "This is my buddy, Brent."

Brent's voice boomed. "That's right, I'm Brent, Tommy boy's old roommate; and as his blocking right guard, I saved his life more times than a swarm of rabbits having sex." Brent stepped back, opened the door wide, and with his thick hand waved, welcoming us into the room. "You're a friend of Tommy boy's, you're a friend of ours."

About a dozen thick-necked guys sat around the room on leather couches and recliners. A banner hung on the wall above a well-stocked bar that read: THE FOOTBALL FRATERNITY. A closed-circuit TV displayed The Citadel's marching band on the field. Each man stood and hugged Thomas as we walked through the room. Their respect for the ex-star running back was obvious and heartfelt.

The room was about the size of a large classroom and was dimly lit, with Citadel paraphernalia covering the walls. It possessed a sweet odor like that of an Irish bar. A white-clothed table overflowed with chicken wings, assorted vegetables, chips and salsa, and of course the southern staple—boiled peanuts.

A handsome middle-aged man wearing khakis, a heavily starched Cutter & Buck sport shirt, and a perfectly pressed blue Citadel vest approached us. He looked as if he could be the world's greatest insurance salesman. He stared at Pat. She was a striking woman. Tall, with shapely long legs, and a smooth, appealing face, she stood upright, exuding confidence. As he walked by her, he asked with a flirty coy voice, "Maybe you and me ought to get to know each other."

Pat lightly tapped him on the shoulder with her hand as if he was a little boy and smiled. "Oh, that is so cute, dude, you actually thought you might have a chance with a person like me, didn't you? Tell you what, give me a call on February 30th and we'll talk."

The guy hesitated, squinted his eyes, and shook his head.

"Huh, what date is that?"

Pat chuckled as she turned away.

Allyson snuggled close to Pat and whispered, "You go, girl."

A loud, coordinated laugh erupted from the men in the room toward their embarrassed and rejected buddy. They yelled, "Busted!" as a small but muscular guy sitting on a couch ordered his obnoxious friend to "Sit the hell down and shut the hell up, asshole."

Thomas whispered, pointing at the guy on the couch. "That's Sparky. He was an All-Conference free safety. He's small, but when he hit you, it felt like a Mack truck."

A heavy man, sitting in one of the leather recliners, with a bulging gut that flooded under his shirt and over his pants pointed toward a large, white refrigerator that stood all alone in the rear corner of the room. He instructed me with a gruff voice, "Have a beer."

I opened the refrigerator door and gawked. The refrigerator had no shelves, no freezer compartment, and contained no food. Its only occupants were a tall skinny silver keg and a stack of thick, frosted mugs.

The large man saw the look on my face and laughed. "Grab a cold mug and fill it up. It's our own brew. Pure nine percent. No pussy beer here. Got to be a man to drink this shit."

As if it had been rehearsed, the men in the room raised their glasses and said in unison, "Cheers and welcome to TFF."

I filled the stein to the brim with beer as foam overflowed the glass, and took a large swig. I nodded and smiled at Thomas. "Good stuff."

The fat man stood, laughed louder, and slapped me on the back.

I felt like I'd walked into National Lampoon's *Animal House.* I anticipated the Blues Brothers appearing at any moment.

The entire team filled their mugs with "The Football Fraternity's" homemade brew. They rearranged their seating and brought out some metal chairs for us all to sit. We sipped beer and watched the TV as the game's second-half kickoff had just taken place.

I liked the TFF. These fraternity brothers welcomed us with open arms. They laughed and joked with each other. These men had been friends for a long time, and it was obvious they knew each other's every wart and flaw. But they were safe in this room. There were no leaks or betrayals.

By the end of the third quarter, I'd refilled my mug several times with the excellent nine percent beer. My head was beginning to spin. I relaxed, allowing my body to sink into the hefty cushions of the couch.

The heavy man with a gruff voice pointed at Thomas. He then looked at Sean and me. "I like you guys. You're not a lightweight like ole Tommy Boy. He could never hold his beer. He'd give us a buick every Friday night his freshman year. As a nob, he'd puke before he'd get two glasses down."

Given his difficulty speaking, Thomas had developed his own personal sign language in order to communicate. He stood and crossed his right forearm over his left forearm with his hands pointing in opposite directions. With his right hand, the hand on top, he held out his index and pinky fingers to simulate the head and horns of a bull. With his left hand, which was underneath, he flapped his fingers up and down as if something was flowing out of the bull's rear. I laughed. Thomas was calling bullshit on his friend's accusation. The entire room exploded in laughter like a pack of hyenas.

The football game ended with a Citadel victory. I'd drunk

more than my fair share of the strong TFF beer. I forced my eyes to stay open as my head spun when I closed them. The fraternity brothers, one by one, hugged each other and staggered out the door mumbling The Citadel's slogan about honor and duty. My dragon boat teammates had left except for Pat, Brooke, Allyson, Sean, Thomas, and myself. We were now all alone in the TFF room. It wasn't like me to allow myself to get close to anyone, and I'd promised myself I wouldn't get emotionally attached to this team. But there was something special about that moment. I looked at each one of my friends and proclaimed, "My famous last words: let's have just one more."

They laughed as we each poured one more glass of beer.

After draining our mugs and pouring yet another, we staggered out of the grand private room of The Citadel's Football Fraternity and ventured onto the football field. The fans had left, and the stadium was empty. We slowly ambled to the middle of the field and collapsed on the fifty-yard line, silently drinking our beer.

The sun was setting over the horizon of the Charleston skyline. The smorgasbord of brilliant colors sobered me. The bright, blinding, orange orb glowed from the base of the earth's horizon, directly into our faces. Piercing rays of sunlight punctured through the clouds like sharp knives. The sky was lit up with vivid shades of orange and purple colors. I felt liberated and safe, with no thoughts of cancer.

As the sun was ending its long daily journey, I thought in the same manner that my new friends and I might be coming to the end of our journey. But one thing I knew for sure—that final day would not be this day. Nope, at least for this evening, the setting sun filled our hearts with a magnificent hope and possibility. A needed pause from our beastly world of disease and treatments.

Thomas stood—barely, wobbling. He started singing one of The Citadel's fight songs. It was the loudest I'd heard his voice.

"All Hail to the Bulldogs,
March to victory
Long live The Citadel, so proud are we.
And yield, we will never.
We're Blue/White forever.
We will fight, we will win, we will conquer in the end,
A Bulldog triumph today."

Brooke's speech slurred as she screamed, which was totally out of character for her normally highly composed personality. "Thomas, what the hell did you do with that money?"

Thomas's voice was gone. He whispered. "What money?"

"The damn money your mama gave you for singing lessons," she screamed.

Thomas fell to the ground with a thud, as we all laughed.

Pat and Brooke stood and wrapped their arms around each other's waist. Their bodies swayed as they announced, "We're going to sing a real song." Their words slurred as they began to sing the national anthem.

"O say can you see, by the dawn's early light,
What so proudly we hail'd at the twilight's last gleaming . . ."

As the word *gleaming* left their lips, they both fell backward slamming onto the thick green sod while continuing to hold firm to each other's waist.

Brooke declared with confidence, "That didn't hurt."

We all fell back on the thick soft turf, lying on our backs with our arms outstretched above our heads. In all my days of coaching, I'd never witnessed such a deep sense of fellowship and team spirit. I listened as my friends horse-laughed. It was cathartic, medicine to our souls. I wanted the night to last forever.

Taking turns, we told stories of our pasts, our families, and youthful embarrassing moments. I cherished every word. The sun had set beyond the horizon, and as the dark consumed us, we stopped talking. No one moved a muscle. We lay there, soaking deep within our spirits our bond of friendship. We just wanted to be together and experience a golden moment of peace and hope.

Sean sat up and broke the silence. "We are brothers and sisters."

Each of us struggled to sit up. We smiled at each other. No one spoke for several minutes.

I slowly peered into the face of each of my new friends. I studied their eyes, smiles, and wrinkles.

In an atypical expression of outward emotion, I said, with the resolve of a man about to go into battle, "No, closer than that."

14

Charleston

Fall 2009

Pride, silly pride. The slayer of kings and the destroyer of noble causes. My pride pushed me, and I pushed my team. During the two months since our successful Beaufort race and our bonding experience at the Citadel football game, the team had begun to lose focus, and I was concerned but conflicted. My teammates were showing signs of weakness and exhaustion, and getting sloppy at practice. The grind of training along with the radiation and chemotherapy poison being pumped into our bodies—was winning. They were discouraged.

I'd relentlessly pressed forward with my win-at-all-cost approach to coaching. Was I pressing too hard? The memory of holding that dying young football player in my arms, of seeing visions of one of my teammates dead in my arms, haunted me, trapping my thoughts in a constant battle of guilt and responsibility.

The Dragon Survivors was a group of sick folks facing a showdown with cancer, a ceaseless master. All we really desired was to live a normal life, to have healthy families, successful careers, and security. But cancer was a deadly thief in the night, and it was now stealing not only my team's health but their willingness to work hard, their hunger to win, and even their belief that they can.

When I was ten years old, my grandmother was diagnosed with stomach cancer. No one in the family spoke about it. It was the cruel, dark secret at family get-togethers and holiday dinners. Her illness and treatments were a huge charade between my elder family members and her doctors. My parents, aunts, and uncles whispered as they discussed her disease as if dying from cancer was a shameful, clandestine event. It appeared my grandmother was completely absent from the decisions that would affect her life.

Receiving a cancer diagnosis in the 1960s was basically a death sentence. It was like being a leper, something that brought humiliation to the family. Maybe the person had committed a great sin or had been cursed by the devil. When my family visited my grandmother's home, I felt like I was already attending her funeral.

In those days, early detection and effective treatment was highly unlikely. Chemotherapy poisoned the entire body, the treatment possibly worse than the disease. I remember my grandmother vomiting almost every time she entered the room. But she was fearless, and I never heard her complain. She never allowed the shame my family members felt to affect her, and she addressed each day with an unadulterated grace. Today, I could have used a huge dose of her poise and bravery.

The fall evenings had cooled from the Lowcountry summer heat, but my agony over coaching had intensified. I sat alone in my home office and covered my face with my hands, attempting to hide my anguish. I was angry with myself for agreeing to be this team's coach. I was angry with Amy for pushing me.

Amy entered my office bringing me a glass of wine. She recognized my distress, and her voice soothed with love as she asked, "What's wrong, sweetheart?"

My hands trembled as I removed them from my face. I tried to stop the shaking but couldn't. Like my grandmother's apparent lack of control over her treatment and life, I felt I was losing control of my future. "I'm scared shitless. I need to quit coaching the Dragon Survivors. I need to stop now."

She sat beside me. "What's wrong, honey? What's brought this about?"

I felt like I'd just swallowed a lead pipe and could barely talk. "I warned you what would happen. You pushed me to coach this team against my will. I told you it wasn't a good decision. Didn't I tell you that?"

She slid closer and tenderly clutched my hand. "Yes, you did. So, what's wrong? What's happened?"

"The team is getting physically weak. These people are really sick. The last several practices have not gone well. Two weeks ago, Pat, who is our lead stroke paddler, would set the correct stroke rate, but then she'd lose focus and slow down. Since everyone follows her stroke, the whole team's timing was awful."

"Is she getting sicker?"

"I spoke with her about it, and she told me since starting her new round of chemotherapy she was having difficulty focusing through her mental fog. She said she'd recently forgotten her mother's birthday, and she worships her mother."

"Chemo brain. Her body should adapt to the new treatment. And the exercise will help," Amy said.

"Those high doses of chemo are tough on the body. After our last practice, I pulled her aside, and we spoke alone. I told her I'd be willing to spend some one-on-one time with her, practicing some focus exercises. I think the concentration drills I did with my football wide receivers would benefit her."

"How did she respond?" Amy asked. "I know at times she's been harsh on your coaching techniques."

"She actually gave me a hug. She seemed to appreciate the individual attention."

"Good. That should make you feel better."

"I'm afraid she's not the only one struggling. Both Sean and Thomas appeared to be very weak. During the 200-meter practice race, I yelled 'Finish,' and their arms looked like spaghetti strings. The boat actually lost speed. I began raising hell with the entire team. And now I'm pissed at myself for losing control and not realizing what was actually happening."

Amy gently rubbed my shoulder. "They're just tired. It's been a long year, and you all have pushed your bodies to your limits, even you. The team will bounce back. Just you wait and see."

"We have less than a year before the Chattanooga races, and we're not ready. I don't intend to lose, and I will not be humiliated. I emphatically told them they weren't working hard enough, their teamwork sucked, and it was unacceptable. I told them to get mentally tougher and physically stronger—no matter what. I firmly reminded them they'd asked me to be their coach—not the other way around."

I stopped speaking as my throat constricted with fear. I forced the words, "But every second I coach, I'm terrified someone will get sick or even worse—die."

Amy hugged me.

"For these people, maybe skydiving on acid would be safer than having me as their coach. I'm quitting. I'll tell them at practice today. Pat can be the coach."

Amy sighed. "Pat can't coach the team. She's preparing for the national team tryouts. Tripp, there's no way she can do it."

"Well, they'll need to find someone else."

"Honey, you know that's impossible at this late date. You're doing great. It's only natural that you question yourself. It'll be okay."

The insidious fear kept creeping up on me. I deeply regretted agreeing to coach this team. It wasn't fair for me to again be placed in this dreadful situation. I questioned if I even had the energy to attend tomorrow morning's practice, much less be the coach. The muscles in my body felt weak, fatigued. I was tired.

Amy softly placed her hands on either side of my face to force me to give her my full attention. "You remember the first time I submitted a painting into a juried art show?"

I nodded.

"And was my painting accepted?"

"No."

"Was I upset?"

"Yes. And you said you'd never paint again."

Her voice became firmer. "And it was your insight that forced me to keep painting. You told me I was a natural-born painter, that being an artist coursed in my veins. You told me I couldn't quit painting even if I wanted to because the hand of God had made me an artist. You do remember those words?"

She sat back and crossed her arms. Her face was stern.

I looked down and bit my lip. Rubbed my eyes. Massaged my temples with my fingers. I then looked up and stared at her perfect face. She was an amazing woman.

"So, you can't quit coaching, either. Like art with me, coaching courses in your veins. You couldn't quit coaching even if you wanted to because the hand of God has made you a coach. And besides, these people are your friends. They're sick with cancer, and they're depending on you to lead them."

I knew her words were true, but her comment gave me the opening I was waiting for to defend my decision. "I have cancer too."

Amy rolled her eyes and sneered. "Don't you dare pull the C-card on me. You can't have it both ways. You can't demand everyone treat you normal like you don't have cancer and then pull this crap."

I stuttered, "Anyway, we may be going to Germany soon for PRRT. It looks like I'm an excellent candidate. The radiation may make me too sick to paddle."

Amy waved her hands in the air dismissing my comment. "Even if we go to Germany, Dr. Aldrich clearly told us you should be recovered enough to paddle and coach. I rarely swear, but you're talking pure bullshit."

I resisted making eye contact as I knew she was right.

Amy grabbed my chin and forced me to look at her. "And what was that courageous statement you so boldly told me when the scan showed your tumors were rapidly growing?"

I tried to shake my head free from her hands but she held tight. "You know what I said."

"I know exactly what you said, but I think you've forgotten. Tell me."

I breathed deeply and sighed and spoke the words. "If I'm breathing, I'm fighting."

Her grip on my chin strengthened. "Now, say it again, like you mean it."

My voice was firm and clear. "If I'm breathing, I'm fighting."

Amy stood and placed her hands on her hip. Her voice forceful. "Don't you ever pull that C-card sympathy crap on me again. We're in this battle together. It looks like we'll be going to Germany soon for treatment, so there's tons of hope. I've walked every step with you, and neither one of us is going to quit. Don't you get into a pity party. Understood?"

The intensity in her eyes shocked me. Amy typically hated confrontation. I felt ashamed.

"Understood?" she asked again, raising her voice.

I nodded and tried to smile. But she was right. I couldn't quit coaching the Dragon Survivors.

***

I gathered the team at the dock prior to loading the boat. They needed to regain focus and commitment, and be reminded to believe in themselves. Our timing was off, and our strokes through the water were weak. We sat in a circle as I began to talk. I briefly reminded the team that they'd agreed to no excuses and that they'd asked me to coach them to victory. But I wanted my words to be an uplifting speech.

"The audacity of your goal of being national champions is

almost unbelievable. The conviction in your hearts is unmatchable. The courage that dwells within your bodies amazes me. You, my friends, are the bravest people I've ever met."

My teammates' eyes wandered. Their bodies sat on the dock more listless than usual. I wasn't commanding their full attention. I raised my arms to emphasize my words. "Let's not shrink from that goal or our courage. I welcome—no, invite the coming tests. Your work and sacrifice must be greater than any team we'll compete against in Chattanooga. But that sacrifice will rule the day.

"I have confidence in each of you. Together as a team we will prevail. But it will be your inner resolve that'll place us on that stage, winning gold. Do you have that resolve?"

My teammates nodded. But I wasn't convinced. They stood and then moved slowly into their seats in the dragon boat. Their legs and arms looked anemic. As we pushed away from the dock, I knew something was wrong.

I wanted to practice a new race start I'd watched a Canadian team perform on YouTube. It might give us an advantage at the nationals. It was much faster than the 6/16 start. And significantly more difficult.

After our warm-up and a few paddling technique drills, I yelled, "Check the boat."

The boat slowly stopped in the middle of the Ashley River. I stood. "I want us to learn a new start. It'll help the bow of the boat to settle and plane on the surface of the water earlier and could cut seconds off our time."

Everyone listened intently.

"The first three strokes will be full and strong. I want complete rotation of your torso. As you await the starter's commands,

I want your paddle blades completely buried in the water and your legs coiled, ready to explode backward. When you hear the horn, give me three full, hard strokes.

"The next six strokes are shorter and faster. They are half strokes and are called ups. We'll do three sets of these six ups. Then we'll transition into our race pace with a strong half stroke, a stronger three-quarters stroke, and finally a very strong full stroke."

The eyes of half the team glazed over.

I pumped my fist in the air. "We can do this, team. Let's give it a try."

Everyone nodded in obedience.

I sat down and repeated the start instructions. "Ready, ready."

Each paddler rotated their torsos and fully extended their arms, holding the paddles above the water well in front of them and outside the canoe. The A-frames looked great. Everyone awaited my orders. I called the race start commands.

"We have alignment."

We buried the blades of our paddles into the murky river. I blew my whistle as the command to start. The first three full strokes went well. As we began the fast-ups, we lost timing, and I heard several paddles clanking against each other.

I screamed, "Check the boat." The boat came to a stop.

I yelled, "Damn it, team, focus. You can do this. Let's give it another try."

I gave the commands and blew the whistle. The first three strokes again were perfect. The first six ups went well. But as soon as we launched into the second set of ups our timing vanished and, as before, paddles clanged against each other.

"Damn it!" I yelled. My frustration boiled over. "Stop the damn boat. What the hell is wrong with you guys? Your concentration is for shit. And you think this team will win the national championship? I don't think so."

Sean stood in the middle of the boat. "We're exhausted. Brooke just started a new round of radiation. Pat is undergoing extremely high doses of chemo. I push myself through pain and the weakness in my leg where the surgeons removed leg muscles to support my gut. Not to mention the rest of the team's cancer crap. You're pushing us too hard."

I stood in the boat. "My tumors are also growing. I'm going through treatment. I told you, when you asked me to be your coach, that I would coach to win. We've all got cancer, including me. And what excuses did I say I'd accept?"

"Fuck you!" Sean screamed, his eyes bulging. "You're pushing too damn hard."

I was taken aback by Sean's coiled intensity, but reflexively, I held firm. "We all agreed—no excuses. Cancer cannot be an excuse. Pain cannot be our excuse. We have no excuses—only the will to win."

Brooke sighed. I could tell she agreed with my statement, but her body was weak. "I'm tired and don't feel well; can we paddle back to the dock?"

I ignored her. "You asked me to coach you to win the national championship. This is how we do it. We paddle through the pain and discomfort. Is everyone on board?"

Sean sat back down and threw his arms above his head in frustration.

"I warned you I'd coach to win. Is everyone on board? Are we a team?"

Everyone lowered their heads and gazed at the bottom of the boat. Their lips pressed tightly together.

"Are we a team?"

Each team member, including Sean, nodded.

I screamed, "Ready, ready!"

Their bodies looked frail as they attempted to rotate their backs.

"We have alignment."

My team's lifeless effort to bury their paddle blades in the river finally convinced me it was time to end this practice.

"Okay, let's head to the dock. Paddles up, take it away."

After we unloaded the boat, Pat grabbed my arm and pressed her finger hard into my chest. "You'd better lighten up on my teammates." She squinted her eyes to make sure I understood the seriousness of her words. "These people are my family. I promise you'll live to regret it if you don't."

I jerked my arm away. "You do want to win, don't you?"

She stepped back. Peered at me. "You truly are an asshole."

As I watched her walk away, I couldn't disagree.

15

Charleston

Late Fall 2009

The night before our team's next practice I wandered along the sand of the eclectic Folly Beach, located twelve miles south of Charleston. Amy would join me in an hour, and we'd grab a bite of dinner.

The rising moon hung low along the sky's horizon and illuminated the pearlescent white sand. The ocean's waves were less daunting at night. The rippling water effortlessly flowing upon the dark, isolated beach fashioned a majestic and peaceful oasis. I heard the hum of a boat motor in the distance and tasted the cool salty mist that hung in the air.

During the day, the pristine beach and surrounding waters bustled with life. They were filled with busy tourists from all over the country, vibrant and diverse locals, fishermen trolling for mackerel, and shrimp boats dragging their outstretched nets to snare the tasty crustaceans. People living energetic and purposeful lives, surrounded by the serenity of the waters.

I felt neither serene nor energetic as guilt swathed my spirit from my harsh treatment of my teammates. But I'd just received a glimmer of hope. The medical team in Germany had approved me for PRRT therapy; my scans verified my tumors possessed a high infinity for the somatostatin analog drug octreotide, which would transport the radiation to my tumors and hopefully destroy them.

As I walked, my thoughts turned to the team. I'd hoped coaching the Dragon Survivors would give me purpose, but my only focus was the team's lack of motivation and effort. My anger provoked the serotonin levels to increase in my bloodstream and caused my head and neck to flush red-hot. My tumors were in full bloom. Why in the hell did I agree to coach this team?

I considered apologizing to the team for my outburst at practice. Maybe I should have been more sympathetic to their physical challenges? After all, I'd lived with the fatigue radiation brought, the pain of intense chemotherapy, and the ever-present danger of an internal infection.

Apologizing didn't come easy for me. My father taught me many hard lessons. One of his teachings was to never, ever apologize—not to anyone for any reason. He preached admitting you're sorry was a sign of weakness, and a real man never exposed his weakness. I never heard him apologize to anyone, especially to me, although he'd fully expect an apology from me or anyone else who'd offended him.

He once beat my sister with his belt for an hour until she apologized to him for what he called "talking back and being disrespectful" Like him, she never apologized to anyone, that I heard. Yes, the fruit doesn't fall far from the tree. And I was another fruit from that tree. In my soul, though, a spring of forgiveness was emerging to break this devastating cycle of hatred and bitterness that'd plagued me since I was a young boy.

Yet the team all had agreed—no excuses. And I'd communicated clearly, I only coached to win. I would not apologize.

Amy's smile seemed to light up the dark beach as she walked toward me. She held a basket in her right hand and a red blanket stuffed under her arm. She set both on the sand, and we embraced. I held her tight against my body. She stared into my eyes. Her love was overwhelming.

"What's in the basket?" I asked.

"Dinner. I thought we'd have a picnic on the beach. I made two turkey Reubens, which I know you love, and a pasta salad with your favorite green olives."

"Sounds wonderful."

"And wine." She pulled a bottle from the basket as her smile widened. "Nickel & Nickel Chardonnay."

"You've done very well," I said.

We walked to the dunes and spread the blanket over the sand. I poured two glasses of the buttery wine. But I couldn't hide my surly mood.

"You look distressed," Amy said.

My jaw clenched. "Just pissed about this dragon boat team."

Amy handed me a plate with a sandwich and salad as she spoke. "I ran into Sean this morning at Harris Teeter, and he told me the team had a meeting last night."

"Good. Maybe they'll get their attitudes right for Saturday's practice."

Her mouth tightened as she spoke. "Don't you think you should lighten up on the team a bit?"

I sipped the wine. My voice became loud. "They asked me to coach to win, and that's what I'll do. And I'll not let this team embarrass and humiliate me. As my dad taught me, the first rule of nature is self-preservation."

Sorrow covered her face as she slowly placed her hand over my hand. "You've been tormented for a long time. Your father was a . . ."

My voice became louder. "Don't go there, Amy."

Her voice matched mine. "You need to go there. We need to go there. He was cruel and callous—a broken man."

"My father did what he had to do to survive. He made me tough. I appreciate that."

Her grip on my hand stiffened as she lowered her voice: "You must deal with this obsession to win."

I pulled my hand away as I gasped, "This obsession to win has provided pretty damn well for us."

Her eyes misted. "Have you really ever lived one happy, satisfied day in your life? Tripp, you need to let go of this crazed compulsion to win at any cost."

I stood and yelled, "So it's all my fault? I came to the beach to clear my head, not be criticized. What . . . you made dinner so you could blast me and my family?"

Amy stood and walked a few feet away from me toward the ocean. "I don't like how you're speaking to me, and I want it to stop right now."

"It'll stop all right."

I'd heard enough. I packed the basket, folded the blanket, and walked away.

16

Charleston

Late Fall 2009

I arrived early for Saturday morning's practice. Brittlebank Park was dusty and not well maintained. The city had recently installed colorful playground equipment, but otherwise, the park was depressingly desolate. I sat alone in my car. I tried to ready myself to coach this morning's practice. The thoughts in my mind were fighting. Should I apologize to the team for my earlier outbursts?

Stepping from my car, I smelled the primordial odor of pluff mud and the fish-tainted Ashley River. It was an odor many find offensive but one I've grown to love. The river was the cradle of life for the many crustaceans and fish. The great salt marshes existed to support the vast systems of rivers. The swamps leading to the marshes acted as filters, sanitizing the winding waters of the Lowcountry rivers.

Daily, the tides of the river ebbed and flowed. Just as the sun rose and set—nothing stood in its way. No one started it, and no one could stop it. The rivers cleansed the earth. I trusted the river. For me, the river's great current carried hope and courage. The ancient waters whispered into my soul: You can do it. You can survive.

Walking down the path toward our dragon boat, I noticed the entire team was sitting serenely on the dock. They were quiet. Everyone peered at me as I approached. I'd decided I wouldn't apologize. "What's going on?" I asked as casually as I could.

Sean stood. "The team met and decided we needed to embrace you as the coach. I need to apologize for screaming at you during our last practice. We all apologize for our lack of focus and commitment."

Pat followed him and spoke in her typical no-nonsense manner. "We, the team, have made a decision. We want to win the national championship, and we will be more focused. We'll rededicate our commitment."

The moment was electric. The Charleston fall air was unusually arid, and the humidity hung in the air like a thick morning fog, making my shirt cling to my chest. I started sweating and stared at my team sitting on the dock. Their obedient submission to my unyielding will stirred painful memories of my days as a high school football coach.

My heart hammered within my chest, and I trembled inside as I remembered holding that dying young body in my hands. I could not disappoint these people—my teammates, my friends.

The fear of failure fluttered in my gut. My stomach clenched and cramped as I considered the responsibility just bestowed upon me by my devoted team—the Dragon Survivors.

Sean grabbed my arm and hugged me. "Enough of this apologizing crap. Let's get in the boat. If we're going to be national champions we need to practice."

The practice was excellent. The team paddled with commitment and enthusiasm. Three dolphins swam around our boat, spewing water from their blowholes. Their smooth, streamlined bodies led us effortlessly through the water. I watched a pelican dive-bomb for a fresh morsel of fish. The stars in the sky had given way to the rising sun. I was convinced a higher power had moved through the threads of my team. After practice, we drifted with the type of exhaustion that brought complete satisfaction and allowed the warmth of the rising sun to revive our tired bodies.

I'd decided not to attempt the fast-paced race start again this morning as I was pleased with the team's practice. Everyone had paddled hard. Each paddler's rotation was perfect, their paddle blades completely buried as they pulled them hard to their hips.

We'd stopped paddling and as the boat floated in the river, I tugged on my brick necklace that was my dad's reminder to never again allow anyone to humiliate me. Bitterness and the fear of humiliation had ruled his life. As Amy had said on the beach the previous evening, he was cruel and callous, a man whose heart had been turned to stone by the harsh rejections of life. Was I to be like him?

I realized for this team to win the national championship; I'd still need to be brutal in my coaching. Could I correctly manage that fierceness? Could I temper my intensity, or would I destroy myself and the team in the process?

After practice, I tied our boat to the dock, but no one exited. I wondered what was happening. Brooke stood from her front seat, hesitated a second, smiled, and then proudly announced. "At our team meeting, we also decided we needed to have a fundraiser to pay for our Chattanooga expenses. Many of us don't have the funds to pay for an entire week on the road."

I said, "No one's mentioned needing money before. I could help."

Brooke said, "That's why. We don't want you to pay."

I laid my paddle on the dock and slowly placed my hand under my chin as I stared at my teammates sitting quietly in the boat. "Okay, and what kind of fundraiser do you have in mind?"

Everyone chuckled. Brooke blushed. Thomas shook his head as if he couldn't believe what was about to be said.

Brooke threw her head back and shook with laughter. "We want to create a calendar to sell as a fundraiser."

"Okay?" I said wondering what this craziness was about.

Brooke smiled. "And use us, our team, as models."

"Really," I said laughing. "And why would people pay for this calendar?"

The team laughed as Brooke answered, "Because we'll all be naked."

My laughter roared. "Are you serious?"

Allyson stood. "We're dead serious. Cancer can't stop us. These bodies are going to take us to victory, and we're proud of them. I have a good friend who owns a printing company and said she'd have us photographed and the calendar printed in just a few weeks." Allyson smiled like a kid opening a Christmas present. "We'll sell the hell out of them."

"Is everyone on board with taking their clothes off?" I asked, in a manner to communicate I had no intentions to take off my clothes.

All heads nodded enthusiastically.

Allyson screamed, "And you'll join us."

Damn! How could I say no? "Well, then let's get naked."

I was elated by their initiative. I was happy with my response. The team had double downed on their commitment to refocus and to win in Chattanooga. My candle of despair was beginning to burn dimmer. The anxiety in my gut relaxed. "So where will we shoot these model-perfect nude photos?"

Pat said, "A different setting than the Lowcountry. One of my old college roommates has a house on a small private lake in the North Carolina foothills of the Blue Ridge Mountains. She's a novelist, and it's her place of solitude where she goes to write. It would be an ideal venue."

I stood, slapped my thigh, and laughed. "Well, let's do it. You've been working hard for the past year and are in good physical shape. I think we'll look great naked."

"I'll line it all up ASAP," Allyson said.

"I'll call my friend. Pick a date and I'll reserve the house," Pat said.

Allyson did a little dance that caused the boat to rock. I thought the boat would flip over. The vibrations of her boisterous voice seemed to skip across the still waters of the Ashley River and across the Charleston peninsula like a smooth pebble.

"Get ready, world, the Dragon Survivors are about to get naked!"

17

Lake Lanier, SC

Late Fall 2009

Lake Lanier was a small, private 130-acre lake that rested in South Carolina just at the North Carolina border. It was like no other lake I'd experienced. The actual lake bed is owned by the county of Greenville, South Carolina. The water that flows over the dam is owned by the small town of Tryon, North Carolina, and provides the drinking water for the town's residents. Individual property owners hold the deeds of ownership of the land that borders the lake, even down to the water's edge.

There is no government entity that has legal jurisdiction to control the lake's water or the land that surrounds the lake. Therefore, the owners do as they like. One very distinctive trademark is the colorful boathouses that were built to extend out over the water. It looked like little Sweden hidden in the glory of the surrounding Blue Ridge Mountains.

The public has no access to the lake, and the only boats allowed on the water belong to the landowners or their invitees. And the tiny lake has no restrictions regarding the size of the boat or motor. If you could get your big-ass bass boat on the water, so be it.

We arrived early at the home of Pat's friend, Mary Beth Malone, and a cool mountain breeze welcomed us. The wind whispered through the tall pine trees and mixed with the chatter of my teammates. The lake's water was black as coal. The brilliant rich foliage of the large elms, grand oaks, and smooth birch trees created a kaleidoscope of color radiantly reflecting off the dark water's still surface.

The mountains' fall morning air was crisp and clean. I breathed in deeply, closing my eyes and welcoming the sharp contrast from the hot and humid Lowcountry. An orchestra of singing birds filled the trees and sang their song to the lone boater in the middle of the lake. I could stay here forever.

The home's backyard sported a breathtaking custom-built infinity pool. The pool's water sparkled like diamonds in the rays of the rising sun. The vanishing edge created the stunning illusion of the pool's water flowing over its walls and directly into the lake. The day was early, but I was ready for an ample glass of a smooth single malt scotch.

Toward one end of the pool, barely beneath the water's surface, were six two-foot-by-two-foot marble stepping stones that crossed the width of the pool. The stones were supported by small concrete columns also located beneath the water. A teammate jovially walked over the stones, crossing from one side of the pool the other. He bragged he was walking on water.

Our photographer, Carolyn, had staged several creative settings for the photo shoot. The first photo consisted of four of our female paddlers standing naked behind a three-foot-by-five-foot white banner with an elaborate drawing of a dragon and the bold red words THE DRAGON SURVIVORS. The four gracious ladies had taken their clothes off in the boathouse. They laughed as they slipped unseen across the dock in the buff and behind the banner, which strategically covered the critical areas of their bodies.

For the next photograph, Carolyn had placed two of our dragon boat's drums on top of the infinity pool's stepping stones. The drums were approximately two feet high and eighteen inches wide. Each drum sat perfectly on two of the stones. She then ordered all of us guys to turn our heads away from the pool and toward the house.

She positioned Allyson and Pat sitting back-to-back on top of one of the drums with their legs crossed and strategically holding a paddle across their bodies so the paddle's blade hid from view their behinds and hips. The paddle's handle was even more carefully positioned to conceal their breasts.

On the other drum, Brooke and another female paddler sat in an identical pose. Carolyn allowed the men to turn around. The ladies looked muscular, delicate, and graceful. They were grand models, and it was a beautiful photo.

I felt privileged to share this special moment with my friends. We horse-laughed with delight. We'd forgotten about our cancer and were full of joy, amazement, and pride. Time stood still for us, even if it was for a short period. Our worlds had become a little brighter. At this moment, innocence and goodness personified our great team.

Carolyn shot several more photos using our woman paddlers as models, and then it was time to break for lunch. Since we'd left Charleston in the wee morning hours, everyone was starved. We stuffed our faces with fried chicken, potato salad, and baked beans.

After lunch, it was time for us hunky guys to pose naked. Carolyn had instructed us to wear swim trunks and said she'd tell us the exact moment to remove them. She carefully positioned five male models on the dock by the boathouse. She instructed the men to place their small waist personal floatation devices (PDFs) around their midsections and then ordered them to remove their swim trunks. These PFDs, which we wore while paddling in case of an emergency, were about a foot long and ten inches wide. Positioned properly, they would sufficiently, but just barely, cloak each guy's family jewels.

The team's largest paddler was Daniel Jones, a stout six-foot, two-inch man of 225 pounds, who stood head and shoulders above the other men. His wife called him Big Daddy. The positioning of his PDF high above the others' created a comical photo. Carolyn clicked several pictures. Everyone hooted as the men shuffled into the boathouse being careful not to allow the PFDs to slip from their strategic locations.

Carolyn then ordered Sean, Thomas, me, and another male paddler to each sit on one of the pool's stepping stones. The crafty photographer set up a six-foot stepladder at that end of the pool. She climbed to the top rung on the ladder and directed each of us to sit. She focused her camera for her next impeccable shot. She looked at the four of us, smiled, and shook her head in amusement.

I had the feeling this photograph was going to be tricky.

One more look through her camera's viewfinder, and then she turned around. With a little chuckle, she instructed us to shed the trunks, cross our legs, and tuck everything important between our legs, so it was completely hidden.

The water was cold, and I hoped that would cause a little shrinkage and make it easier to hide my privates. Each of us sat proudly and refused to look at the other as we tucked our private parts between our legs. This was personal stuff.

Another important factor when dealing with naked men was to always look straight into their eyes. Never down. The worst thing that could happen to a man was to be caught looking at another man's junk. So, each of us continued to stare directly at the camera. I squeezed my legs together and made sure everything was securely hidden from the camera's peering eye.

Carolyn asked, "Is everyone ready?"

We all grunted, "Yes."

She turned around, still smiling. After another quick peek through her camera's lens, she lifted her head and offered us encouragement. "You guys have some very nice curves."

She looked at me. "You going to wear that necklace?"

I nodded. "I never take off my necklace."

She again shook her head as if we were all idiots. Maybe we were. Her camera began clicking, and when she finished taking her highly embarrassing pictures, she stepped down the ladder, folded it closed, and walked away laughing.

The four of us guys were left to put on our swim trunks while taking great care to maintain eye contact. I finally looked at Thomas, he looked at me, and we simultaneously broke out in boisterous laughter.

Thomas asked, "What's so special about that ugly necklace you wear? Looks like a little piece of rock to me."

I pulled my swim trucks up my body. "One day I'll share with you the meaning of, as you call it, my ugly necklace."

The photography session was over. I would wait with great anticipation to see the final product. I hoped people would want to purchase a calendar showing the bodies of an older, and a bit scared, group of models.

I wandered inside the house. The library was Mary Beth Malone's writing retreat and was home to many books. The decomposing paper of old manuscripts released a distinctive aroma. I loved that earthy, woody odor of a timeworn book. I removed an old copy of Ernest Hemingway's *A Moveable Feast* and held it close to my nostrils. I closed my eyes and could see Papa Hemingway walking the 1920s Paris streets. I imagined sitting in Gertrude Stein's living room with Hemingway and the other expatriates of that Lost Generation, discussing books and art, food, and drink.

The image reminded me of my first experience of the magic of books. I was an inquiring eight-year-old third grader. Every Wednesday, our teacher would escort the class to the school's library. On my first visit, I checked out a small hardcover book titled *Men of Iron* by Howard Pyle.

The book told about noble fifteenth-century knights and their valorous rules of chivalry. The author nobly described these courageous men jousting on horseback, carrying large wooden lances with a sharp metal point. They aspired to spear their opponent with their lances or knock him off his horse. The knight's task was difficult. With his left hand, using his thick metal shield, he must protect his heart and steer his horse. His right hand firmly held his lance while pointing its tip toward his enemy's head. I loved to read about chivalry and honor. It defined the kind of man I wanted to be. The novel ushered my mind into another world, into the magical realm of the writer's imagination.

I wondered what thrill it would be to one day write such a story myself.

The friendly chatter of the group cooking in the adjacent kitchen filled my ears and awakened me from my trance. The sweet aroma of shrimp boiling grabbed my attention. I was hungry and needed a glass of wine. Eating and drinking with my friends made me feel like I was touching a part of the divine.

Pat entered the library and sat down beside me. "It was a fun day," she said.

"It was a great day," I said.

She twisted the ring on her finger and her eyes darted back and forth. She was nervous. Not characteristic of Pat. She finally spoke. "I need your help."

I was surprised as she was highly independent and self-reliant. I respected Pat immensely, but at times she and I struggled with each other's strong personalities. But it pleased me she wanted my help. "Sure, whatever you need."

"The month before we go to Chattanooga, I try out for the US Senior Women's National Team. I told you I've been having difficulty concentrating. I can't maintain a strong direct focus for more than a few minutes. It's the chemo."

I listened intently to her every word.

She placed her hand over her heart. "This tryout is really important to me. Would you help me with my focus?"

Her request honored me. "Let's meet early one morning next

week, and I'll share a few mental exercises that may be helpful."

Pat leaned over and gave me a rare hug. I welcomed it.

"Thanks," she said as she left the room.

After an immensely satisfying day, I wanted time to myself. I'd planned a solo fly-fishing adventure. Casting a line in a clear mountain stream and hooking a rainbow trout was close to the top of my list of great accomplishments. It'd be just me, the bobbing of my fly atop the river's water, and an ever-ingenious trout attempting to eat dinner while cleverly evading my expertly disguised trap. I would sleep well tonight in anticipation.

***

I stood in the middle of the cool water of the Tuckasegee River, one of North Carolina's streams rich with mountain trout. I stared down the river at an oasis that was lined as far as I could see with large oaks and tall, skinny, pine trees. It looked like a multicolored tunnel leading me to a safe haven. The blinding yellow sun rose, causing the sleepy world to wake. The fog slowly lifted from the water, like steam roiling from a boiling pot. The river, like a snake, coiled its powerful currents, caught the glistening waves of sunlight, and sparkled like the scales of the trout I was eager to catch. The only noises were birds softly chirping and the river's current gently flowing over the smooth rocks.

I'd donned my waist-high waders and my old fishing vest that was covered with an array of barbless hooks and colorful flies. The line in my rod was threaded and ready. My reel was loaded for an active morning. I'd be happy hooking a nice-sized brook or brown but dreamed of a twenty-inch rainbow.

Casting a fly rod was like playing a delicate musical

instrument. It had its own enchanted rhythmic motion. Brute strength was useless. It was all about timing, tempo, and technique. Just like paddling a dragon boat. I made a nice loop with my line behind me and shot it forward. The fly at the end of my line gently settled on the water's surface just above a small eddy behind a cluster of rocks. I mended the line and began to feather it back through my fingers.

I allowed the fly to float past the rock and into the eddy. That's the place the cunning trout found refuge from the river's current. They swam facing upstream in order to efficiently snag and quickly swallow a bug floating down the river. I repeated the action several times, hopeful my diligence and patience would pay off.

With a new cast, the fly made its way onto the clear water like a leaf slowly floating to the ground. As soon as the fake insect hit the water, my rod snapped downward. I gave a sharp tug upward as the pole bent forward. The multicolored rainbow shot straight out of the water. Adrenaline flooded my body. The trout's frame twisted, and its open mouth violently shook, trying to spit out the hook. I carefully pulled in some line, being thoughtful not to pull too tight to hurt the fish. I delicately drew the line through my hand to reel in my catch.

The tints of red and blue of the fish's body glistened in the water as I netted my trout. He twisted and squirmed to free himself. He wanted to live. He swam to live. I pulled the hook from his mouth softly as I placed my hands around his body. I admired my catch and then lowered him back into the water. I opened my hands and let him go. He swam away, again living freely.

I thought as I watched my shiny, scaled catch swim away that I, too, needed to live freely. Over the past year and a half since my cancer diagnosis, I'd forgotten how—instead, I'd worked hard at learning how not to die. And as Amy said, maybe I'd been a tormented man for a long time.

My glistening fish had taught me a lesson A calm covered my body with my next thought. It was a revelation I desperately needed. I closed my eyes as I meditated on the words floating through my head. The words were like the melodic lyrics of a new song of hope:

I needed to live to live, and not to live trying not to die.

18

Charleston

Late Fall 2009

Pat's life for the past eight years had been like a roller-coaster ride. Chaos had bombarded her in the form of life-threatening ovarian tumors. She'd embraced her plight with grace like an autumn-flowering shoot. She never despaired and seemed to be in total control of her emotions. Until now.

She'd recently purchased an OC-2, a lightweight twenty-foot-long outrigger canoe made for two people, and it was the perfect vessel to practice focus drills. The rear paddler controlled the boat's direction by operating the rudder with foot pedals. The paddler in the front seat was free to focus on technique and form.

Pat met me at Brittlebank dock early Sunday morning the week after the hilarious naked photo shoot. I had great anticipation to mentor Pat and strengthen our relationship. She was a team captain, and her never-say-die attitude inspired us all.

When she arrived, I was shocked by her appearance. She'd cut her thick blond shoulder-length hair very short and dyed it red. Although the hairstyle hardened her face, she appeared both powerful and attractive.

"What did you do?" I asked.

"I needed to refocus my life, and I wanted a new look. You don't like it?"

"I like it a lot. It looks stunning."

She nodded.

"You ready?" I asked.

Pat grabbed her paddle, "Always."

I laughed. "Before getting into the canoe I want us to sit cross-legged on the dock facing each other."

We sat down, crisscrossed our legs, folding our feet under the opposite knees, and resting our hands in our laps.

I instructed, "Close your eyes. Think of nothing but this moment. Eliminate all other thoughts, and imagine yourself at the time trial's starting line, sitting in the outrigger canoe. Hear the starter's horn. Lock your head looking forward and visualize your first stroke. Strong. And the next stroke and the next. Feel yourself breathing, filling your lungs with oxygen between each deep perfect stroke."

Pat visualized the entire time trial paddle for the next two minutes. We opened our eyes and peered at each other.

I said, "We train our muscles to be strong and create endurance by the exertion of physical exercises. We teach our bodies to act automatically by performing repetitive workouts and drills. Focus is like any other muscle. It, too, must be trained and developed."

Pat breathed calmly. She concentrated on my words.

I continued, "Once you clear your mind of the garbage, there is one thing you must do and one thing you must not do to learn how to focus."

She smiled. "And what are those?"

"You must expect to excel. I taught my wide receivers on my football team that when they lined up for the play, to see themselves, at that very moment, already catching the football. Their entire focus must be on the end result, which is the reception of the quarterback's pass."

"And the thing I must not do?" she asked.

"The thing you can't do is to allow yourself to ever become frustrated. You will fail. If my receiver dropped a passed ball, we taught him to immediately become refocused. There is no time for regret or self-pity. If you miss a stroke or don't get maximum rotation or extension, then refocus on the next stroke and make it perfect."

Pat nodded.

"Let's get into the boat, and I want to take you to a special place for the next exercise."

We paddled about a mile up the Ashley River, veered left, and paddled up a small tributary called Oldtown Creek. We navigated the canoe for another ten minutes when we saw the sun bristle against the golden wood of a large sailboat. The water became shallow, so we paddled slowly. The ship was a replica of a seventeenth-century cargo vessel. Similar ships carried goods, foodstuffs, and even livestock throughout the eastern seaboard more than three hundred years ago.

The ship was moored at Charles Town Landing, the original site of the initial English settlement in South Carolina in 1670. Charles Town Landing is one of only a few original settlements that still exist in the United States.

I felt tranquil at the sight of the reflection of the vessel's oak, cedar, and pine wood on the water's smooth surface. I imagined sailing in the Caribbean off the Barbados coast transporting sugar and rum, living a much simpler life. Would I trade the rigorous life of those sailors with their cramped living quarters for a cancer-free body? Maybe.

But for now, the beauty of the wooden boat moored in the narrow, shallow creek surrounded by thick, green marsh grass and moss-covered oak trees allowed me to forget my illness. We stopped paddling.

I looked directly into Pat's eyes. "The brain is a trainable organ. You need to create a mental structure in your mind to house your desire. I want you to close your eyes again. Visualize inside your brain that you are building a highly fortified structure. Now see the structure complete. And that building contains nothing but the image of you winning the time trial."

Pat asked. "How do I do that?"

"You must rechannel your fear and focus on your race plan," I said, as I reached around her body and held both her hands in mine. "Imagine you're sitting in your boat, surrounded by a protective white light. The white light is forcing all negative thoughts from your mind. Don't think about winning or losing but only of the majesty of each perfect paddle stroke. Move into a more spiritual realm and unlimited place; I'd tell my football receivers when they entered that unlimited space, their hands and the ball became one. In your case, you, your boat, your paddle, and your body will become one. Imagine the white light protecting and guiding each stroke."

She closed her eyes and sat silent for several minutes.

Pat slowly opened her eyes and looked at me. She smiled and in a low, calm voice, she said, "I could see it. The white light leading each stroke of my paddle." She squeezed my hand, "Thank you."

We began to paddle back to the dock. The water was calm, the sun warm on my back. Each smooth stroke of the paddle seemed effortless. But an inscrutable shadow surrounded my thoughts. With each stroke, I was plagued by hypocrisy regarding the advice I'd given Pat.

Maybe I should channel more protective white light into the darkness of my life.

19

Paris, France

Spring 2010

Amy and I had decided to spend a week in Paris, celebrating life, prior to our trip to Germany for my PRRT treatment. I prayed the romantic and cultured city of lights would allow me to express my love and gratitude for her abiding commitment and graceful elegance in dealing with my illness. The past two years had been difficult; and whoever said being a caregiver was an easy task was delusional.

I needed—no, wanted—to share with Amy my deep love, respect, and devotion. I envisioned us strolling slowly along the romantic Seine River, consuming brilliant French wine and food, and making constant love. By the end of the week when we left Paris for Germany, I wanted Amy to have no doubt of my undying love and appreciation.

We'd flown all night from Charleston to Paris, slept little, and lost six hours of time. We grabbed a cab from the airport to the Hotel Regina, which was located in downtown Paris just opposite the Louvre. Our high-floor suite had an exquisite view of the Eiffel Tower. I envisioned making love to Amy with the tower's enchanting blue glow shining through the window of our dark room and over our naked bodies.

The bellhop led us to our suite, arranged our luggage, and offered tips on how to enjoy Paris. As he left, Amy pulled back the long, thick, satin curtains of the large window. Her eyes widened as she stepped back. "What a view. The Eiffel Tower is absolutely stunning. Thank you."

I moved my body behind hers and held her tight. I kissed her neck as we gazed over the Tuileries Garden and the Louvre. I gently kissed her cheek and caressed her breast; she leaned her head back toward my face. "Not now," she said. "Let's get some sleep, see the city, and make love later tonight."

We slept for six hours, showered, and dressed to explore the city that had inspired Hemingway and Balzac. "Could we walk to the Eiffel Tower?" Amy asked.

"Absolutely."

Her smile was sly, and I knew it well. I anticipated a delightful evening. "We'll act like a couple of real tourists, take a selfie standing in front of the Eiffel Tower and frustrate a real Frenchman by trying to impress him with our horrible French."

Her eyes glowed as she spoke. She slowly ran her fingers along my face. "Then we'll find a wonderful French restaurant to eat dinner and come back to our room and make love."

"You're on. Or maybe we can reverse the order of events," I said.

She laughed as she forcefully pulled me forward and out the room's door. "I'll give you credit—you are persistent."

We left the hotel and walked in the direction of the Eiffel Tower. Holding hands, we casually strolled through the sandy gravel paths of le jardin des Tuileries and crossed the Seine River. We left the Paris city map in the room to make our trip more adventurous. Paris's thousands of trees were in bright bloom. The cool night air gently blew through their leaves and branches and onto our faces. April was a magical time to be in this romantic city.

We walked along several cobbled streets for more than an hour, laughing and not paying much attention to the direction we were heading. We finally realized the tip of the tower appeared to be getting farther away—not closer. We concluded we were lost.

I asked a well-dressed older Parisian woman: "Excusez-moi! síl vous plaît, comment vais-je en ville Eiffel Tower?"

She laughed at my broken French. "Monsieur." She then spoke with perfect English. "Turn right at the next street, go five blocks, turn left, and then straight ahead."

Amy and I both laughed. "Thank you," I said.

We followed her directions but our legs were tiring and our stomachs began growling from hunger. We hung a left and found ourselves walking along a pleasing avenue of merchants and shops.

L'avenue de Saxe was a large and busy street surrounded by the most stunning old buildings. It was bordered by two rows of beautiful plane trees. The homes had elaborate sculptures and exquisite decorations on the doors. We came across an almost ceaseless frontage of amazing small shops and stores.

Clothing stores, bookstores, restaurants, and all types of medical offices. We watched local businessmen and women in their small workplaces talking on their phones. Shop after shop displayed excellent French wine, cheeses, and a plentiful assortment of breads and meats.

Local residents walking the street peered through the windows of the bakery shops watching the bakers spin and weave new delicacies. The pleasing aroma of baking bread and roasting meats floated from the ovens like an invisible dew and filled the streets. Men and women sat outside the shops at small, round tables, laughing as they dipped bread in olive oil and drank wine.

Amy pulled me into one of the cozy shops. "I have a new plan. Let's buy a bottle of Burgundy, a loaf of hot bread, some meat and cheese, and go back to our room. We'll drink, eat, and make love."

Her plan sounded splendid. "Let's do it."

We purchased a bottle of red wine from the French Burgundy region, a generous cut of a delicately cured French ham, lavish slices of Comté cheese, which is the French cousin of the delicious Swiss Gruyére cheese, a baguette, and a small bottle of the local extra virgin olive oil.

We marched to our hotel and settled onto our room's balcony. I sliced several pieces of bread and thoroughly moistened them in the deep-green olive oil. I combined a small piece of cheese and ham on top of the thinly sliced bread. We ate and drank very slowly. It was only the two of us, and we wanted no other.

We made love. We lay naked on the plush bed and fell asleep. I awoke about an hour later, and seeing Amy lying next to me naked made me realize God had blessed me more than I deserved. Thankfulness rushed through my body like the Seine River flowing under the Pont Neuf. Her naked form also raised a more primal sensation.

I gently touched her breasts. She groaned slightly. I kissed her lips, neck, and breasts. With her eyes still closed Amy moved her body against mine. My longing was for her to know she was the only woman my heart desired, my touch to communicate her body was the only body I craved, and she would be, that night and forever, my only lover.

I exalted in the fact she'd generously given her perfect body to me. We made love again and slept like two baby lambs.

***

It was no surprise that when my artist wife stepped from her morning shower she proclaimed, "You do realize where our first visit will be, don't you?"

"To see the Masters," I said.

"The wonderful impressionists, Monet, Manet, Degas, Renoir, Van Gogh. I'm so excited. The Musée d'Orsay opens at nine o'clock, and we will be first in line. And Notre-Dame in the afternoon."

"We'll be the first," I said, offering a smile. "Great evening last night."

Amy cut her eyes toward me, showing me her sumptuous, sly smile that answered, yes, it was. I momentarily wanted to skip the art museum. But I knew that wasn't going to happen.

The Musée d'Orsay, one of the largest museums in Europe, was located on the left bank of the Seine River and housed the world's largest collection of impressionist and post-impressionist art masterpieces.

As promised, we were first in line and entered the grand museum promptly at nine o'clock. The building was an old train station. A massive and ornate clock that marked these timeworn European train stations still hung high above the opulent glass ceiling just inside the museum's entrance. Amy was mesmerized.

I followed her around like a puppy for about an hour as she studied the paintings but soon realized she'd prefer to be on her own. I found a comfortable seat and watched my wife study the works of her heroes from afar.

For thirty minutes she stared at Vincent van Gogh's *The Church at Auvers.* Another forty-five minutes studying Edgar Degas's *L Àbsinthe.* She stood, for what seemed like an hour, in front of Gustave Courbet's *The Painter's Studio.* I could tell she was examining their intricate brushstrokes. As she always said of her own artwork,, "You've got to lay it and leave it."

She approached me close to noon. "I'm done. My mind's saturated and full of ideas. I can't take in anymore."

"You hungry?" I asked.

"Starving."

We found a small open-air café across from the Hotel Regina located on rue de Rivoli at the intersection of rue des Pyramides. We ate turkey baguettes and drank a glass of wine while overlooking the gilded statue of Joan of Arc.

"You still up for a visit to Notre-Dame?" Amy asked.

"Sure."

A joyful melody crescendo through the wooden arches as a choir sang as we entered the cathedral. We sat in a wooden pew and listened. The perfect harmony of the voices seemed angelic. When the chorus stopped singing, we browsed the basilica.

Amy pointed to an abundant number of lit candles resting on tiered tables in a secured corner of the church, a place where parishioners would pay to light a candle and say a prayer.

She encouraged, "Light a candle and say a prayer for God's healing and guidance for next week's treatment in Germany."

I studied the box in which to pay money to light a candle and grimaced. "I don't think I need to pay money for God to hear my prayer."

"It may help," Amy said, frowning at my attitude.

I stepped back and closed my eyes. "I don't think giving money or lighting a candle will make any difference to God. I believe He's already heard my prayer."

Amy huffed. "You sure can be pig-headed."

I walked away. "Maybe so, but I have my convictions."

"And at times, I have no clue where all those crazy thoughts come from," Amy said, following me.

But I did appreciate the majesty of the grand cathedral and the holiness I sensed from the many visitors as they worshipped. It was a place of hallowed ground, and I did whisper a fervent prayer for my treatment.

We ate dinner at a first-rate French restaurant that featured steaks cut from local grass-fed cows. The meat was tender and juicy. We enjoyed the succulent flavors of our dinner for two hours. After dinner we strolled along the quais and surveyed the vendors' supplies, searching for a rare book but to no avail. Although tired from a full day's activities, we again made love. Afterward, we cuddled close for a restful night of hard sleep.

I really liked Paris.

Tomorrow we would visit Normandy, the site of amazing human courage, and then we'd be off to Germany for my body to be pumped full of radiation. I prayed I'd have the same courage those heroes had displayed more than sixty-five years ago. And wondered if maybe I should have lit a candle at Notre-Dame.

20

Normandy, France

Spring 2010

I stood staring at almost ten thousand white crosses along the Seine, marking the plain but imposing graves of nobleman. I held Amy's hand as I recalled reading Dwight Eisenhower's speech to these distinguished men before they embarked on what would amount largely to a suicide mission.

He told them "the hopes and prayers of liberty-loving people everywhere" marched with them. He declared to these brave men that "the tide [of the war] has turned" and "the free men of the world are marching together."

I sat on the ground and said nothing.

"What are you thinking about?" Amy asked.

"I'm thinking about Saul Lerner. Do you remember Saul? My business partner on the first subdivision I developed."

"Of course, I remember Saul. He was a wonderful mentor to you."

I continued to stare at the crosses and spoke as if I was alone. "He was more like a father than a mentor, and he's been on my mind all day. He encouraged me to be strong when the housing bubble was expanding like crazy and we couldn't rent apartments as everyone was buying a house. You remember how I struggled to pay mortgage payments."

"How could I forget? It was an awful time."

"But Saul supported me through the entire nightmare." I hesitated and stared at the sky. After a few minutes, I asked Amy, "Did you know he lost his entire family during World War II?"

Amy sat beside me on the bench. "I never knew that. How?"

"When the Nazis occupied Hungary, Saul's family—his father, mother, and two sisters—were deported to the Auschwitz concentration camp. I'll never forget the pain in his eyes as he told me the story."

Amy touched my hand. "He really loved you."

I finally looked at her. "Saul told me his father was a strong and honorable man. The kind of man I wished my father had been."

Amy appeared surprised by my comment about my father.

"Saul told me the moment they stepped off the packed freight train, and without warning or reason, his father was shot in the head. Can you imagine witnessing your father being killed as you stood next to him?"

"How terrible," she said.

I stared back at the river's black water. "Both his sisters were killed in the gas chambers. He said his mother's grief-stricken heart one day just stopped pumping blood. But Saul was highly intelligent and had endeared himself to one of the German officers, the one who supervised the Jewish prisoners working in the mines that were located a few miles outside the concentration camp. He eventually became the driver of the officer's horse-drawn wagon."

I pulled my attention from the river and again looked at Amy. "Do you remember his business partner Benjamin Weiss?"

She smiled with her mouth and her eyes as she nodded.

"Benjamin's family lived next to Saul's family in Budapest. Benjamin's entire family was also deported to Auschwitz. Benjamin was one of the laborers in the German mines. One day as Saul sat on the wagon and the German officer inspected the work at the mine, Benjamin approached him. Saul said he didn't recognize him as his face and clothing were covered completely with black coal dust.

"Their private encounters continued for several months, and Saul learned from Benjamin the mine had a secluded second exit that'd been boarded closed. Saul devised a plan to escape and instructed Benjamin to begin digging a trench under the boards just large enough for the two of them to slide underneath. Benjamin dug a small amount of dirt each day for three months.

Amy creased her brow as she listened intently. "I never knew any of this about Saul. He was an amazing man."

"Saul was a private man of few words. But one day when I was at his home reviewing a development plan, I asked him about his family. He said nothing for what seemed like an eternity. I thought I'd pissed him off. But he finally started talking and shared with me this amazing story. He began the story with 'My son.'"

Amy squeezed my hand. "He always saw you as his protégé. Maybe the son he never had."

"Maybe he was the strong father I never had." I smiled. "Saul once told me that people loved diamonds, and I was his diamond in the rough. He emphasized the word *rough.*"

Amy smiled as if she agreed with Saul.

"The German officer conducted daily inspections of the mines, and every afternoon he and the guards would gather just inside the mine's entrance to report on the day's production of coal. If the amount of coal excavated exceeded that day's quota, they would partake generously in the superb vodka they'd stolen from Poland. At times, the group would linger long into the dusk of the evening.

"Once Benjamin had the trench dug, Saul patiently waited for the evening when the officer and his guards overserved themselves on the vodka so he could slip away from the wagon. One evening, after a highly productive week, the captain passed out and slept.

"Saul found Benjamin, and they hurried to the mine's boarded exit, and being starved and extremely thin, they easily slid under the boards and escaped into the surrounding mountains. Saul knew they only had an hour or two at the most before the officer would wake and realize he was gone. He told me they traveled all night and all of the next day before they stopped to rest. They heard search parties with dogs barking close by."

"What a courageous escape," Amy said.

"He said it took them a month to walk the thousand miles, mostly at night, to Paris. Benjamin had an uncle who'd emigrated to the United States and started a thriving clothing business. The uncle arranged transportation from Paris to America.

And you know how successful they became."

Amy's looked at me wide-eyed—spellbound. "What a wonderful story. It was a special moment that he chose you to share such a private and personal story. What do you think he was trying to teach you?"

I intently stared back at the river. "One word: exemplar."

The tone of Amy's voice communicated confusion. "What does that mean?"

"Saul told me, from the time he could remember, his father's favorite expression was an Edmund Burke quote: *Example is the school of mankind, and they will learn at no other.*" A tear formed at the corner of my eye. "Saul's lip quivered as he shared with me what his father told him just before he stepped off the train and was killed: to always be an exemplar. He quietly told me that word drove him daily. Helped him make wise decisions."

I looked at Amy. She looked woeful and lamented, "What a wise, brave man."

"Saul instructed me, as his father had instructed him, to be an exemplar. He told me to be an example that others would follow." I stopped talking and took a deep breath. "I thought I was being a good example by working hard, being successful, and showing people I wasn't a failure. But I'm beginning to think those aren't the examples he meant. To be honest, I'm not sure what he really meant." I looked away from Amy. "But I'm afraid I've failed my trusted mentor. I've not been a good example for anyone."

Amy squeezed my hand tighter. "Saul would be very proud of you. Just like a son. He saw a quality within you that you've never been able to see yourself. But you will one day."

I stood and stared silently at the site of heroes. I thought of the great general's words that the war's tide has changed. I reflected on the Cooper and Ashely Rivers in Charleston. How they ebbed and flowed twice a day. Since I was a young boy, anger had flowed through my mind like those rising Charleston tides. I felt as if I'd been swimming against the tide all my life, fighting against everything and everyone. Maybe I needed to heed Saul's wise words and become a worthy example, by letting go of my anger.

I question deep with my soul if that was possible.

21

Bad Berka, Germany

Spring 2010

The nurse led Amy and me through a wide hallway in the modern German hospital called the Zentralklinik. The main lobby's elegant skylight allowed bright sun rays to illuminate the clean, waxed, shiny floors. It was a beautiful East German Sunday afternoon.

Hauling the majority of the heavy luggage—we'd packed enough for weeks—I breathed heavily. Amy and I were both exhausted. We'd ridden for hours on a train from Paris to the East German town of Weimar, the home of Goethe, the author of the tragic play, *Faust*. In Weimar, we forced our luggage into the trunk of a cab and traveled to Bad Berka.

At the hospital, after walking down several hallways we finally found an elevator and rode to the third floor. Amy sighed with relief. "We can relax when we get to your room."

We approached two sets of thick, double glass doors which the nurse opened the first set of doors with a key. As Amy and I started to enter the nurse raised his hand. "This is a highly restricted area, and only patients can proceed."

Shock covered Amy's face. Her eyes swelled with water.

"Where is she to go?" I asked. We hadn't checked into a hotel yet.

His look was intense. "Maybe her hotel or somewhere to eat but she's not allowed in the radiation unit."

I raised my voice. "No, no, she's going to stay with me in my room until the tests begin."

The nurse raised his voice. "Impossible."

Tears flowed down Amy's face. She was exhausted, scared, and now angry. "I can go to the hotel, Tripp."

I looked at the nurse and yelled, "That's a mile away."

Amy gritted her teeth, attempting to control her emotions. "I'll take a cab."

The nurse stepped forward and in typical German earnestness said, "Mr. Avery, I need to take you to your room."

I hugged Amy and didn't want to let her go. She pulled away, kissed me, and walked back down the hallway toward the elevator. My heart raced with fear as I watched her walk away. The nurse seemed oblivious to our pain.

The nurse closed the glass doors, and we stood in another small foyer. In front of us was another set of thick, glass doors. He rang a bell and the doors flew open. Damn, two foyers with double doors. They must be killing people in this place. This double-foyer entryway protected people outside our unit from the powerful radiation that was about to be flooded into my body.

We walked into the sterile private ward, and he led me to my spartan but comfortable room. It was unlike any hospital room I'd seen in the United States. It was a room for two patients with small beds and no television, bleak but spotless and functional. Only one nondescript picture hung on the wall. I was five thousand miles from home and felt very alone.

As soon as the nurse completed his instructions and left, I called Amy. "You okay?"

Her voice sounded more hopeful. "I checked into the Hotel Hubertushof, and the room is fine. Bettina, the owner, speaks no English, but we communicated using a dictionary. What a crazy experience. But I'm fine. How about you?"

"All's good. They'll test my kidneys and heart tomorrow. Since the radiation is eliminated from my body through my kidneys, they need to make sure they're functioning properly."

Her voice rattled. "It scares me thinking you could have a problem with your kidneys and not be able to have the treatment."

"Don't worry; my kidneys are fine."

"Call me in the morning and let me know the test results."

"Will do."

"In the meantime," she said. "I plan to get some rest, and tomorrow I plan to explore this little German village."

"Have fun and be careful. I love you a ton and will call you in the morning."

Monday morning breakfast at the hospital was classic German—cold processed meats and cheese. It was awful. If these doctors don't radiate me to death, I thought, I'd die of starvation.

A nurse entered my room and handed me my medical chart. She was short and stocky, and wore her hair in a tight bun on top of her head. I smiled, but she didn't respond. She inserted a large IV needle that looked like a small knife into my arm, when I asked, "Do you live near the hospital?"

She looked at me and clenched her jaw without speaking.

I continued my inquiry. "You have family living in Bad Berka?"

She pursed her lips and sneered with a strong German accent. "Mr. Avery, I have no time for your funnies."

My eyes widened with surprise at her snappy response. I felt even more alone and wished like hell Amy was with me. Nurse Ratched gave me directions to the ward where the effectiveness of my kidneys would be tested.

A gamma camera scanned my kidneys and provided images used to assess my renal function. A blood sample was then drawn to test my kidneys' tubular extraction and my glomerular filtration rate. PRRT could damage kidneys, but the risk was low. After the CT scan and learning my renal functions were excellent, I called Amy.

"How was your morning?" I asked.

"Weird. I slept great, took a shower this morning, dressed, put on my makeup, and walked the city. It took all of fifteen minutes, but I walked it several times."

"That doesn't sound so weird."

"It was the men," she said in a raspy voice. "They looked at me in an odd manner."

My heart raced. "Were you hurt or in danger? Do I need to check out of this room and come down there to kick some German butt?"

She laughed. "No, I'm fine. But the women here wear little makeup and have funky-colored hair. Since I was dressed nicely and wore makeup, I think the men thought I was a prostitute."

"No shit?"

Her laughter increased. "Yeah, the men would smile oddly at me as I crossed the street or waited on the street corners. The women gave me dirty looks."

I joined her laughter. "Now I know how we can pay for this trip."

Her tone more serious as she ignored my comment. "I learned a lot about this beautiful little town, Bad Berka. It's a small resort village with about eight thousand people. The Zentralklinik hospital is the major employer. Wealthy European families vacation here to cross-country ski in the winter or hike the trails in the summer. It's really a beautiful little town."

"Sounds nice," I said.

Amy's voice was more upbeat. "The village has several German restaurants overlooking a lovely small canal. I'm going to try one for lunch."

The pitch in my voice rose. "Wonderful, and I can't wait to go with you when they release me from this prison they call a hospital room."

"Tell me about your test results."

"My kidneys work great, and the treatment is on track. I have my first of two Gallium-68 scans tomorrow, the PRRT treatment the following day, and then forty-eight hours of quarantine."

Her voice was subdued. "I'm praying the treatment kills every one of those ugly tumors."

"Yeah, me too."

"I'm going to eat lunch, have a glass of wine, and relax. I love you and sure miss you."

"Yeah, rub it in. My breakfast looked like it was sprouting fur. And I miss the hell out of you."

Lunch was the only hot meal of the day at the Klinik. When I returned to my room, a food tray rested on the room's desk. As I lifted the cover, I was appalled. I think the fish was herring served in some sort of cream sauce. It looked like cat food. I took a bite. It tasted like cat food. I'd found my formula to lose that extra ten pounds after all.

That afternoon, Dr. Aldrich, chairman of the department of nuclear medicine, stopped by to introduce himself. Nurse Ratched followed him. The doctor was tall, slightly heavy, with a distinguished white beard. His wavy, thick, white hair made him look like a Roman god. He spoke perfect English.

He thoroughly explained the treatment plan and possible side effects. "Your nurse will be glad to accommodate your every need," he said. Her harsh look communicated clearly: I shouldn't make many requests.

Dr. Aldrich said I'd be weak for several months from a significantly reduced level of red and white blood cells. The weakness concerned me, as the Dragon Survivors' trip to Chattanooga for the national championship competition was only three weeks away. I needed to be strong.

The next day brought more blood tests, a liver ultrasound, and the specialized Gallium-68 scan. The Gallium-68 scan offered a considerably better picture regarding the number, size, and activity of my neuroendocrine tumors than a CT or MRI scan. This initial scan would serve as a benchmark to determine the treatment's effectiveness. I began to relax, knowing Amy was finding her way around Bad Berka and felt safe.

Wednesday was the big day for the PRRT treatment. It was less complicated than I thought. I began drinking mineral water early that morning, then was given amino acids through my IV to protect my kidneys. After two hours of having my kidneys flushed with the amino acids, Dr. Aldrich and Nurse Ratched entered my room, pushing a large square lead box that sat on a table with wheels. A blood-pressure cuff was strapped to my arm and the treatment began. The IV administered two types of radiation: Yttrium-90 and Lutetium-177. The treatment took about twenty minutes, and the amino acids were continued afterward for another two hours.

The simplest way to understand how PRRT works is to think about the analogy of a magnet and its ability to attract iron shavings. Neuroendocrine tumors, with their positive somatostatin receptors, attract the somatostatin analog chemical which is injected through the IV and carrying radioactive material. My tumors would attract this analog in the same manner a magnet attracts the iron shavings. The radioactive material is absorbed into the tumors and hopefully kills them.

My forty-eight-hour quarantine began. I wasn't allowed to leave my room. I was nauseous and had no appetite. Which, considering the food, was a good thing. I began to feel weak. To help eliminate the radiation through my kidneys Nurse Ratched insisted I drink three liters of water as quickly as possible.

I was also anticipating a message from Pat, informing me of the results of her time trial. I was confident she'd do well. But knowing she'd made the national team would reduce my anxiety. I slept ten hours that evening.

The next day I felt stronger, but the nausea had worsened.

Several times I stuck my head out of my room to see if Nurse Ratched was watching. I thought I might escape to scrounge the kitchen for some edible food. Each time, I'd receive a stern scowl and a serious grunt from the old battle-axe nurse as an order to return promptly to my room. Hell, I just wanted to find a decent morsel of food to eat.

Nurse Ratched finally told me she'd scheduled a Friday afternoon appointment for the post-treatment Gallium-68 scan and an evaluation visit to review the therapy's results with Dr. Aldrich. I'd finally be released from my mandatory prison-like quarantine and be able to see Amy.

Thursday evening's meal was the worst. It consisted of a mystery meat, more bread, and cheese. I was having outbursts of anxiety. I wanted to scream, laugh, and cry at the same time. My stomach growled with hunger. I remembered seeing a McDonald's restaurant on our taxi ride from Weimar to Bad Berka.

I called Amy and before she could speak, I barked, "I'm starving, you've got to get me a McDonalds hamburger."

She barked back, "There's no McDonalds in Bad Berka!"

Desperation filled my words. "I saw one during the cab ride from Weimar."

Amy's voice softened. "I know you're starving. Let me see what I can do. Otherwise, how are you feeling?"

"I feel like Jack Nicholson in *One Flew Over the Cuckoo's Nest.* Nurse Ratched is watching my every move, making sure I don't leave this dastardly room."

"Are you holding an axe, with your hair sticking straight up and your eyes bulging wide open?"

"Funny, just get me a Big Mac and some fries."

"I'll do my best."

"No, get me two Big Macs."

"Like I said, I'll do my best."

About two hours later my favorite nurse brought a large bag that sported two golden arches into my room. It contained two Big Macs and two large fries. I inhaled them in seconds and could have eaten five.

I called Amy. "Thank you so much. Now I'll survive."

The high pitch in her voice expressed her exasperation. "I called four cab companies before I found one to take me to Weimar. The McDonald's was about twenty miles away and cost forty euros—that's sixty US bucks. So, I hope you enjoyed them."

I grunted. "I'd have paid a hundred bucks. Thank you so much. I can't wait to see you tomorrow."

I heard a small sniffle. "Me too. I miss you terribly."

The next morning, standing in my room feeling like a track star waiting for the starter's gun, I watched the clock on the wall tick down my forty-eight-hour lockup. I was ready to blast out of my room like a lion stalking after an unsuspecting prey. Amy and I had agreed she'd be waiting outside the double foyers. I'd set the alarm on my phone, and as soon as I heard a beeping sound, I pranced from my room with my head held high and directly past Nurse Ratched's station. We offered competing smiles.

I was ecstatic when I saw Amy waiting. I used the key fob they'd given me to open all the doors and hugged my wife. They'd warned me to stay away from little children and pregnant women, but she was neither. As I hugged her tight, I felt a wave of nausea swarm through my body. I released Amy from my bear hug, found the nearest bathroom, and lost the delightful hamburgers from the previous evening.

I washed my face and rinsed out my mouth several times. When I returned from the restroom, we held each other for a long time. We kissed as if it was our first kiss.

After the scan, Dr. Aldrich welcomed us to his office. Amy and I both shook nervously like two scared elementary kids sitting in the principal's office. I prayed the therapy had worked.

Dr. Aldrich slid the scans across his desk. "Your uptake of radiation was good but not great. You should experience a good response in decreased tumor size and tumor stabilization."

"By tumor stabilization, you mean they should stop growing?" I asked.

"Yes, for a period of time. Some tumors will begin to grow again after a few months and others not for many years."

I swiped sweat from my face. "And my blood counts?"

"Your white and red blood counts are low. You will need to be very careful concerning any infections, and you will experience extreme anemia, nausea, and muscle weakness."

I thought about my dragon boat teammates and our upcoming competition. Nausea and weakness would be a problem. "Can I do anything to regain my strength quicker?" I asked.

Dr. Aldrich handed me a copy of my scans. "Eat well and rest. I'd like for you to return in nine months for restaging and a possible second treatment. But I promise you have many years to live."

The three of us talked for another fifteen minutes regarding the treatment and side effects, and then Amy and I left.

"You okay with the results?" she asked.

"I am. I'm just dog tired, but I realize this cancer is a chronic disease. But if I'm living and with you, I'm good."

She smiled and hugged me. "As you say, if we're breathing, we're fighting."

My phone vibrated. A text communicating Pat had been selected to paddle with the US Senior Women's National Team. I felt a surge of pride.

"Damn right. Now let's go home."

22

Charleston

Summer 2010

Our team had practiced three days a week through the winter months as the weather permitted and religiously during the spring. Each practice seemed to be harder than the last. For interval training between practices, some had adopted a strict running schedule, while others chose exercise regimens such as CrossFit.

Today would be my team's last practice before embarking on our trip to Chattanooga, the final test of our tedious preparation. Twenty people from various backgrounds were coming together to train for a common goal—winning the gold medal and a trip to Hong Kong to represent the United States. Some of my teammates had never excelled at a sporting event but now were part of an outstanding team.

It'd been two weeks since Amy and I had returned from Germany, and my weekly blood counts were not showing much improvement. My white blood cells remained dangerously low, and my red blood cells and hemoglobin were still at the anemic level. But I was determined. I would help the team in Chattanooga. I'd paddle like hell.

Our calendar sales had been strong, raising enough money to pay for the team's transportation and lodging. We sold calendars to friends and family. We set up booths at local farmers' markets and festivals. We unashamedly peddled the photos of our cleverly clad naked bodies to anyone who'd listen to our spiel. I guess getting naked pays off. Our bodies were sending us to Chattanooga in more ways than one.

It would be a short practice. A five-minute warm-up and a few race pieces to set our minds. But first I wanted to share some thoughts with my teammates. We gathered on the dock prior to loading the boat. I asked everyone to stand in a circle.

I set a boom box in the middle of the circle. "Before practice we have some celebrating to do. I've held this information for this moment. I'd like to announce that our esteemed teammate Pat Selinsky has been selected to paddle with the US Senior Women's National Team."

The team screamed with delight and tapped their paddles against the dock. Pat stepped back.

I yelled above their screams. "When I start the music, I want each of us, starting with me, then Sean and moving to his right, to jump into the middle of our circle and dance a jig of celebration for Pat.

I hit the boom box's play button.

Celebrate good times, come on . . .

There's a party going on right here . . .

I started hopping up and down. I banged my paddle against the dock trying to stay in time with the music. I looked like a galloping hyena. I danced for about ten seconds and jumped out of the middle of the circle as Sean sprang into the circle and began to dance.

As Sean left the circle, Allyson leaped in and danced like a professional. Then Brooke. Finally, the entire team danced celebrating Pat's success.

Pat had stepped a few feet away from the circle. We all stopped, looked at her, and held our paddles high in the air. It was the first time I'd ever seen Pat cry.

After we stopped dancing, I walked to the middle of the circle and spoke to the team. "We've set a high goal. And of course, the higher our goals, the more is required from the depths of our inner souls. The more intense our desire to win. This weekend will be three very difficult days but ones we'll remember for the rest of our lives. The teams we'll compete against will be talented, and they've also trained hard. We're going to race against the best of the best."

I looked at Thomas and he offered me a broad grin. His jaw squeezed tight with intensity, with the resolve to be a champion. He was ready.

I continued my speech. "Our minds must be disciplined the same as our bodies. You, me, all of us must master that all-knowing and all-powerful inner monologue. That voice of fear, self-doubt, and the feeling of unworthiness. Evict those destructive thoughts from your brain. Don't allow the voice that is screaming you can't do it control your thoughts . . . your body. Transcend your concentration to that of supreme focus and a calm confidence."

I motioned for everyone to close the circle. Each team member stepped forward and was keenly fixated on my words. "Remember the pain of our practices and the agony of our fight against the cancer that's trying to steal our lives. Thoughts have consequences. Now close your eyes and visualize yourself crossing the finish line ahead of the other boats. See yourself standing on the podium receiving the gold medal."

I breathed hard. "Emerson once wrote that thoughts are the seeds of action. Do you see it? Do you see it? Now open your eyes. Let's go do it."

Without my saying a word, the team reverently loaded the dragon boat, everyone sitting quietly in their assigned seats. Brooke and Pat were the stroke paddlers in the two front seats, our big men were in the middle of the boat, and our smaller paddlers in the back. We paddled a five-minute warm-up and stopped.

I was tempted to again try the faster start of ups but refused the temptation. "Let's do two 200-meter races and one five-hundred-meter piece. But don't stop at the mark, as I want us to continue to paddle with all our might for an additional twenty meters past the finish line. The races will be won by the team that can finish strong. I know you can put more power into that paddle."

I roared the commands: "Ready? Go!" As if a single mighty being with forty arms, our dragon boat team responded with a solid first stroke in the water, followed by five powerful strokes that left their marks in the craft's wake. I screamed, "Up, up, up!" and the racers obeyed in a furious blur of motion. Together bent in resolute determination, the Dragon Survivors glided across the water, not one paddle too fast, nor one too slow. And then, seemingly in a blink of an eye, the practice race was over, and I immediately cried out, “Paddles up.” Instantly the team reacted in military fashion, raising their paddles in perfect unison, anticipating yet another start.

All three practice races were strong. Even being anemic, I felt strong. Each time, we paddled past the finish line with power. Our race times were competitive. I was pleased.

My team, the Dragon Survivors, was ready.

23

Chattanooga, Tennessee

Thursday, July 22, 2010
6:30 p.m.

Filing off buses, eighty dragon boat teams made their way through the crowds of spectators lining the banks of the Tennessee River. Much had been done in preparation to welcome the best dragon boat teams in the nation to Chattanooga, Tennessee. The festival's opening celebration promised to be spectacular, starting with a parade called the Dragon God Ceremony.

The temperature was one hundred degrees, and even though I am from Charleston, I felt like I'd walked into a burning oven. I wiped sweat beads from my forehead. Perspiration formed underneath my shirt. A sizable group of people gathered around a large fan. I stood with my arms outstretched allowing the fast-moving air to cool my body. July in Chattanooga was always hot, but today's heat broke records. The humid air shimmered and rose off the river's still water.

The ceremony had begun as hundreds of performers, many holding paddles, escorted the sacred dragon head to the race site. White doves were released and flew high into the clear blue cloudless sky. Wearing large straw hats, a group of paddlers dressed in black shirts and pants waded into the river and began to reenact the search for Qu Yuan's body. Slowly and rhythmically, they slammed their paddlers against the water in exaggerated sweeping motions.

Musicians playing loud cymbals, heavy gongs, large drums, and horns walked the river's bank as folk dancers performed. Paddlers from every team marched to the docks and loaded into the multicolored boats. Each team carried a flag that represented their club. We pushed off the docks and paddled a short way out into the river. The steerspersons slowly moved their decorative canoes close and formed a semicircle around the dock.

The announcer regally, one by one, called the names of each team to the cheering competitors and spectators. The warmth of my blood rushed through my veins as I heard the inspirational words *The Dragon Survivors from Charleston, South Carolina,* blast through the speakers. My teammates enthusiastically raised their paddles and provided the crowd with a perfectly choreographed wave with their paddles. I wish Amy could have been here to witness the festival's beauty and pageantry, but she had an art show in Charleston.

Teams had traveled from all over the country to compete in the many different divisions, including the ever-popular breast cancer division. Twelve teams, from Florida to California, were competing against us in the Grand Masters Mixed division.

An earth-shaking drum roll came from the premier Philadelphia team, whose drummer silenced the crowd with an awesome display of talent. His first five hard hits on the drum echoed across the river like thunderous gunshots. As he completed his display of percussive talent, everyone broke into applause.

The boats made their way back to the loading docks, and we were greeted with more applause from the spectators in recognition of each competitor's hard work and dedication. After we docked the boat, my teammates made their way to the vast island of tents in the park area that were set up for each team.

Strolling along the river's bank, I witnessed four young boys, about twelve years old, laughing and jumping around. Upon a closer examination, I saw another boy, about the same age but smaller, sitting on the ground, hiding his face with his hands.

I ran to him. The young boy was crying. The other kids were poking at his clothes and laughing, jesting, and making fun of his small size. I jumped in front of the four boys. "What's going on?"

The four young bullies were all handsome, with neat haircuts, wearing GQ shirts and shorts. Our country's future bankers, I thought. The leader confidently said, "Look at what he's wearing. It's stupid. A plaid shirt with checkered pants. He's a doofus."

I wanted to punch the little brat in the nose but resisted. "Hey, buddy, you kiss your mama with that ugly, nasty mouth?"

He looked at me and scowled. "What's it to you, old man?"

I ignored his comment as I remembered my days growing up in the mill village. We'd routinely be rude to our elders. And eventually, some adult would get fed up with the disrespect and pop a kid across the lips. We called it getting slapped damn in the mouth.

With bloody lips, we'd run home yelling to our daddy to go beat the old man up. But typically, that complaint would garner us another slap across the jaw for being an insolent little jackass. Eventually, we learned to keep our mouths closed and to carefully choose our words.

The four boys again proceeded to pour their scorn on this disgraced young lad. I yelled loud enough that everyone within a hundred feet could hear. "Dammit, leave this guy alone."

The boys jumped backward, and as I raised my hand to slap one of their mouths, the gang's leader screamed, "Hey, mister, we're just joking around."

I heard a man's husky voice behind me. "What the hell's going on?"

I turned and stepped within inches of his face and asked as nervous sweat poured down my face, "These hoodlums belong to you?" My heart raced with the humiliating pain of my own past.

He stepped closer. "Yeah, two of them. What of it?"

I tightly clasped my fist ready to teach somebody an important lesson when I was jerked around by a strong arm. It was Thomas. He grunted, "Let's go."

The hoodlums' father yelled, "You better get him out of here before I kick his ass."

I struggled to release myself from Thomas's grip but to no avail, as he was too strong. He pulled me back to our team's tent. My heart continued to race.

"Those kids need to be taught a lesson," I said.

Thomas groaned, "Not here, not now." He then laughed

and whispered. "I hate Bonnie's at a meeting in Atlanta as she would have loved watching me restrain you. Usually, she's the one stopping me from doing something stupid."

I sat in a chair underneath our tent and breathed deeply. After several minutes, my pulse rate slowed, and I stopped sweating. What the hell was I thinking? Getting into a fight the evening before our great competition?

Our spouses and friends had lined the border of our tent with coolers full of water and Gatorade. They'd graciously set up tables in the middle and covered them with all types of fruits, energy bars, loaves of bread, jars of peanut butter, sandwiches of all types, and numerous vegetable trays.

The sense of a festive celebration filled the thick, balmy air as the teams gathered underneath their tent. Paddlers, families, and friends. The sun was setting over the lake. It'd been a long, grueling day, and we were tired. Ready for a well-earned night of restful sleep.

But without notice, an unexpected wave of anxiety flooded my body and my thoughts. What was happening? I tried to hide my panic but was unsuccessful. Sean and Thomas approached me and put their arms around my shoulders. "Relax, Coach, and don't worry; we're not going to let you down."

I smiled, but the truth was, to my utter surprise, that I was more worried about letting them down than about winning. And even more, I was concerned about their safety.

"I'm concerned. This heat can be dangerous," I said.

Sean slapped me on my back. "Just be yourself, the great coach that you are, and we'll be just fine."

I said under my breath, "That's what worries me . . . being myself."

I hoped my pep talk to the team would soothe my anxiety. I asked everyone to gather close. "I've brought for each of us a stick-on tattoo of the mythical creature, the phoenix." Their startled looks amused me. "The bird is a symbol of strength and resilience. He dies in flames and then resurrects himself, arising from the ashes of the same fire that killed him. Each of us, in our own way, have risen from our plight of cancer to once again fly. Take a tattoo and in the morning put it on the shoulder of your right arm and come ready to race. No—come ready to *fly,* like the phoenix."

24

Chattanooga

Friday, July 23, 2010
8:30 a.m.
Finish of the First 200-Meter Race

Morning came, as did our first race. Four beautifully ornate boats pulsated through the water along the racecourse. We'd had an excellent start and were currently neck and neck for the lead with the defending national champions, the Leathernecks. The divine dragon was with my team. Cancer would not win this race. The Dragon Survivors were paddling like real dragons—the godlike rulers of the water. After adjusting his colostomy bags, Sean regained his timing and stroked with abandon. We were twenty synchronized silhouettes paddling down the Tennessee River. This was dragon boat racing at its highest level. It was poetry on water.

The Leathernecks were a team of retired Marine veterans who lived in The Villages, a huge central Florida community. They were strong, disciplined, and committed to winning. They chanted, "U-rah, u-rah," with each paddle stroke. We needed to not allow their mantra to distract us from our race strategy.

Our drummer, perched on the boat's bow in front of the brilliant dragon head, was our focus. She was the heartbeat of our boat. Each paddler became a shadow of the next, their blades moving up and down like pistons in the water.

Our steersperson kept us moving in a perfect straight line between the floating buoys, although I could feel him struggle as the wind picked up and caused the waves to increase. Our stroke paddlers in the front seat, Pat and Brooke, led the team as their arms moved in perfect unison with the drummer's beat.

When we passed the course's midway buoy, we were tied with the Leathernecks and were several feet ahead of the other two boats. We were about to learn if our intense yearlong training had been enough. Did we have the stamina to push ahead during the final stretch? I felt my face and neck flush with heat as my body tested my tumors.

As we reached the buoy marking the final fifty meters, our drummer yelled, "Finish, finish!" The muscles in my shoulders tightened. I tried to relax but couldn't. I wanted to win. I pushed through my body's radiation-induced energy drain. My arms felt like water-filled spaghetti noodles.

Each paddler extended their reach into the water like the stretching of a rubber band. We completely buried our paddle blades to fully load them with water. We forced them hard, back through the river with all our might, propelling the slender canoe forward. Our boat picked up speed.

Pain shot through my arms and legs. My heart throbbed within my chest as I gasped for each valuable breath. My body weakened. I needed some red blood cells. It would have been a perfect time for some Lance Armstrong doping. We increased the rate of our strokes with our drummer's final scream, "Finish now!"

I didn't look to the left or to the right. My eyes were open, but all I could see was the drummer pounding her mallet against the skin of the drum. I heard deep breaths and grunts from my teammates. My muscled were in overload.

A few more strokes.

One more stroke.

I had to finish strong.

I had to win.

I heard the drummer yell, "Let it run," which meant to stop, as we'd crossed the finish line. Had we won? My heart raced. My lungs craved fresh air. I lowered my head into my lap in complete exhaustion. I felt a pat on my back and heard the words, "Great race."

Our steersperson turned the boat to head back to the dock. The temples in my forehead pulsed in and out as my heartbeat wouldn't slow. The flushing worsened. That's when I heard the announcer's glorious voice blare through those loudspeakers: "First place from Charleston, South Carolina, the Dragon Survivors!"

My body's heat cooled as our boat pulled alongside the dock. We celebrated, offering each other high fives and hard fist bumps. We'd just beaten the defending national champions. It was only the first race, but it was an excellent start.

Hopefully we were on our way to winning the gold medal and a trip to Hong Kong.

25

Chattanooga

Friday, July 23, 2010
8:40 a.m.

Race volunteers assisted us from our boat and onto the dock. I welcomed the help, as my body was tired and weak. My team reveled in our victory as we walked back to our tent. I marveled at Sean's toughness as he'd dealt with his specially-made ostomy belt during the race. I grabbed Sean's shoulder to get his attention. As he turned toward me, his massive smile shone brilliantly. I shouted at him, to be heard above the team's loud celebration: "So proud of you. I've never seen your colostomy bag come loose before, but you hardly missed a stroke. Great job, especially in your condition!"

Sean's smile disappeared. His strong hand grabbed the collar of my shirt and pulled it tight around my neck. I gasped for air. His face distorted with anger. His intense response shocked me. "Don't you ever look at me as a lesser person because of my cancer. Listen carefully. I'm not a person dying from a terrible disease. I'm an individual, the same as you or anyone else living each day to its fullest. Don't you dare show pity toward me."

I twisted my head and jerked my neck away from his grip. I breathed deeply. "I didn't mean to . . . I mean I just wanted to say I'm proud of you."

Sean stepped closer. His eyes penetrated mine as if he was peering into my inner self. His words were serious and authoritative. "What are you afraid of, Tripp? Losing? Being humiliated? Not being good enough? Who's hurt you?" His stare grew more intense. "You need to find the courage to face your demons. Your real illness isn't cancer."

The back of my neck turned hot. "Damn, Sean, I was just trying to give you a compliment. You don't have to attack me."

He grimaced, nodded, and walked back to the team's tent. I slowly followed him. What the hell had he meant I needed courage to face my demons. Hell, I had more courage than five Seans. Creating my company, making it successful, dealing with vicious New York bond attorneys, ruthless Boston investors, and several severe economic downturns. I had plenty of courage.

The team continued their boisterous celebration as I approached the tent, still ruminating over Sean's comments. They were giving each other big high fives, hugging, and a few were running around the tent. They were ecstatic, and that attitude concerned me.

We needed to maintain our hungry appetite for victory. We

must now focus on the next race. We had plenty of strongly competitive races ahead: two additional 200-meter races that afternoon and two 500-meter races tomorrow. Not to mention Sunday's challenging finale, a 1000-meter race.

I needed more essential red blood cells to carry oxygen through the veins and arteries of my body. My normally strong, athletic legs felt paralyzed with weakness. Stress had caused my hormone-producing neuroendocrine tumors to jump into overdrive. Hot flushing in my face and neck intensified. I walked to the dock to watch the other races. The temperature exceeded one hundred degrees. The heat had become a dangerous factor.

Spectators sheltered their bodies with umbrellas and sat in front of huge fans seeking reprieve from the sweltering air. My anxiety for my team's safety grew with each increased degree in the temperature. My hands were too sweaty to wipe the perspiration dripping from my face.

Four canoes had just finished racing and docked. As the paddlers were being helped from the boats, a shaky female paddler's face was white as a ghost. Her legs wobbly. Suddenly her knees buckled, and she collapsed like a felled tree onto the wooden dock.

An emergency medical crew sprinted to her and began an IV. The woman had heat exhaustion and was severely dehydrated. Her collapse heightened my concern for my team. Our bodies were already weakened from radiation, chemotherapy, and surgeries. Our immune systems were compromised. The hundred-degree heat scared me. I prayed I'd not made a huge mistake leading this team of sick people to compete in this heat.

I walked to the river's roped-off swimming area and slid into the water to cool my hot body. I knelt so the water rested against my chin. After about ten minutes of sitting still with my eyes closed, my energy began to return.

I returned to our team's tent and strictly ordered my teammates to stay out of the sun and drink plenty of water. I wanted them hydrated to the point their urine was perfectly clear. I found a shady spot and lay down on a towel. The ground was hard from the lack of rain. I closed my eyes and prepared my mind for the next race. Allyson startled me as she sat down beside me.

"Do you have many friends?" she asked.

I hesitated to answer her odd and intrusive question. Why did she care about my friends? It was true I didn't let many people get close to me, but I considered myself a good friend. After pondering not answering, my curiosity got the best of me. I sat up and confidently replied, "I have many friends. My work associates and the coaches and players from my days as a high school coach. Why do you ask?"

She leaned backward and supported her body with her elbows. She suspiciously lowered her eyebrows and requested, "Tell me a story about one of your good friends."

I narrowed my eyes. "What do you mean?"

She cocked her head to one side as if she was testing me. "A story about you and one of your good ole buddies. You must have one."

This conversation was becoming weirder by the second. But I'd go along. Play her little game. "A few years after Amy and I were married, one of my coaching buddies, let's call him Donovan, asked me to help him with his son. Donovan had married his college sweetheart just after their freshman year of college. Soon after graduation, they had a son, Justin. But his wife had begun to use drugs and wasn't much of the settling-down type and consequently was a terrible mother. Shortly after Justin's birth, she disappeared, vanished like Jimmy Hoffa. No one had a clue where she'd gone, and my friend was left to raise Justin alone."

Allyson sat up a little on her elbows. "How terrible. A mother has to be awful or really sick to abandon her child."

"But Donovan was an excellent father and was granted full custody of Justin. Life went along as normal, school, baseball, you know, the usual stuff, for seven years without a word from the mother. And then, one night out of the blue, she called, wanting to see her son."

Allyson sat up and locked her arms around her knees. "Did Donovan agree?"

"He was torn. She lived in Denver with a truck driver, and he knew nothing about her life. But Justin wanted to meet her and, after all, she was his mother. Donovan considered her request for two weeks. He and I discussed his decision. He met with a counselor and finally agreed to allow Justin to visit his mother."

Allyson stroked her chin with her hand and shook her head back and forth. "I don't think I could have done that. Not after seven years of silence. That must have been a difficult decision."

I leaned forward. "Excruciatingly difficult, and it scared him to death. Donovan and the counselor spoke with Justin's mother and her live-in boyfriend. His ex-wife had several old friends assure him she'd straightened out her life and quit drugs. Donovan and the counselor felt Justin would be safe. And he believed it was important to honor his son's wishes and that it would be good for him to meet his mother. So, Donovan purchased a round-trip plane ticket and sent him to Denver for a week's visit with his mother."

Allyson's eyes widened. "Did you think the mother was trustworthy?"

"I didn't, but I understood Donovan's rationale. He confirmed Justin had arrived safely in Denver. His son called the first four evenings but not the fifth or the sixth. Donovan tried to call to confirm Justin had made the flight home but got no response."

Allyson leaned forward. "He must have been scared shitless."

"I promise you he was more than scared. He was afraid she'd kidnapped him and taken off. Donovan called me crying. He wanted us to drive nonstop to Denver—as it would be faster than flying—grab Justin, and head straight back to Charleston. We'd take turns driving."

"And did you go?"

"Of course, I went. We left Charleston at five o'clock in the morning and drove seventeen hundred miles without stopping except for gas. We alternated driving and sleeping every six hours. We arrived in Denver at six o'clock the next morning."

Allyson's gaze was fixed upon me. "Did you find his son?"

"We found her house and knocked on the door. She opened it wearing a skimpy nightgown and all drugged out. Her boyfriend never got out of bed. She said that after spending the five days with their son, she felt so guilty for abandoning him, she started using drugs again. She'd pumped her body full of heroin. She even propositioned us for sex if we'd let Justin stay with her for a few more days. We hurriedly grabbed Justin and hit the road."

"Thank goodness," Allyson said.

"On the return trip, we stopped in Memphis to eat and sleep. We returned safely to Charleston, and neither Donovan nor Justin ever heard from her again. I later became Justin's godfather, and he's like a son to me today. Justin now has a son of his own, and I visit them every year."

Allyson stood. "Well for goodness' sake, you are a good friend after all. I think maybe, after hearing that story, I just might be able to place my trust in you."

I smiled and my eyes opened wide. "So, you're just now going to trust me? Allyson, I've been coaching you for more than a year."

"I don't easily trust people."

"Why not?" I asked.

Allyson hesitated several moments before she spoke. "Prior to my breast cancer diagnosis, my life appeared from any outside observer to be perfect. My husband was a successful and respected Charleston attorney. We lived in a large house on the Wando River in Mount Pleasant. I served on several nonprofit boards, including for the Spoleto Festival."

I lifted my eyebrows. "I didn't know you were on the Spoleto board. Very cool."

"It was all cool until surgery took my breasts and the chemo and radiation treatment made me very sick and all my hair fell out. I felt awful and looked worse. That's when my husband informed me he'd been having a four-year affair with a law partner. Of course, she was young, blond, and had big boobs. Just like your friend's wife, he left in the middle of the night. I'd never felt more alone or abandoned. I prayed to die."

I held out an open hand to her. "A true asshole."

She grabbed my hand. "Thankfully, God didn't answer my prayer."

Her story humbled me. "What happened? Now you're one of the happiest people I know."

Her eyes crinkled with a tear. "Kent happened. Since he's

twelve years my junior, I was shocked when he asked me out for dinner. I'd had reconstructive surgery and spent many hours in therapy, but I was still emotionally damaged."

I learned toward her. "I like Kent. We've fist bumped and laughed several times after our practices. He seems like a good man. And he has the best-looking beard I've ever seen."

"He's perfect, and he does have a great beard. He hadn't shaved his beard since he was seventeen until . . ." Tears ran down her face. "And . . . and when my cancer returned, I was horrified. I was convinced he'd leave me." Allyson's countenance changed She smiled and sat upright. "And what did Kent do?"

I was into Allyson's story. "What did he do?"

"Instead of running away, he arrived at the hospital after my surgery to remove the affected lymph nodes with no beard, a shaved head, and no eyebrows. I didn't recognize him."

"I bet. He shaved his beard?" I asked.

Allyson picked up a napkin from one of our tables and wiped the tears that ran off her chin. She laughed. "Not only had he shaved his beard, he'd shaved his entire body. And he's a hairy man."

I laughed. "His entire body?"

She laughed louder. "I made him strip, totally naked, right there in my hospital room. I had to see for myself. I'm talking mammoth man grooming. Funniest thing I'd ever seen."

I tilted my head back. "That's cool, but I don't think I could ever shave my entire body."

Her smile turned to adoration. "He told me he did it to prove to me he'd never leave. He knew well my fear of abandonment and that every man in my life had deserted me. And he knew that I knew how much he loved his beard."

I wanted to speak but I had no words.

She continued. "But Kent did more. I was scared and depressed. All I could think about was more treatment, more surgery, and losing Kent. I couldn't shake it."

"Believe me, I understand."

"This man, who I've never seen darken a church door, gave me a stunning framed white napkin with a portion of a Bible verse he'd cross-stitched on it. I didn't think he even knew what cross-stitching was or anything about the Bible."

"What was the verse?"

"In beautiful red letters it read, *Think on things that are true, right, admirable, noble, pure, and lovely . . .*"

My anxiety calmed.

"Then he leaned over the hospital's bed and whispered, 'And you are the loveliest person I have ever seen or known." She chuckled. "Crazy for a silent-type, burly, hairy man, huh?"

I laughed. "He wasn't hairy anymore."

She laughed. "No, he wasn't. He was just a beautiful person. Anyway, you understand why I have difficulty trusting people."

"I do."

"But I do think you're a good man."

She stopped talking. Her eyes appeared serious as if she had something to say that she didn't want to say.

"What? What else?" I asked.

She breathed in deeply, held the air for several moments, and slowly exhaled. She looked at the ground and then finally at me. "A good man with a serious flaw."

I was confused. "What do you mean a serious flaw?"

She stood and hugged me. Nodded. Smiled. "That one you'll need to figure out on your own."

26

Chattanooga

Friday, July 23, 2010
1:00 p.m.

We had forty-five minutes to loosen up and prepare, prior to marshaling for our next 200-meter race. I gathered the team and led them in calisthenics. After ten minutes of jumping jacks, leg raises, sit-ups, and push-ups, we all scattered to individually stretch our old muscles. It was critical to avoid injury. I was rested and felt stronger.

When the announcer called our team to marshal, I grouped us all into a small circle. "We had a great first race. We beat the defending national champions. I'm very proud of you. But remember, we collect cumulative points for each race. If we finish less than third place, we receive no points for that race."

Everyone's gaze was fixed upon me. "This race is very important. The winning team collects five points, second-place team receives three, and third place one point. It is also possible to earn up to two bonus points on the grueling final 1000-meter race if we win by a large enough margin. It's common to have a letdown after a big victory. We cannot allow that to happen. During this race, concentrate on one perfect stroke after another. Don't think about winning or losing. If we're focused, we'll be fine."

The team appeared to be focused. I hoped so. "We're racing three slower teams in this heat, so we should be fine. Focus, focus, focus." We raised our paddles into the air and screamed, "Thrive, Dragon Survivors, thrive!"

The marshaling area was located near the loading dock and underneath a large white tent to shelter the teams from the smoldering sun. The area was designed to organize the teams and ensure races ran smoothly and the festival's schedule remained on track.

The head marshaller, a woman holding a clipboard with many papers attached, instructed each team to line up in accordance with how we sat in the boat. Her voice was firm but cordial, and she seemed smart and highly organized. We and the other three teams diligently followed her orders.

Brooke and Pat, our two stroke paddlers, who sat in row one, lined up first—Brooke on the right and Pat on the left. The team then lined up behind them from row two back to row ten. The marshaller led us in this exact order to the dock and to our boat. For safety reasons, we carefully stepped into the slender canoe one row at a time, beginning with row one.

After each paddler had gotten into the boat we paddled to

the starting line. I noticed the team seemed lethargic. Their arms and legs appeared heavy and tired, as though they had weights strapped to them.

We were slotted in the first lane, which was the closest to the river's bank and had the shallowest water. Lane four was the farthest distance from the shore and consequently the water was deeper. The deeper the water, the less draft on the boat, and the faster it would move. We'd been in lane three for our first race. We readied ourselves for the starter's commands, but I was troubled and couldn't clear my head.

The starter's horn blasted. The first six strokes of our start were perfect. But then we sputtered. Our timing was off. I heard two paddles clang together. What the hell?

I screamed, "Settle," hoping the team would relax into a smooth and in-sync race pace. But we didn't. We were falling behind the other teams. The steersperson tried to help and yelled, "Settle, settle, timing."

But no encouragement or instruction seemed to get my team to function like the well-oiled machine we'd become during the past eighteen months of practice. The more effort we exerted to move into sync, the more our timing worsened. Two other boats increased their lead.

We flailed down the river's racecourse looking like a drunken octopus. To the onlooking crowd, we must have appeared to be a bunch of idiots. As the team's coach, I was humiliated and madder than hell.

We struggled to finish in a miserable third place. The results of this race jeopardized our chances of winning the gold medal. Even though I'd been worried about the heat, I hadn't thought the team would completely fall apart. Shame burned in my gut.

I was so angry I could barely see straight. I should have known better than to put myself in this humiliating position.

How should I respond to this embarrassing loss?

The team silently paddled back to the dock with their heads hung in despair like a group of people who'd fallen into a giant abyss. We unloaded the boat and slowly walked back to our team's tent. The Dragon Survivors were a defeated team. I allowed the team to sit without saying a word for thirty minutes.

I finally walked to the middle of the tent. My anger flared, and I kicked the lounge chair against the table of food. The chair collapsed. Food splattered onto the ground. No one spoke or looked at me. You could have heard a pin drop onto the thick, soft grass.

"What the hell just happened? That race was total chaos. A complete cluster. Where was your focus? You, the team, and especially me as your coach, are an outright embarrassment to everyone watching."

Sean stood, his face beet red. His jaw muscles were clenched tight. He was about to talk, but I had no intention of being interrupted. "Sit down, Sean," I harshly instructed and continued my chastisement. "This mental letdown stinks like a pile of horse crap. We practiced a year and a half, sacrificed time away from our families, suffered through treatments, and for what—this crap."

My shirt was soaked with sweat. I felt light-headed like I was swimming underwater with no escape. But I wasn't finished. "We set our goal high. And now we've put ourselves in a tough position to win gold. We'll need to win all the remaining races to be national champions." I stopped speaking and stared at each team member. I had their undivided attention. "Wasn't that the goal that you asked me to coach you to achieve?"

My initial concerns to coach this team had been confirmed. It was a huge mistake. I warned Amy. I was also pissed at her. The temperature was one hundred two degrees, but I felt as if I was walking over a thinly frozen lake. I could hardly breathe. "I suggest we fold up this tent and head back to Charleston before someone gets hurt and you turn me into a total disgrace."

Brooke stood; her eyes moist. "We can still win if we come together as a team. We are a team—a team that loves each other."

I sighed, looked away, and shook my head. "This is an odd way to show love. It's time to show real love. Stop this crazy endeavor to kill ourselves."

I walked away. I strolled to the river and stood in front of an orchard-stone retaining wall that supported the river's bank. The rivers had been a source for life for me, but now it was my nemesis. Damn! My heart raced. I ripped off my soaked shirt. I held my brick necklace in my hand. I wanted to disappear, to end this madness. This humiliation.

***

"What the hell are you doing?" I heard Sean's voice ricochet off the stone wall.

I ignored him and continued staring at the river. I had no intention to answer.

He powerfully grabbed my arm and twirled me around to face him. Sean and Pat both stood in front of me. Sean repeated his question with rage. "I asked, what the hell do you think you're doing?"

I ripped my arm from his grasp and stepped back. "Saving us a ton of heartache and embarrassment," I said.

Pat approached and moved to within an inch of my face, maddened, her face as red as her hair. "We deserve better than this. We're not a bunch of pawns in the war of your fragile ego. It's as if you're possessed by some schizo demon. One day you're a great coach and the next a crazed person. Maybe it *should* be you that goes home."

I was blind with anger. "You don't have a clue about me or what I've endured. We practiced eighteen months for this crap. Was this team ever serious about being national champions? Do they understand what it takes? Because it's not the way we just raced."

Pat's muscles tightened as if she was being squeezed in a vice. She yelled, "It was *one* shitty race. We can overcome and still win gold. I know these people, and they are neither quitters nor losers."

I yelled in return: "Not a group of national champions, either."

Sean grabbed Pat's hand from blasting into my face, his arm muscles rippling. He was breathing hard. He stared straight into my eyes. "I guarantee you this team can and will do better. We can't quit now. It would destroy some of these folks."

My voice was firm. "Give it up, Sean. The team has lost their focus. We need to go home and stop humiliating ourselves. Or worse, in this heat, someone hurts themselves or becomes deathly sick. Admit it, going to Hong Kong was a foolish dream. Hell, some of us may not even be alive next year. We need to go home and focus on our families, not some crazy pipe dream."

Pat jumped at me and this time successfully slapped my face. Sean pulled her back. She yelled, "Don't you dare tell me what I can or cannot dream. Or when I'll die. You don't have the right to speak about our deaths. Lying on The Citadel football field, you said we were closer than brothers and sisters. What the hell happened to you? Who abused and destroyed you as a child?"

I couldn't swallow. I remembered my dad slapping my face. I recalled my boyhood bedroom window and the calmness it spawned in my spirit. I stepped back to ease the tension.

Pat calmed down. "This team is a family, and families don't abandon each other."

Sean raised his right hand and held up his index finger. "One more race. If we don't come together, then we go home."

My voice cracked as if I was begging. "Sean, Pat . . . look at us. We're sick. Continuing to race in this heat could be dangerous. Brooke was seriously weak after the last race. You guys look bad. I feel like shit. Be realistic."

Pat placed her hand on my shoulder. "One more race. That's all we ask."

I sighed hard but was glad we'd calmed down. My heart told me I should agree with Pat, but my brain screamed in disagreement. I was afraid my ugly past would repeat. I'd not only be a danger to myself but to the whole team. But they'd survived mountains of adversity to get here, and I couldn't deny their request.

"One more race."

27

Chattanooga

Friday, July 23, 2010
3:30 p.m.

I was prepared for our final 200-meter race. I'd decided to allow the team to muster their own motivation for this race. No inspirational speech before this race. I hoped, deep within my heart, this team would rise up on its own desire to win. Accept the challenge and overcome.

Since I'd accepted Sean and Pat's request to coach the Dragon Survivors, I'd felt an enormous pressure to build confidence and the winning attitude in my teammates, helping them believe they could be national champions. My current dismay was my belief that I'd failed.

The unrelenting temperature still exceeded one hundred degrees. Our bodies continued to be frail. I'd pushed this team hard over the past year and a half. Maybe I should have created a safety net for the failure of reaching our goal as national champions. It would have been easier to adopt the approach to encourage the team to do their best and not worry about winning. But that attitude did not exist in my bones. I wanted to win at all cost.

"Dragon Survivors, prepare to marshal!" blared through the festival speakers. On the outside I appeared as calm as an owl. But on the inside, my stomach was flipping somersaults. We marshaled, and again I resisted the extreme temptation to provide a motivational speech. But I said nothing.

We walked to the dock, loaded the boat, and paddled to the race's starting line for the day's final 200-meter race. The other three teams in this race were a team from California that wasn't competitive; a team from Chicago, the Windy City Dragons, who were currently in second place; and a competitive Philadelphia team called the Thunder Dragons. If we finished third or last, our chances of being national champions would mathematically be impossible. The best medal we could win would be silver, and that was if we won both of Saturday's 500-meter races plus Sunday's 1000-meter race. I forced myself to submit to that possibility. A silver medal would have to be an acceptable accomplishment.

We had alignment, and the starter's horn blasted. The team nailed the start. Our stroke paddlers, Pat and Brooke, led the team in a perfect stroke rate. We settled into our race pace with impeccable timing. After 100 meters, we held a safe lead on the California and Philadelphia teams but were neck and neck with the Windy City Dragons.

Our torsos fully rotated with each stroke, just as we'd practiced. Each paddler's reach was fully extended, and they slammed their paddles deep into the water like the blades were harpoons attempting to kill that great white shark.

We de-rotated our upper bodies, lengthening our back muscles for maximum leverage. As our paddles became parallel with our hips in the boat, the team snapped them from the water as if we were pulling a sword from that sheath and rotated again forward. Just like we'd practiced. Our legs powerfully flexed, driving hard against the bottom of the boat and propelling us forward. We repeated the mighty stroke, one after another.

Our faces were locked in the boat staring forward. We looked neither to the left nor to the right. Our muscles relaxed between strokes, wasting no energy. The boat surged forward with each rip of our paddles. I felt as if I was floating on top of the water. The team had total commitment to each stroke and absolute focus. My strength returned to me. I felt young—like I'd never had cancer, as if my body had never been pumped full of poisonous radiation.

I couldn't resist the temptation and cheated and looked at the other boats. With only fifty meters to go, we were three boat seats ahead of the Windy City Dragons, and the other two teams were far behind. The desire to win big overwhelmed me and I screamed, "Deeper, deeper . . . power!"

Endorphins circulated in my brain as I witnessed twenty teammates perfectly focused on one thing—victory. The amazing sight captivated me. We were now a full boat length ahead of the Windy City Dragons. The other teams were nowhere in sight.

Feeling like the coach of the team again, I screamed, "Finish!"

Our highly decorated, ornate dragon boat surged forward. I heard the announcer's words blare through the speakers: "The Dragon Survivors from Charleston, South Carolina, are putting on a paddling clinic."

It was a perfect moment. The dream of every athlete. The moment when every muscle works in perfect unison where your body transcends the sporting event. When your effort seems effortless. It's the ace baseball pitcher's perfect game. Or the basketball sharpshooter hitting ten three-pointers in a row.

We didn't stop paddling until we were fifty meters past the finish line. Finally, we allowed ourselves to stop and raised our paddles high into the air. There was no doubt which team had won the race.

We'd at last achieved the team unity I'd so strived to obtain. Twenty brave paddlers working together as one for more than a single race. The team performing as a unit fusing together their physical, mental, and spiritual parts.

Could we maintain this unity?

28

Chattanooga

Friday, July 23, 2010
5:00 p.m.

The victory of the last race positioned us in a close second place to the Leathernecks. After our triumph, the team was refreshed and energized. My teammates and I celebrated. We basked in hope. Not just hope for a dragon boat race victory, but hope for tomorrow. Hope for a miracle. A hope for our bodies to be healed.

The day's racing was complete, and the cancer survivor ceremony that had become a vital part of every dragon boat competition would start at dusk. But for now, all the festival's paddlers would relax. Enjoy their friends and families. Eat and drink. Teams had brought charcoal grills to cook hamburgers, hot dogs, and chicken breasts. Some teams had local restaurants deliver food, but everyone celebrated life.

The heavy aroma of burning charcoal blending with the scent of roasting meat tranquilized my mind from the stress of the day's events. The fresh culinary odors mixed with the sweet fragrance of the flowing river calmed my soul. Hundreds of people mingled, laughing and hugging and sharing stories about the day's races.

The scene reminded me of my family picnics when I was a young boy. Several times a year, my parents would take my brother, sister, and me to the creek at the foothills of the Smokey Mountains. We'd spread blankets over the same large boulders. My mother took great pride in preparing the meal: southern fried chicken cooked with real lard, homemade potato salad, and sweet fried cream corn. The meal smelled so wonderful, we were lucky we didn't get attacked by every bear in the woods. Those days were some of the best for my family—just too rare.

Dad told stories about growing up poor as a sharecrop farmer and moving every two years from farm to farm. He hated changing schools so often, so he quit in the tenth grade. He'd talk about plowing a field with a hand-held plow pulled by a horse or milking a cow by hand. My sister and I hung on his every word. Those family times branded a restful peace in my mind that I longed to experience again. The days were simple and primitive. A rare time of harmony and order.

Breaking into my reverie, the master of ceremonies announced the cancer survivors' ceremony was about to begin and asked all cancer survivors to make their way to the dock. It was time to celebrate life. The cancer survivors' ceremony was a vital part of a dragon boat festival. As we walked to the dock, a reverent silence hovered over the entire park area. In one manner or another, cancer had touched all of our lives, either personally, a family member, or a close friend.

The sport of dragon boating had become especially popular with breast cancer patients and survivors. The upper-body exercise and team esprit de corps had proven to be instrumental in recovery and the tolerance of treatment. There are few sports that allow a person of any age or level of athleticism to participate competitively. Dragon boating was such a sport.

In fact, the sport had become so popular with breast cancer survivors, a separate racing division had been dedicated just for them. These women possessed a pugnacious determination to live and compete. Their never-give-up attitude inspired every life they touched. They paddled through sickness, hair loss, disfiguring surgeries, and depression. Their untainted passion was only surpassed by their love and dedication for their teammates.

Participants and spectators lined the banks of the Tennessee River to observe the ceremony. The somber, respectful hush was awe-inspiring. As each cancer survivor stepped into a boat, a festival volunteer handed them a white or red rose. We paddled the boats close to the river's bank and faced the spectators. Our steersperson pulled the canoes close to each other. Gunwale next to gunwale. Each somber paddler took the hand of the person next to them in the adjacent boat and pulled the canoes even closer. We hung our heads and offered a silent prayer for the paddlers who'd died during the previous year. Tears streamed down the faces of these real-life heroes.

Whatever God each person worshipped was present. The water, the air, our boats, had become holy ground filling our hearts with love and hope. A breast cancer survivor shared her story. Another woman sang a song about the preciousness of life.

A hallowed silence descended over the river and the park, consecrating the value of each life. In one magical, orchestrated moment, the cancer survivors tossed their roses into the river, signifying their veneration for every person who'd lost their battle with cancer. The roses floated in perfect silence along the river's current, offering us a renewed faith in tomorrow. I felt safe in the river. I prayed for healing.

The boats paddled slowly back to the dock. We continued basking in the wonder of life and the power of friendship. As the heat continued to intensify, I noticed Brooke had stopped paddling. Her face was pale, and she stared listlessly into the sky. She stumbled and almost fell as we exited the boats onto the dock.

As everyone embraced and cried walking up the dock, I grabbed Brooke around the waist to help her walk. "Are you okay?" I asked her.

She nodded and grabbed my arm for support. Her voice was weak. "Just need some water and to lie down."

We slowly strolled back to our tent to pack up and end the day's activities. I gathered the team around. It was time for my speech. "It's apparent we have the ability to win the gold medal. Currently, we're in a close second to the Leathernecks, so we can't afford another mental letdown like we had in today's second race."

Allyson smiled at me. I sensed she now had trust in my words.

"I'm proud of how you responded and the comeback from our loss. Celebrate today's achievements, but tomorrow be ready for two grueling 500-meter races. I'm going to push you hard toward that gold medal. Do I have everyone's commitment?"

Heads nodded with enthusiasm.

"Get a good night's rest and be at our tent at six o'clock in the morning—ready to compete."

My teammates walked away with a renewed skip in their steps.

Everyone except Brooke. She was standing about fifty feet away and staring at me. I witnessed pain and fear in her eyes. She appeared as if she could hardly stand. Her husband, Clawson, gently put his arm around her back to support her weakened body. He held her tight against his waist to assist with each step toward their car.

We'd won the day's final race but I wondered at what cost.

29

Chattanooga

Friday, July 23, 2010
8:00 p.m.

My hotel room, which was within walking distance from the festival site, was large as hotel rooms go. The room had a sitting area that looked out onto a concrete patio which was only a few steps from the swimming pool. The furniture was pleasant, although the lamps were rickety and cheap. Admirable reproductions featuring Glenn Miller's big band and the swing song "Chattanooga Choo Choo" hung on the walls. The room was comfortable and quiet, but its best feature—a cozy, king-size bed.

I was too exhausted to watch television, and butterflies swirled in my stomach as I thought about tomorrow's tough

500-meter races. Brooke's physical condition worried me. Her body was weak from the radiation treatments and dehydrated from the extreme heat.

I lay on the bed with my hands covering my face as I listened to music playing on the radio. Two 500-meter races would challenge our endurance. I wasn't sure that I myself wasn't too weak. The heat, our cancer, the surgeries, radiation, and chemotherapy that were taking its toll on my teammates scared me. I questioned: Even if we won the gold medal, how we could ever endure a trip to Hong Kong?

My eyes slowly closed as I listened to Nat King Cole and his daughter Natalie sing their iconic computer-generated duet, "Unforgettable," when I heard a soft knock on the room's door. My heart raced. What was wrong? Who was sick? My hand trembled as I opened the door.

Relief immediately rushed throughout my body. Amy smiled as she blurted out, "I thought you'd never answer the door. I knocked three times."

She stepped into the room and placed her luggage in front of the closet. We embraced and kissed. "I was listening to music," I said as I stepped back and stared at her beautiful face. I grabbed her and again kissed her. "Man, did I need to see your smiling face tonight. You surprised me!"

She gently rubbed my cheek with her soft hand. "I came to be with you for the balance of the competition. You know my special intuition. I knew you needed me. What's going on? How are you feeling?"

"I'm tired and weak, as if my bones could break at any moment. Our final race of the day was our best ever, but I have a god-awful feeling in my gut that something's wrong. Like everything's about to blow apart."

The song ended, and the room fell silent.

Amy looked worried as she grabbed my arm and pulled me out the door. "Come on, we're going to walk to the river."

The air was still thick with the heaviness of deep southern humidity, the kind that made it difficult to breathe. Amy's short but shapely legs skipped like an antelope, pulling me along behind her as if on a leash. I could still smell the BBQ grill's hot coals smoldering as we approached the river and our race site.

She marched straight toward the river, pulling me along step for step. A full moon was rising in the sky and shining across the water. Its radiant reflection seemed endless. The bright stars glowed like candles and lit our path. A few stray paddlers sat on benches overlooking the river and talked about the day's events. An old man sitting on a bench stared at us, I'm sure wondering why such a petite woman was so aggressively pulling a rather large man.

I gazed at the river. It'd been my friend. But the hard-flowing currents of the water could also be cold and dangerous, an indifferent killer. Amy could see in me what I couldn't. The shroud I'd worn since a young boy to protect my inner self was also like the river—cold and dangerous. We stopped walking at the water's edge. She waved her hand, pointing at the river. "You love the river. It's given you life and joy. Let it now be your light of success, not the source of your demise. Lead your team as your heart is gently speaking, not as your brain is screaming."

My mind understood her words, but my heart did not. My anger flared—she was the one who had coerced me to coach this team. I wearily sat on a bench, not wanting to think about my past. I watched the wind ripple the dark but moonlit water.

Amy sat next to me. "Many times, I've heard you compare the waters of the river to the blood within our bodies. You remember the sewer leak that contaminated the Ashley River a few years ago?"

I nodded, wondering where this story was heading.

"The river had to be cleansed before it was again useful. It's the same with blood. If the integrity of our circulatory system is compromised, we can die. It needs to be treated with antibiotics or other measures to make it healthy." Amy touched my hand. "It's also the same with our spirit . . . our hearts. You have allowed anger and bitterness to contaminate your soul. Maybe you're pushing your team too hard for your own benefit."

I closed my eyes. My words were harsh. "It's the only way I know how to survive or coach. Plus, you're the one who, against my better judgment, convinced me to coach this team."

She squeezed my hand harder. "I know your heart. I see your kindness and gentleness. But you rarely allow others to see you that way. And when you do, you refuse to allow it to last. You're double-minded. Pulled toward compassion one day and bitterness the next. It's exhausting."

The muscles in my jaw tightened. I had no desire to have this conversation. "You don't understand. My pure existence depends upon me hanging on to my anger and bitterness, like a feral cat clutching a piece of food in a dumpster. It's my protection."

Amy released my hand and rubbed my face. "I watched you refuse to help Allyson in Beaufort when Pat asked you to talk to her about being nervous. She needed you, and you had the ability to help. Be the example your great mentor Saul requested you to become. Be that exemplar. Let go and help these people. Help yourself. Cleanse your spirit."

I again thought of my dad slapping my face and telling me to never let go of my anger. "It's the way I am—the way I coach."

Amy slid closer and wrapped her arms around me. "Would you try? For me?"

"I'm not sure I can . . . even for you."

30

Chattanooga

Saturday, July 24, 2010
6:00 a.m.

I woke at six o'clock, showered, shaved, and kissed Amy goodbye as she slept. She had a morning call with an art gallery and planned to arrive at the festival site after the first race. I walked to the race venue. Anxiety swirled in my gut as I considered the day's 500-meter races. Our first 500-meter race was scheduled for 8:45 this morning and the second 500-meter race at 2:00 in the afternoon. I found a quiet spot near our tent to sit and prepare my strategy.

I'd promised Amy I'd try to let go of my anger and bitterness, but I wasn't sure I could. They had served me well for many years. I'd decided to coach this team today in the only fashion I knew. Push and push hard. I'd think about changing when we returned to Charleston.

Sean was first to arrive. He was relaxed and cheerful. He asserted, "I've got a good feeling about today. We're going to do great."

I grimaced. "I wish I shared your optimism. I'm concerned about Brooke. She could hardly walk last night after the cancer ceremony."

Sean's voice became more subdued. "I did see Clawson helping her walk. Have you seen her this morning?"

I shook my head. "No, and Pat also looked weak. If we're going to win today's daunting 500-meter race, we desperately need our two stroke paddlers."

Sean sat down next to me. "As a kid, my father taught me the value of thinking negatively. He faithfully preached if you prepare for the worst, when it happens, you'll not be disappointed. I mastered the great art of negativism. I could say, 'Yeah, but' with the best of negative folks."

I smiled.

Sean laughed. "It became a joke in my family that I had the tendency to be just a little bit pessimistic. Although, I've always preferred the title of realist."

I laughed as Sean's satirical sense of humor caused me to relax.

"Go ahead and laugh," Sean said. "But I've had to learn a few hard lessons. When I was first diagnosed with stage IV cancer, from all I could read, my chances of surviving were nil. The most likely outcome was death within a year. The best I could hope for was two years. I've never been particularly religious, but I prayed hard for the second outcome."

I chuckled. "Sorry, I didn't mean to laugh."

"I figured I needed to change my thinking if I was going to live longer than one year. I knew I was sick before my diagnosis. But denial is a wonderful coping skill. I made excuses to explain the pain in my body. I was just having a bad day or I was working too many hours. And of course, the biggie . . . it was stress related, although at times denial can help you get out of bed in the morning. But eventually, I had to face my cancer head-on. I had to start finding solutions rather than excuses. And I had to become an optimist instead of a . . . well, let's say a realist."

I understood what Sean was saying, but I needed to think about the day's races. I stood and began to walk to our team's tent area. "So, tell me, what are you trying to say?"

Sean's smile disappeared. "I've watched you over the past year and a half, and you seem to be in denial of some pretty serious issues. But like me, you can't live in denial forever. You'll eventually have to let go." His smile returned. "You know, *la vida loca.*"

As Sean finished speaking, more teammates appeared. Good, this conversation could end. Anyway, I wasn't in denial. It was called self-preservation. Although I realized I could be harsh, but at least I admitted it. Thomas and Pat walked toward us. Sean patted my back and smiled. Pat attempted to walk erect and strong, but she looked weak and tired. The team was present with the exception of Brooke.

We scattered into small groups to loosen their muscles. We made small talk and tried to relax. I saw Brooke's husband, Clawson, briskly walking in my direction. The threatening look on his face screamed fear and rage. Clawson was a stocky muscular man with a thick Geraldo Rivera–style mustache that covered his upper lip.

As he approached me, he stuck a stiff finger into my chest and proclaimed, "You're trying to kill my wife. She's sick with cancer and undergoing severe radiation. I'm terrified for her safety and have forbidden her to paddle today. Do you understand?"

I stepped back, as I had no desire to confront this hurting and irate man. I could smell the tension in his body. His face contorted with exhaustion and fear. He looked as if he might throw up. He continued his rant. "Her port is irritated, and I'm afraid she'll develop phlebitis. I don't understand what you guys are trying to prove. Is a gold medal worth your life?"

Possibly this frantic man was the only sane person among us. I raised both my hands above my head in a gesture of surrender. "No problem. You're her husband, and you know her. We can race with nineteen paddlers. Allyson can join Pat as a stroke paddler."

He blew a large breath of air directly into my face and walked away. I'd seen that look—in the mirror—many times. Rage was a familiar friend, and I knew it well.

Cancer tested all of us and our families in every manner. A successful surgery only to be followed by the words, "The tumors have returned." A treatment that provides hope that the tumors have shrunk and then the great disappointment when you learn the cancer is growing again—now with a vengeance. News of a cure but then hopes of remission dashed. And—finally the dropping of the dreaded oppressive anvil—"The cancer has spread." Cancer sucks and that's the absolute truth. But we must keep going.

I moved Allyson from seat three to seat one to paddle in the stroke position. I rearranged a few larger men in order to maintain the boat's weight balance from left to right and front to back. Racing a grueling 500 meters with only nineteen paddlers would be challenging. But now, we must continue competing.

The announcer called for the Dragon Survivors to marshal. We tightened our PFDs, gathered our paddles, and as a team made our way to the marshaling tent. As we were lining up, Brooke appeared, wearing her life jacket and holding her paddle.

My mouth twisted open in disbelief. "What are you doing?"

She moved Allyson back to her normal place in row three and stepped into position as the stroke paddler. "I'm here to race."

"But Clawson said—"

"Clawson loves me and is scared to death I'll die. He left the hotel without me. I had to take a cab. Do you know how hard it is to find a cab this early on a Saturday morning in Chattanooga?"

No one spoke. I just stared at her.

"What?" she said. "I make my own decisions."

I closed my eyes in despair. My mind's eye could see her collapsing in the boat or worse—dying. I placed my hand on her shoulder. "Brooke, I can't allow you to paddle. You're not well, and it's too dangerous."

Brooke faced me and the team. "Coach, it's not your decision. I'll abide by how the team votes; if they think I'm too weak to set the race pace, I'll not paddle."

I sighed and stepped back.

Brooke peered into the eyes of each of her teammates. "A woman learns to appreciate her life when she almost loses it. If I dwelled on the fear and suffering that are inherent with cancer, then I'd be a miserable person. I also understand that to say this disease will never get me down, well, that's delusional. Balance is my key—living in the moment."

She looked around. "A friend recently asked me with great sincerity how could I keep going, knowing I may have an incurable cancer? I thought about answering her question with one of our clichéd responses. Like, 'I have faith' or 'They'll find a cure.' You know, our positive attitude will save the day. But each of us are very aware all that is bullshit. The reason I keep going every day is I make a conscious decision not to live in the past or the future. I try my damnedest to balance my anger and negativity with hope and faith. I've learned to take life minute by minute. Is everything okay? Right this minute? Yeah, I'm doing okay today. Will all be okay tomorrow? No way to tell. But today, I'm okay, and at this very moment I plan to race with my beloved teammates."

Before I could say a word, Thomas grunted. "I vote she paddles."

Eighteen paddles simultaneously were lifted high in the air—a unanimous approval for Brooke to paddle. All the paddlers moved back to their original positions.

Brooke must have brought an angel from heaven with her. The first 500-meter race was perfect. At the halfway marker, we were neck and neck with the Thunder Dragons from Philadelphia. And then it happened. Like a mystical wind Brooke screamed, "Power . . . finish!"

Brooke's eloquent body appeared to be like that of a graceful dancer pirouetting across a Broadway stage. Her frame was one smooth fluid motion. Her stroke increased in rate and power. The team responded. After we crossed the finish line of the grueling 500-meter race, our margin of victory was our greatest of the festival.

31

Chattanooga

Saturday, July 24, 2010
9:00 a.m.

Walking back to the tent area after the race, the team moved slowly. The zip in our steps, especially after such a victory, was missing. We dragged our feet sluggishly, and our eyes drooped with gray circles. The cancer, the treatments, the heat, and the grueling races were taking their toll. Fear tightened the muscles in my chest. Could we continue at this pace? We'd won the first 500-meter race but again—how costly was the victory?

I tried to relax and savor the victory, sitting underneath our tent with my teammates. But my anxiety robbed my joy. I was light-headed and nauseous. I needed to cool my body in the cool river water. I studied Brooke's lack of motion as she reclined in a chair. Her skin was pale, and she breathed heavily.

Fatigue overtook my legs as I walked to the banks of the great Tennessee River. The heat index exceeded one hundred and ten degrees. I became dizzy and fell to the ground. My scorching face and head felt like I was in a furnace. My chest pounded, and my face was as red as a matador's cape. I wheezed for air. Thomas and Sean lifted my fragile body and carried me to my car. They forced me to drink an ice-cold Gatorade. Thomas reclined the passenger's front seat and turned the air conditioner to full power for me to rest and my body temperature to cool down.

In the NET world, it's called a carcinoid crisis, a life-threatening condition where a rapid release of hormones, particularly serotonin, are secreted by the tumors, and overtake the body. Sean placed a cold, wet towel over my face. The car's air-conditioner vents blew frigid air onto my body. I closed my eyes and sat still. I'd decided, this was it. We had to stop this insanity before someone got seriously hurt, especially me. After about thirty minutes, my body temperature cooled, and my heart rate settled to normal.

I texted a message to Sean and Pat to meet me at the river's bank. Sean walked up first. "What's up, Captain?"

I bit my lip. "Let's wait for Pat."

He clasped his hands behind his back in self-assuredness. "Sure.... Can't wait for the next race. The last one was remarkable."

Pat approached us, moving slowly. It wasn't her typical strong gait. She almost stumbled and fell as she walked over a small tree root. She was silent, but her gaze communicated concern.

Amy arrived and began to walk toward me. She abruptly stopped as she recognized the serious look on my face. She discreetly moved close enough to hear the conversation.

I stared at Pat. My voice cracked with apprehension, as I desired to make my best effort to be gracious with my comments. "I realize I've pushed our team hard, and I'm afraid I've made a mistake. This team isn't healthy." Again, I wanted to be diplomatic and give the team—and, of course, myself—an amicable way to quit while saving face. "I've overdone the Lombardi coaching card, and I now realize that winning isn't everything. You are my friends, and as your coach, I need to protect you."

Sean stepped forward and narrowed his eyes. "What the hell do you mean? Are you recommending we quit? Is this because you nearly passed out?"

I lowered my head in an effort to tactfully respond. "No, I don't want the team to quit, but I also don't want any of our teammates to be physically harmed. I could never live with that on my conscience."

Pat rubbed her eyes and slouched but said nothing. She looked like a hungry Lowcountry alligator ready to pounce on its prey.

Sean raised his hand in the air. His knuckles were white. "Don't be an idiot; it's too late to think about quitting. We practiced sick for a year and a half. We've paddled and suffered through treatments that poisoned our bodies. All of us knew we were sick when we signed up for this gig. You told us no excuses. We're big boys and girls. We came to win, and that's what I intend to do."

My voice was calm. "It's time we thought rationally. Our goal is admirable, maybe even heroic, but we're sick. What we've already accomplished is miraculous. I'll not allow anyone to be harmed on my watch."

Pat spoke clearly and with authority. "Your watch? Who the hell said this team was your watch?" She stumbled as she stepped toward me. "You are—"

I interrupted her sharply. "Look at you. You can hardly walk. And I just collapsed not more than thirty minutes ago." I pointed toward our team's tent. "Look at Brooke. She hasn't moved from that chair since the last race. And Thomas, his feeding tube looks bad, and I'm worried it could get infected." I stepped away from Pat and pointed toward Sean. "You've had cancer scaped off your sciatic nerve and had what you call the big scoop surgery. You're paddling with a colostomy and an ileostomy. Listen to me—colostomy bags, feeding tubes, chemotherapy, radiation, and surgeries—what the hell are we thinking? It's one thing to paddle recreationally. But to push this hard day after day in this heat to be competitive?"

Pat now stepped with an inch of my face. "Don't you ever interrupt me again. I've endured ports in my veins, puking at work, not being able to have sex because my body ached from head to toe, chemo brain, and dealing with the reality I could die any day. And now, I've got to put up with your bullshit. Quit . . . I don't fucking think so."

Amy frowned. It was obvious she was disappointed with my words.

Sean grabbed Pat's shoulder, pulled her back, and looked at me. "You've brought the team this far; let's finish the course."

Pat barked. "As Thomas said, this may be our last chance to win. His and our final victory. I'll be damned if I'm walking away. I fully intend to have that gold medal placed around my neck."

I felt as if I'd been punched in the face. Did I have the courage to continue this dangerous quest? The discouraging voice within my head screamed, *Don't do it. Someone will die and it will be your fault. You'll be disgraced for the world to witness.*

Pat's voice calmed. "As Maya Angelou said, 'Life is not measured by the number of breaths we take, but by the moments that take our breath away.'" Pat paused and looked at me as if she understood my fear. "Let's go win. Let's take everyone's breath away."

I thought of my mentor Saul's message. Be an exemplar. I wanted to be a good example. Was this my time for healing? Or, was it a time for more shame to descend upon my life? I didn't like putting myself in such a vulnerable position. But my soul knew the correct response. My heart pounded, knowing I couldn't quit. I stared at Pat, nodded slowly at Sean, and looked at the ground. Damn, damn, damn.

Without looking up, I said softly, "Let's go prepare the team for the next race."

32

Chattanooga

Saturday, July 24, 2010
10:30 a.m.

Sean and Pat walked back to the team's tent area and left me alone standing by the river. My legs were still weak. I sat down and prayed I'd made the correct decision. Winning the gold medal and representing the United States in Hong Kong would be a huge accomplishment.

"You know death is the enemy until it isn't." Thomas's faint voice as he walked up behind me was barely audible but powerful.

I just wanted to be left alone, but Thomas was intent to talk. And talking was difficult for Thomas. He stood next to me. I leaned toward him to listen to his words.

"'*Twas grace that taught my heart to fear, and grace, my fears relieved.* It's a great song, and grace shows up in many different ways. My grace was cancer. It taught me to live—to live without fear. All my life I'd been fearful. Frightened of the past. Afraid to face the future. But now I live for today. I live to be here, with you, my friend."

I wasn't sure I understood Thomas's words and had no response. Who isn't afraid? My philosophy had always been, I'll control the events in my life and, by doing so, control my fear. But there was nothing about having cancer that was controllable.

Thomas asked, "Tell me, why are you so afraid?"

I studied his eyes. They spoke peace and contentment. His eyes told a story of a man of much inner thought and self-reflection. I just wanted him to go away. I was both mentally and physically exhausted.

He grabbed my brick necklace. "Tell me why you wear this gosh-ugly necklace."

I hesitated. An image of my father appeared in my mind. I took the necklace from him and stared at it. The words flowed from my mouth without effort or my understanding why I was telling this man my story.

"When I was ten years old and starting the fifth grade, I wanted to be popular and fit in with the other boys. I was a good athlete and could run fast. Because the other boys wanted me to play on their team, they invited me to join their club. They called themselves the Blacklight Boys. Each of the boys had a blacklight in his room, illuminating cool psychedelic posters. These were the school's popular guys."

Thomas grinned.

"I was poor, and they were rich. I wore crappy clothes, and they wore stylish shirts and sharp-looking pants. My mother gave me crappy haircuts, and they went to professional barbers. I desperately wanted to belong to the Blacklight Boys Club."

Thomas snickered.

"The head of the club, Babe, told me they needed to inspect my room and approve my blacklight and posters. Friday afternoon of the first week of school, a group of five very cool and well-dressed Blacklight Boys Club members arrived at my house to perform their inspection."

Thomas's gaze was fixed on me as he intently listened to every word.

"My dad told me buying a blacklight was a complete waste of money, but my mom could see my intense desire to belong with this group of boys. She secretly bought me a blacklight and some great psychedelic posters. I worked hard all week, installing my blacklight in the perfect location to light up the entire room. My fluorescent posters glowed, and my room looked great. Babe was a tough guy, and his father owned the local newspaper. They thought they ran the town. When he and his entourage arrived at my family's small, rough, mill village house, Babe began laughing. I initially thought he was happy, but he wouldn't even go inside my house much less look at my perfect room. Between the other boys' roars of laughter, he loudly proclaimed he'd never allow someone who lived in such a small, dingy house to join their club. The boys arrogantly rode their bikes away, still laughing. It seemed as if I could hear their laughter for miles."

Thomas grunted as his smile vanished.

"That's when my dad gave me this necklace."

"What does the necklace mean?" Thomas asked.

"After witnessing my humiliation, my dad, who was a hard-hearted brick mason who rarely spoke to me, went into the backyard and chipped this small piece off a brick. He wrapped it in this cloth and attached the leather strand. He clenched his fist, slammed it hard onto the kitchen table. He angrily told me: 'Those boys will never be your friends. You do not belong with them. Just as their fathers have shunned me, those boys will shun you. Wear this necklace as a reminder of your pain and humiliation.' He grabbed my face with both hands and told me words I'll never forget: 'Let this necklace serve as a wall of bitterness to protect you from those people. Never forget it is your hate that pushes you every minute of every day to prove yourself.'"

Thomas grimaced. "Your dad was a damaged, angry man."

"He was tough, but he did what he had to do to survive. But there's more to the story. Those fine, upstanding, rich boys excluded me for years. But they and their parents still wanted me on their high school sports teams, as I helped them win and look good. But I was never invited to their large neighborhood homes for after-the-game celebration parties. Once, I attended a party, but their looks and sneers made me feel like dirt beneath their feet. I swore to never feel that way again."

"That's terrible," Thomas said.

I clenched my jaw. "It was okay as it motivated me to be the best. When I was offered a football scholarship, I left that dingy town and never looked back. My hate and bitterness worked out pretty well."

Thomas slowly rubbed his chin like a wise man pondering a statement. "Are you sure about that? Sounds like you to took some major league baggage with you when you left that dingy little town."

I sneered, "Pretty damn sure. I won two high school football state championships as a coach and have made lots of money. I'd say I've shown the Blacklight Club Boys and ole Babe a thing or two."

Thomas's smile widened. Almost a smirk. "Bank accounts and trophies . . . how about friends? Where are your friends?"

"You're my friend," I said.

"Where are your friends outside of this team?"

I was growing weary of this conversation. "I've learned to live on my own. I don't need all this sissy grace and fake friends. My dad taught me a real man needs to live like a man. He didn't need anybody."

Thomas stuck his finger hard into my chest with such pressure it caused a bruise. I jerked my body straight. I felt my heart beat in my neck. He forcefully instructed. "You do need grace, and you already have all the grace you'll need." He pushed harder on my chest. "Here in your heart. It's not sissy, and you need friends. Soon you'll understand. Soon you'll see the light."

Thomas stopped speaking. Suddenly, I heard Allyson scream from our tent area. I saw Pat lying on the ground. Thomas and I rushed to her. Allyson was yelling, "I think she has heatstroke. She could die. We need to get her to a hospital."

Amy ran toward her. Pat's skin looked shriveled and dry. Her eyes were sunken in their sockets. I checked her pulse, and her heart was racing. She appeared to be having a seizure.

Thomas lifted her into his strong arms. I ran to his car and opened the door. He carefully set her in the backseat, and I turned on the motor and the air conditioner. Thomas gently held her.

The image of my young football player dying in my arms rushed into my mind. My heart pounded in my chest like a pile driver. It didn't feel full of grace. It was filled with fear. Would Pat die?

Amy drove and when we arrived at the hospital, the emergency room physician immediately checked Pat into a room. After about ten minutes, Brooke and Allyson arrived. We stood stunned in the hospital's sterile hallway.

The emergency room doctor finally approached us. "You have a severely dehydrated young woman. Her electrolytes are abnormally low. I've started an IV, so she should gradually improve. Have her drink lots of water and eat food high in fluid, such as watermelon, oranges, and yogurt. With several days of rest, she should be fine."

We breathed with relief. As we entered her room, I was surprised to see her spry, smiling, and sitting upright in her bed.

Pat howled and threw open her arms when she saw us. "Gave you guys quite a scare, huh? I'm feeling much better now and don't worry for a second. I'll be fully hydrated and chocked-full of energy for our next 500-meter race."

My shocked stare was fixed upon this superwoman. At least she thought she was a superhuman. Damn, who are these people? Maybe they're aliens from another planet sent here to test me. These crazed idiots wouldn't stop. "Hell no, you're not paddling in the next race. You're in the hospital with a big-ass needle stuck in your arm feeding you fluid so you don't die. I'm pulling the plug on this team—now."

As I turned to walk away Thomas blocked me.

I clenched my fist. "Don't do this, Thomas."

He lifted his chin and didn't move a muscle. He stared

directly into my eyes. "We must race. Pat will be ready. Soon you'll understand and see the grace that has brought you to this place. We didn't come to win; we came to survive. There will be no quitting."

Pat spoke loudly, "We all know cancer sucks. Chemo sucks. It all sucks. I don't deserve to be dying, and it's not fair my future has been ripped away. But let me tell you, I refuse to become obsessed with what has been stolen from me. I'm here now, and the benefit I'm seeking is worth it. All I have is today, and I'm grasping it. Tomorrow may be another story, but I'll not give up today."

I pushed Thomas aside and mumbled okay as I left the room. Amy followed and screamed for me to stop. I kept walking. Even if it killed me and them, we had two races left, and it was time for me to double down. I'd show them how hard I could push toward a championship. No more Mr. Nice Guy.

But I'd refuse to be humiliated. I shoved my brick necklace beneath my shirt. If something really bad happened to any of them, they couldn't blame it on me. I'd offered fair warning.

33

Chattanooga

Saturday, July 24, 2010
1:00 p.m.

The Dragon Survivor's final 500-meter race was scheduled to begin in an hour. The team was exhausted. They'd begged me to continue racing, and now I wouldn't accept any excuses for losing. It would be win at all costs.

I thought about my speech before the next race. I would state clearly my expectations. It would be obvious to this team and to anyone watching that I'd done my best. If the team lost and embarrassed themselves, I couldn't be blamed. I would not be the loser. After all, I had a whole other life where I was highly successful and respected. The disgrace of losing and possibly losing big would fall on the team. Maybe we'd arrived at the end of our road. I'd go home holding my head high.

I rested for the next hour, isolating myself. I recalled my initial exposure to the sport of dragon boating. Brooke so enthusiastically introducing me to the team. Pat, the expert international paddler, teaching me the proper stroke technique. Sean, the miracle man, fighting like hell to live. And Thomas, my inspiration. We'd come a long way but were still far from our goal.

We'd squeezed practices in between chemotherapy and radiation treatments. We were just a group of normal people trying to accomplish something extraordinary. We'd laughed, cried, and dreamed together.

Thirty minutes prior to the team marshaling I walked to the tent and instructed everyone to begin stretching to loosen their muscles. I would do everything perfectly. My words and my coaching would be above reproach. The team's mood was somber and weighty.

I gathered the team underneath a large oak tree. I strutted in front of them for a few minutes. I looked at Pat, and then Thomas, and then Sean—and then Brooke, and then Allyson, and finally each of the others; I really looked. I realized that it was the first time I'd genuinely looked at my teammates without judging or feeling judged. Just looked. Each of them looked back at me, hopeful, determined, strong. But there was something else in their eyes. There was no judgment from them. Only compassion, hope, and that spark of life that made them who they were. And it was as if they were offering a piece of that to me. I stopped walking and looked up into the sky.

The speech I'd prepared left my thoughts. It seemed as if a force from within my body, one that I'd never experienced, took over my brain. Words began to flow from deep inside my soul I didn't know existed.

"Vince Lombardi said there is no room for second place. Everything we have worked for and every inch of our striving has been critical. Now is our time. Time to defeat the Leathernecks."

For a brief moment, a peace like I'd never before felt filled my mind. I stopped talking. What was happening? A new emotion. A flicker of a sensation that I was at the exact place at the exact time that had been divinely destined. For a trace of time, I sensed a wholeness—without anger or bitterness.

I refocused on my teammates. My ad-libbed speech continued. "Our time is precious. What will we do with it? How do we get to where we want to be? We're tired—sick. Cancer may kill our bodies, but it can never kill our hope. It can't rip away our courage. Life is standing in the corner, throwing rocks at us. But we know the faith that exists within our guts. Trust that faith. Today we will confront our cancer and win. We will be in the same heat as the Leathernecks. If, no, when we win, we still have a shot at gold."

The peaceful feeling that had briefly overtaken me left as quickly as it had arrived. I didn't understand what had just happened. It wasn't the speech I'd intended to give. I'd planned to say something like I've done all I can do. I've coached all I can coach. I've done my part and now it's up to you. Do you have the want and desire? Can you dig deep within your bodies and give it all you have? Are you true champions? Those would have been words that would place the burden on them and not me.

The loudspeaker announced, "Dragon Survivors, please report to the marshaling tent."

My teammates stared at me without making a sound,

waiting for my instruction. My inspiring words had disappeared. I reverted to my prepared speech. "This race is on you, not me. It's time to see if you have within you the spirit of a champion."

We silently marshaled, loaded the boat, and paddled to the race's starting line. The team's strokes were weak. I was weak and tired. Fighting against all odds had shattered our strength. I buried the blade of my paddle deep into the water and readied myself for a punishing two and a half minutes.

All heads were looking straight ahead and torsos were twisted, leaning outside the canoe's gunwale. I pressed my foot hard against the bottom of the boat for my first stroke's maximum leverage. The start had to be perfect if we were to win the race.

The starter's horn blasted. Brooke and Pat, our stroke paddlers, were in perfect unison. Each paddler on the team had flawless extended rotation. Their reach and stroke recovery were full and in harmony with each other. The team looked strong.

I saw the drummer's eyes look with concern at the steersperson. No words needed to be spoken. The boat in the lane next to us, the Leathernecks, was rapidly pulling ahead. The heat pounded on our backs as the drummer yelled, "Power." Our boat didn't surge forward as normal.

I heard the spectators lined along the river's bank screaming. The river smelled musty and polluted. I felt nauseous. Pain rippled across the faces of my teammates. The river was no longer my friend, my lifeblood. It had aligned itself with the cancer that was trying to destroy my body. The majestic colors of our boat looked dark and depressing.

At the race's midpoint, the Leathernecks had a commanding lead. Then the Windy City Dragons passed us. Our drummer yelled to no avail, "Deeper, stronger. I need more power!"

The bow of our boat stagnated. Our strength was gone. The cancer and tumors that ravaged our bodies had seemingly bested us. But I wanted more and was determined to push the team. Between each breath and stroke, I screamed, "Power, power, power!"

The dragon god would not perform a miracle today. There would be no white doves released celebrating our victory. The drummer continued vigorously to pound and scream, but our fragile bodies could not respond. Our paddles struggled through the now-heavy water.

Our loss was sharp and cutting. Finishing a distant third place made the path to a gold medal almost impossible. The coveted reward for our long and difficult training had appeared to vanish. Our spirits were bloodied, our hopes battered, and I was pissed. The magical inner dragon spirit of the Dragon Survivors was nearly dead.

34

Chattanooga

Saturday, July 24, 2010
2:30 p.m.

I didn't speak as I disembarked from the canoe and walked past the spectators and other competitors. I hated to lose. I despised the way people looked at losers. Every part of me was scorned when others looked at me as a pathetic failure. I shuddered with pain from our loss. The festival officials posted the race results near the announcer's table. I went over to see the team's time and overall ranking.

We were still in second place in the overall standings, and I loosely calculated that if we won tomorrow's final one-thousand-meter race by a significant margin, we could still win the gold medal. I wrote down all the race times for the Leathernecks and the Dragon Survivors and then left the table.

Given our extreme physical fatigue, I maintained little hope of winning tomorrow's final 1000-meter race. I'd do my best to prepare the team for the eventual outcome.

Walking toward our tent, I heard boisterous celebrating from another team. I moved closer. The Leathernecks were singing and dancing, reveling in their victory. A paddler screamed above the music: "We've got the Charleston team beat now. They're not as strong as we thought. Just one more race, and we're on a boat to Hong Kong." Another paddler laughed as he spoke: "The Dragon Survivors finished third. They're all but eliminated to win gold. Ladies and gents, I think we can start celebrating."

Another team member opened a bottle of bourbon and poured shots. "Ready your glasses for a toast."

I moved a bit closer to hear but remained hidden behind another team's tent. The Leathernecks' coach entered the tent and raised his arms to quiet the team and get their attention. Silence pervaded as he spoke. "We're in first place, and the Dragon Survivors are second. For them to gain enough points to win the gold medal, they must beat us by two and half seconds in tomorrow's 1000-meter race."

A woman screamed, "That'll never happen."

The coach continued, "We cannot and will not underestimate our competitors. I have full confidence in each of you and your resolve. Together as a team, we will prevail. Winning this festival is our fate. We will not shrink in our courage or our goal. I welcome the coming race."

The entire Leatherneck team stood and raised their paddles and shot glasses of bourbon and yelled a simultaneous

"Ooh-rah! Ooh-rah!"

My body burned with contempt.

As I turned to walk back to our tent, I bumped into the Leatherneck's coach. He shot out his right hand like a rifle. "I'm Bob King, the Leatherneck's coach. Sorry, old chap, about your loss, but your team put up an admirable battle. Especially considering all those folks in your boat having cancer. The courage of your team is the talk of the festival. You should be proud to go home with a silver medal."

I straightened my back with ferocity. Like the mighty lion about to pounce on its prey, I looked aggressively into his eyes. For failure did not course in my veins. I rubbed my necklace. I spoke with power and might. "The festival isn't over yet . . . *old chap.* We have one more race."

The coach patted me on my shoulder like I was a child. "Got to love that never-quit spirit," he said. I clenched my fist tight, ready for battle, after hearing those words.

He walked away just in time to spare me being arrested for assault. I was determined more than ever to win at all costs.

My blood boiled with rage and indignation.

35

Chattanooga

Saturday, July 24, 2010
2:45 p.m.

After calming down from my interaction with the Leathernecks' coach, I'd rerun the numbers. And rerun them again. We would need to beat the Leathernecks in the final race by two and a half seconds for a bonus point, which meant that we weren't out yet! We could do this! I could lead them to do this! In every dark hour, there is a hero. I would be my team's hero. I'd push this team to victory as if our lives depended upon it.

We'd master our fast start and surprise the Leathernecks. No one would expect a team to do a fast start on a long endurance race. If we established a commanding lead, maybe my team could muster the strength for one more miracle.

I asked my team to gather in a tight circle underneath our tent as I had something to say.

The team was quiet and hung their heads in defeat. They stared at the ground like they were looking straight into the belly of hell. The horrendous loss had annihilated their dream. A cloud of depression weighed heavily upon everyone.

As I moved to speak, I was surprised to hear Sean cut me off, but I was even more surprised at his words. "Gang, we've given it our best shot. Our sick bodies have had enough. It's time to call it quits and go home."

Allyson confirmed Sean's sentiments. "It's the hand we've been dealt. We did our best and should be proud. Even if we don't race in the final race, we have enough points to win the bronze medal. Not bad, considering."

I said in a firm voice, "I'll be damned if we're going to concede now. I asked you to quit yesterday, and you refused. I just endured the Leathernecks' coach's harassment and watched his team celebrate winning the goal medal. Hell no, we're not quitting now. I didn't come to Chattanooga to be humiliated by a bunch of sore losers."

Pat blurted, "Sure, blame the team. Protect that fragile ego. You truly are a royal asshole."

Brooke stepped forward. "We only have one remaining race. I know all of you are worried about me, but I assure you I'm fine. We may not win gold, but we didn't do all this work and endure all this pain just to quit. I vote we paddle the final race."

Thomas spoke slowly and softly. Everyone was quiet. "We're going to paddle the final race and finish this competition. And all of us are going to leave it all out there on that river. No matter the outcome, I will never quit."

Thomas raised his head higher. His weary face wrinkled with seriousness as he continued speaking. "If we win the next race, we will qualify to represent this great nation—the country I fought in Vietnam to protect—in Hong Kong. I realize the odds of me being alive in a year are less than fifty percent, but I must try. We must try. Fate has brought us together. Cancer may steal my life, but I refuse to allow the evil bastard to rob me of my victory with this team."

Thomas's comments didn't surprise me as I knew he'd never quit. I also realized he might not survive to make a trip to China.

Sean pointed his finger at me. "It's time for some gut-wrenching honesty. You don't want to concede or quit now because you'd be humiliated as the coach of a bunch of quitters. Before, you had the excuse of us being sick. You're all about saving your precious reputation."

Pat turned to Sean. "Don't try to reason with this jackass. Who cares what he thinks? But I do care about Thomas. And if he votes to paddle, I vote to paddle."

Allyson moaned and looked at Pat. "I'm concerned about you and Brooke. Racing isn't worth your health. I love you guys and couldn't live with myself if anything happened to either of you."

The truth was, I'd be devastated if anyone was harmed or died. My thoughts were out of control.

Brooke said, "I'm good to race. It's only one thousand meters."

Allyson said, "If Brooke's racing, then I'm in the boat."

Pat looked at Sean. They both nodded an affirming yes.

Each team member nodded their head in agreement.

I moved to the center of our small circle. "We have a chance for the gold, if that's what you all want." I looked around. Nobody said a word. I continued, "It turns out that if we beat the Leathernecks by at least two and a half seconds, we will win. I ran the numbers." I raised my voice. I had everyone's attention. "Normally the start for a 1000-meter race is slow, and we build the rate as the race progresses. But if we're going to defeat the Leathernecks by two and a half seconds, we'll need a commanding early lead. To do this, we're going to use my fast start."

Pat spurted out. "That's ridiculous! A fast start will exhaust us, and we'll not be able to finish. And we're already weak. Plus, the start on a long race makes no difference. It's all about timing and stroke rate."

I knew she might be correct, and I felt like a moth heading straight into a bright light. But I had to win. "I understand we're weak, but I believe if we develop a large lead, we can hold on to beat the Leathernecks." I hesitated and peered at my teammates. "You all agreed to follow my instructions."

Veins throbbed in Pat's neck as she turned away.

Sean asked with a calm voice, "What do you want us to do?"

I narrowed my eyes. "To practice the fast start—this afternoon. Get some rest and meet me at the dock in two hours."

Pat stepped toward me. "Are you full of shit? You want us to go out in this heat and practice a start that isn't even going to work in an endurance?"

I stepped toward her. "In Charleston, all of you agreed to follow my direction. You agreed to do it my way. I've lined up a steersperson, and that's her only available time. The practice will be short and we'll have tonight to rest."

Pat turned away and kicked a chair.

I looked at my teammates. "Any more questions?"

The team was silent.

"Rest and meet at the dock at five o'clock."

***

We loaded the boat at five o'clock and paddled to the middle of the river. Amy watched from the river's shore. We checked the boat. The river was calm but steamy. The heat rose from the water's surface like flames erupting from a burning building. We wiped sweat from our faces. My shirt stuck to my wet chest.

This race start was like a master chef measuring the precise ingredients for a recipe. It had to be perfect, or it would be a disaster. I stood from my seat in the boat. My instructions were crystal clear.

"Remember, the first three strokes are long, slow, deep strokes to get the boat moving from a dead stop. After we complete these strokes, the drummer will yell, 'Up!' We then begin our first set of the short, fast half strokes, the ups, to cause the boat to quickly plane on top of the water and propel us forward."

The boat was quiet. I commanded their full attention.

"On the ups, do your maximum rotation and slam your paddle into the water at the halfway point of your normal forward reach. Pull your paddle hard through the water but exit at your midthigh instead of your hip. We do six of these quick half strokes, and the drummer will yell 'Up!' again. We repeat these six strokes and then do one more set of the six ups for a total of three sets of up strokes. Understood?"

Everyone nodded they understood.

"After the third set of ups, we transition into our standard race rate. The transition is one additional half-stroke, then a deeper three-quarter stroke, and finally a hard full stroke. Hopefully we'll have a commanding lead, and we'll shock the Leathernecks into a panic. Our stroke paddlers, Brooke and Pat, will establish the race rate that we'll maintain until I yell 'Finish.'"

Practicing starts are challenging. It requires a lot of energy as the team must move the boat from a dead stop. Considering the heat and the team's weakened physical condition, I needed to be careful. I looked at the drummer and nodded for her to yell the race's starting commands.

"Paddles in the water," she yelled. "Ready, ready. We have alignment." She blew her whistle.

The first three long strokes were perfect. The drummer yelled, "Up." The first set of ups was flawless. The drummer again yelled, "Up." During the second set of up stokes the team lost timing. I heard paddles clanging against each other.

"Stop!" I yelled.

The team quit paddling, and we brought the boat to a complete stop.

"Do it again!" I yelled.

The drummer repeated her commands and blew her whistle.

Same result. We lost timing during the second set of ups.

I again yelled, "Stop!" Anger rang through my voice.

Same starting commands from the drummer. The team nailed the first three strokes. The first and second sets of ups were spot on. But we lost timing during the third and final set of ups. I slapped the side of the boat in frustration and yelled, "Stop the boat!"

Everyone was breathing hard. Sweat ran down our faces. My heart raced. The heat bore down on us like a hungry hawk.

Thomas's face was contorted. He grimaced as he attempted to rearrange his body on the wooden seat. He appeared to be in pain.

I asked, "Thomas, are you okay?"

His exaggerated nod communicated he was fine. He didn't look fine.

I said, "Let's take a ten-minute break, and we'll try again."

Adding this practice after racing two excruciating 500-meter races was risky. But we had to nail this start if we had any chance of beating the Leathernecks. We sat still and quiet in the boat for ten minutes.

I instructed, "One more time, and let's nail it."

The drummer provided the race's starting commands. "Paddles in the water. Ready, ready. We have alignment—" The whistle.

The first three strokes were perfect. First set of ups—textbook. Second set of ups—impeccable. The third set of ups was like magic as each paddler was in perfect timing. It was a symphony of motion in seamless harmony.

I heard an awful scream. It was Allyson. "Something's wrong with Thomas!"

We stopped the boat. I stepped three seats forward and grabbed him. Thomas grunted in extreme pain. He swallowed hard and immediately vomited in the boat. We paddled hard back to the dock.

Sean and I helped Thomas out of the dragon boat and carried him to my car. We drove as if we were transporting a woman in labor, blowing our horn while running through every traffic signal on our way to the hospital. My second trip to the emergency room that day.

I trembled in panic. I couldn't think about Thomas dying.

I dried my cold, clammy hands with a towel as we entered the hospital. My gut cramped with tension. This tragedy could not be happening to me again.

***

Raw fright quivered in Amy's voice as she ran into the hospital. She found me sitting in the emergency room waiting area with Brooke, Pat, Sean, and Allyson. She hugged me tight. "I just heard about Thomas and called Bonnie. She's on her way. Is he okay?"

I held Amy close against my body. I felt like I'd been thrown from a moving car. My entire body winced in agony. "We don't know, but he was in a lot of pain. The doctors transferred him to another section of the hospital. It doesn't look good, and I'm worried."

"Luckily Bonnie was in Atlanta. She purchased a first-class ticket and should be here in a few hours," Amy said.

We all sat in uncomfortable chairs and said nothing. We were too scared to talk. I prayed.

About thirty minutes later the doctor entered the room. A short, bald, older man wearing small wired-rim glasses. He looked smart. His demeanor was icy. "Mr. Avery?" he asked, looking around the room.

We all stood simultaneously.

"That's me," I said.

Amy and Brooke stood beside me.

The doctor peered into my eyes. "Mr. Huger is a very sick man. His feeding tube has developed an infection which could be fatal. We're administering a massive dose of a strong antibiotic and gave him medication for pain. He's sleeping. We should know more in a few hours."

I stuttered—afraid to ask. "But he's going to be okay?"

The doctor hesitated and pulled his glasses down slightly over his nose. "We hope."

Brooke asked, "Does he have significant edema?"

The doctor glanced at Brooke as if assessing her medical training. "Luckily, he does not. He must be in excellent physical condition. I expected his body to be swollen like a balloon."

Brooke closed her eyes as if she was silently expressing a thankful prayer. "Wonderful," she said as she shook the doctor's hand. He nodded and walked away.

Pat, Brooke, Sean, Allyson, Amy, and I walked like zombies out of the hospital and into the parking lot. Pat stopped walking, turned toward me, and stepped forward like a cat ready to pounce on a rat. "I hope you're satisfied. Your fragile ego may have killed my best friend. You once showed me how to see the light. Yet I wonder if all you see is total darkness."

With those words, my teammates walked away. Amy and I stood alone looking at each other. Worried. There was no playbook that taught how to coach a team of people dying of cancer.

I closed my eyes. I saw clearly the face of my young dying football player as I held his head in my hands. I could see his burning desire to be accepted and appreciated as he peered into my eyes. I understood that desire.

What had I done?

36

Chattanooga

Saturday, July 24, 2010
7:30 p.m.

Amy and I didn't speak as we drove away from the hospital. I finally broke our silence. In a low, weak voice, I said. "I'm not ready to go to the hotel room. Let's just ride."

"Where? She asked.

"Anywhere, I don't care."

"Lookout Mountain is not far. I understand the view is spectacular."

I grunted. She drove to the famous mountain and parked. In the dark, we carefully hiked along an uneven rocky path to Sunset Rock, a large boulder surrounded by large majestic oaks.

We took short steps, and my leg muscles burned with pain from the day's events. But the breathtaking view was worth the agony as it soothed my remorse for agreeing to coach this team.

I thought about Thomas and prayed he'd recover. The sun was already below the sky's horizon, so the tourists had left. Good, as I needed to be alone. We sat on the rock, and I yearned the gentle evening breeze to take away my fear of Thomas dying.

The lights in the valley twinkled and I could see the Tennessee River in the valley. The million-year-old limestone Sunset Rock emitted a rustic odor like the scent of rotting dried wood. I reflected on the mountain's original inhabitants. A hundred and fifty years ago, the self-reliant Cherokee Indians roamed unrestricted and lived as free as the buffalos, a freedom I now longed to experience. To be set free from the great burden of coaching this godforsaken team.

I imagined I could see the physical borders of the seven states allegedly visible from my perch. I pictured brave but misguided men killing each other on the grounds of this renowned Civil War battlefield. Brother killing brother. Families torn apart. Was I killing my brothers and sisters? Tearing my dragon boat family apart? Had I pushed them too hard?

I remembered Dr. Simpson's words, "You have cancer." The words that changed my life. And when my oncologist told me my liver tumors had doubled in size and nothing could be done, get your affairs in order—well, those were fighting words. The course of my life would never be the same. Shock, anger, pain, and regret—I'd experienced all these feelings.

I held my brick necklace tightly in my hand. The cancer had caused my bitterness to grow like the tumors. Statistics show only one in five people with stage IV cancer will survive. How could I become the twenty percent? The one survivor rather than one of the other four poor bastards? I thought the cancer of bitterness was more deadly that my real tumors.

Who can bear the stress? Blood tests every six weeks. Scans every three months. Tumor markers going up. After a treatment, my tumors would shrink only to grow again. I'd carefully planned my life, and it didn't include cancer. And it certainly didn't include coaching the Dragon Survivors.

My Sunday school teacher taught me that the opposite of love was hate. But now I disagreed. My father said it was indifference. I didn't think so. I believed the opposite of love is fear. Love fills the gaps of needs in our lives. Love creates meaning from the meaningless. But fear creates an emptiness, a void of nothingness. Fear is the great thief of the universe. Fear had given birth to my anger. Anger was my protection. My defense. I used my anger to disguise my fear.

After the surgeon removed the tumors outside my liver, I yearned for my body to be healthy again. Maybe I'd been misguided, and it was my mind that needed to be healed. I'd never needed camaraderie or lots of friends. Truthfully, my only friends had been Amy, my work, and my relentless need to prove my worth. I wondered if some great power had led Brooke to be my nurse and tell me about the sport of dragon boating. Could this sport, this team, be the impetus that leads me to the answer of my eternal question, Why me? In contrast to Sean, I didn't compare having cancer to winning the lottery.

Amy broke our silence. "Are you okay? I'm terribly worried about you."

I nodded. "I'm okay."

I shook my head to rid my mind of these menacing thoughts.

All these questions about myself and my fragile ego. I wasn't the problem.

Amy scuffled through her purse and pulled out a small white envelope. She gingerly handed it to me. "I brought you a gift."

I opened the envelope. It was an old Polaroid picture of my boyhood home. The mill village house. In the middle of the picture was the magical window of my room. A stream of light beamed from the heavens and reflected off the window's pane. "Where did you get this picture? I've never seen it."

"From an old photo album your mother gave me. The picture was stuck behind another one and last week as I was reorganizing your bookshelves, I found it. I thought you would enjoy seeing it."

I saw, in my mind's eye, myself as a young boy standing in front of the window, peering out over a town that'd branded my psyche with insufferable anger and impenetrable bitterness. I heard the bully Babe laughing at me as he and his Black Light Boys rode their bikes away, mocking me and my house.

I remembered, being a high school star athlete, scoring touchdowns, and making hard tackles only to receive snarky looks and humiliation from my uppity teammates and their families. That look—that look that said I didn't belong was branded into my soul. I owed a debt to Babe and the people of that little town. Without them, I'd never have developed the hate and anger that had become my motivation to succeed at all costs.

I'd tried to bury these memories, but the pain was as intense as ever. I'd just wanted to belong, to fit in and be accepted. And since, I'd fought every day of my life to never again have the need to belong. And now I belonged to a team that might destroy me. Their weaknesses had caused me to be a failure.

A recurring childhood nightmare flashed into my thoughts. In this dream, I was lost and couldn't find my way home. I ran up and down the street, but every house looked the same. The houses were dark with no lights. The front doors were closed and locked. I could smell the sweet aroma of dinners being cooked in the homes' kitchens. I heard laughter inside the houses, but no one would open the doors. I banged loudly on the front doors, but no one answered.

Eventually I'd become exhausted and sit in the middle of the street like a terrorized dog. I wanted to die. People with no faces walked on the sidewalk, and they couldn't see me. Cars, all black, drove past me without stopping. The world ignored me sitting alone in the middle of the street.

Eventually anxiety would paralyze my body as I sat in the street, and I couldn't move. The terror of being alone and ignored for the rest of my life would suck the air from my lungs. I'd gasp to breathe. Suddenly the laughter inside the houses would stop, and the cooking aromas left. I'd open my mouth wide to scream, but I could make no sound. I only wanted to find my way home to be safe and loved.

The dream always ended the same way. My father would mysteriously appear and lift my paralyzed body from the street. He'd be holding my brick necklace in front of my face and shout, "Your hate is your protection. Your bitterness is your suit of armor."

Then, I'd wake.

I looked at the picture. The sight of my boyhood room's window made me nauseous. My hands began to shake. I grabbed Amy's arm to keep from falling off the rock. My vision blurred. My heart raced.

Any squeezed my arm, and her grip was tight. "Are you okay?"

I wanted to stay on this mountaintop forever to hide and escape my fate. I could convince myself that all was well and I had no worries. I could believe I belonged at this place on this rock. I could throw away my necklace.

I turned to Amy and said, "I need to see Thomas."

She forcefully grabbed my arm. "Tripp, you're destroying yourself. You need to immediately and emphatically apologize to your team. For many years you've been a broken man. My heart is crying, no, screaming for your healing. You're a better coach and person than this."

I stood and aggressively pulled my arm from her grasp. "I don't need this shit right now, Amy."

She stood, "It's exactly what you need. You—"

Without a word, I walked to the car, opened the door, and sat in the driver's seat.

I watched Amy's long slow strides to the car. Every step roared with a livid indignation.

But I had to see Thomas.

37

Chattanooga

Saturday, July 24, 2010
9:30 p.m.

The air was thick and heavy like my heart. I'd dropped Amy off at the hotel room. She raced from the car without speaking. I faced a harsh wind as I approached the hospital. The light from the moon allowed me to see the fog had crept off Lookout Mountain toward the river. A sharp pungent sensation of nausea gripped my stomach. I felt combustible, as if I could explode at any moment. I needed to find the words that would bring peace to my friend Thomas. Words that would also release my guilt. But how can words remove guilt if your hands are bloody?

I gagged as I entered the hospital with its odor of sickness and death. I wanted to sprint away and find clean air. The smell intensified like my guilt as I walked the sterile hospital hallway toward Thomas's room.

Thomas was sleeping as I opened the door to his room. He looked terrible, like a man who'd been beaten with a bat. His breaths were shallow and quick. His eyes sunken in his face. His body appeared frail and weak.

Sitting next to the bed holding his hand was his wife, Bonnie. Her tall, slender frame leaned over his body. She was an eloquently handsome woman with shoulder-length, wavy gray hair. Tiny lines radiated from her tired eyes. The red stylish dress she wore made her look rather majestic. She politely smiled when she saw me.

A clear plastic bag hanging above his bed pumped antibiotics into his infected body.

"How's Thomas?" I asked her.

Her lips appeared soft but weary as she answered. "I just arrived, but I can tell he's not doing well. The nurse at the desk said he has a very dangerous infection. I'm praying the antibiotics kick in soon."

"How are you doing?" I asked.

Her voice sounded long-suffering, like a warrior who'd been deployed for many years. "I've written this book many times. I have no idea how many hours I've spent sitting quietly next to his hospital bed, watching him sleep. I could never allow him to wake up and not see me. I wasn't with him the evening after his last surgery when the doctor told him his cancer had returned. I'll never forgive myself for that moment of weakness."

She appeared as if she was about to cry but didn't. Her tears had all been shed. "Although I wasn't in any mental state to have offered much support, I feel better knowing I'm here for him if he needs anything. I believe it helps him regain his strength, knowing I'm by his side. The real horror is my overwhelming sense of helplessness. I just want to make him healthy again."

I breathed heavily from exhaustion. I wasn't sure how I was still standing. My body ached with both pain and shame. "Please forgive me for forcing Thomas to practice that difficult start. I knew he was too exhausted."

She looked adoringly at Thomas. "No need to apologize. You didn't force him to do anything. I'd have liked to have seen you try to stop him. Thomas will never give up."

I appreciated her words. "But I should have stopped him."

Bonnie lifted her head and looked me in the eye. Her words clear and precise. "You don't know Thomas. He will never surrender this battle without a fight. He'd have surgery, and we would believe his cancer was gone. Then the cancer returned, and he'd have a new treatment and we'd think it was gone again. And it'd come back. A yo-yo has more stability than our lives have had for the past ten years. But never, not once, has he given up."

"I'm sorry, I didn't mean to—"

She interrupted me. "Let me tell you a story about Thomas. As a teenager he was nationally recognized by the National Field Archery Society as one of the nation's most prominent archers. He's continued competing throughout his life and has rarely lost. His first surgery was a piece of cake. After a few short months he was back shooting at targets. But the cancer returned and spread throughout his jaw and down his neck. His second surgery was significantly more severe. The surgeon had to remove the majority of his right trapezius muscle, which is the muscle you use to move your shoulder blade and which supports your arm. Since Thomas was right-handed, we figured his archery days were over."

I laughed and said sarcastically, "What did he do, train himself to shoot lefthanded?"

Bonnie laughed louder. "That's exactly what he did."

I stopped laughing. "He is one determined man."

Bonnie rubbed Thomas's hand. "He turned the house into a makeshift gymnasium. He did pull-ups on the door frames. He'd do push-ups standing against the refrigerator. He set up an archery target in the backyard to practice."

Bonnie chuckled and rolled her eyes. "And then he almost killed me. His determination has always blinded him. He learned the targets for left-handed archers at competitions had a different angle than for right-handed shooters. The only way he could create this same angle in our backyard was for him to shoot his arrow across our driveway. As you know, the drive is winding and you can't see a car arriving until it's at the house."

I nodded. "I've driven that driveway and it's definitely a blind drive."

She continued, "One afternoon as I arrived home, parked, and got out of my car, an arrow buzzed within an inch of my ear. I thought I was dead. We all learned from that day forward to blow the car's horn as we approached the house, or otherwise, your life could be in danger."

"Did he ever compete shooting left-handed?"

"You know it. After a year he qualified for the local NAFS tournament—shooting left-handed."

"Did he win?"

Bonnie threw her hands back, tossing her shiny silver hair.

"Of course he won. Thomas always wins." She stopped smiling, "Everything but this cursed cancer."

She looked away as she spoke. "The most difficult adjustment is the ability to set future goals. It's something I wrestle with daily. I wonder what my life would have been like if cancer hadn't become a permanent resident in our home. Would I be stuck in the same job? Would we have traveled more? Second-guessing your life can drive a person crazy. I try not to think about those questions but some days it's pretty damn hard."

A tear flowed down her face. "From time to time I go out to dinner with friends. I work out three times a week, and I make sure I have time for long, hot showers. These all help, but I feel guilty enjoying myself when I know Thomas is in so much pain."

I was unable to move. Her words gripped my mind like a mental vise. I whispered, "And I almost killed him."

She was crying and her lips trembled as she spoke. "Thomas says death is your enemy until it isn't. When is that time exactly? Will we know when we are there? When death has arrived?"

A loud noise snapped me from my hypnotic state. Thomas slammed his hand against the wall behind his bed. "That time hasn't arrived yet," he said.

Bonnie tenderly kissed him. "No, it hasn't."

"We're sure going to miss you being in the boat tomorrow."

He grinned. "Who knows, I might just be there."

Bonnie rubbed his forehead and laughed. "Always the jester."

His voice strengthened. "We nailed that damn start before I went bonkers on you."

I stepped close to his bed and held his hand. "Yes, we did. But we'll be just fine with nineteen paddlers. A thousand meters is a long race."

Thomas lifted his head. "When these kick-ass antibiotics kill this infection, I'll be okay. Sooner rather than later. Wait and see."

Without warning his head lunged forward and fluid spewed from his mouth and covered the entire bed. Bonnie pushed the nurses' button, and I reached for him as he started to seize. I held his head in my hands just as I had with my young football player. I stared, wide-eyed. Thomas was going to die.

The nurse ran into the room and pushed me aside. Bonnie looked at her and said, "These strong antibiotics make him sick. Please get something to stop the vomiting and to calm him so he can rest." Bonnie then looked at me. "You better leave."

I ran out of the hospital and into a thick grassy area and fell to my knees. The storm was approaching, and it was very dark. I wanted to cry but couldn't. I didn't know why. I felt as though I also had an appointment with death. If not with my body, then certainly with my soul. I could see my demise as clearly as if I was looking out of the window of my boyhood home.

I would never be a part of the club. I didn't deserve to belong.

38

Chattanooga

Sunday, July 25, 2010
10:00 p.m.

As I knelt on the hospital's lawn, I tried to pray. But there was no prayer inside me. I couldn't connect with God. My path forward was blocked with confusion, anger, and bitterness; confusion about what I was supposed to do now, angry at the team for putting me in this position, and bitterness at the world.

Everyone had accepted the risks. They all realized the physical challenge this endeavor would be for our sick bodies. All of us had cancer, not just Thomas. No, this tragedy couldn't be placed in my lap. I coached this team just as I would any other team. If Thomas dies, it wouldn't be my fault. Even Bonnie had said so.

I rose from my knees and grabbed my necklace. I was surrounded by every manner of darkness inside and outside of my body. Bitterness was my only constant companion. It lived in the marrow of my bones. Bitterness had served me well.

I drove to the river. The moon flickered between the now fast-moving clouds and lit my way. Exhaustion consumed my muscles. As I left my car and approached the river, I found an abandoned life jacket and lay down, resting my head on it. I stared at the troubled sky, listening to distant thunder. I would never give in to Pat's accusation that the infection that threatened Thomas's life was my fault.

I'd fallen asleep when I heard Amy's voice. "Are you okay? I've been walking around the park looking for you. I was so worried. How is Thomas?"

I snapped, "This damn team is killing me. How in the world did I get rooked into coaching a bunch of sick losers?"

Amy sighed as she sat next to me. "They're not losers, Tripp. As you've said, they're sick and doing the best they can."

My words were curt. "Well, you sure as hell can't blame me. These people are lucky to have me as their coach."

Amy frowned and leaned away from me. "What's gotten into you? You're wrong about your teammates."

I shouted loudly, "What the hell do you know about coaching? You've never played a competitive sport in your whole damn life."

Her jaw clenched tightly. She bit her lip. "I don't deserve your abusive treatment. And, I'll not tolerate it. Why do you think being rude and mean will help this situation?"

I rolled my eyes. "Because it's true. You know nothing about coaching. I'm the one who's won two state championships. I was recognized as the coach of the year. If this team was as committed to winning as I am, I wouldn't be in this situation."

Amy's tone softened as she tried to reason with me. But her words were frank. "I love you with all my heart, but you're wrong about the team being the problem. Tripp, you are the problem. Your anger and bitterness are not only destroying you but also the team."

I laughed sarcastically. "Like I said, what the hell do you know about coaching? What, did you just come down here to make me feel like an ass? Damn, Amy, what kind of person does that to the one they love?"

Amy sternly pointed her finger in my face. "You're just like him."

"Like who?"

"Your awful dad. I don't need to make you feel like an ass, as you've already mastered that feat."

I felt as if my head was exploding. "I'm nothing like my dad," I yelled. "If I'm such an ass, then why are you still here?"

Amy stood. Indignant. "You've never been cruel like him, but you've crossed the line. And you were just a high school coach. You didn't win the Super Bowl."

My face flushed. "If you love me, you'll stand by me, not give me this shit. After all, it was your idea for me to coach this team. All this is your fault."

Amy jabbed her finger into my chest. "You belligerent jerk. You'll not blame me for your problems. No, this is all about you. You talk about being a man, but you're nothing more than a spoiled rotten kid."

She hesitated and drew in a deep breath. "Don't even think about coming to the hotel. I do not want to see you or talk with you until you decide what kind of man you're going to be. A graceful, civilized, thankful man or a barbarian destroying everyone and everything in your scorched path."

For a moment, the fear of losing Amy paralyzed me. My mind went numb. But I was the one who was right. How could she blame me? How could she leave?

"I'll leave you here to wallow in the stench of your own bullshit." She threw the picture of my boyhood home at me, and she screamed as she walked away, "Study that picture. Maybe you'll see your ugly self in your precious window. I pray you'll see the problem isn't the team, but the problem is you. And don't come back to Charleston. You're not welcome there, either."

Amy left. In a blind rage, I threw the life jacket into the river and started walking fast. I crammed the picture in my pants pocket. I saw a young couple laughing and dancing in the flickering moonlight. Why are they so damn happy? I walked past a woman beggar sitting on a bench under a streetlight, holding a cardboard sign with the word *HOPE* written with a red crayon.

It started to rain. The parched ground eagerly soaked up the water. I was wet. And I was angry and all alone—just like my dad had been.

39

Chattanooga

Sunday, July 25, 2010
1:00 a.m.

The wind became gusty, causing the rain to swirl in the dark sky like a spinning top, as if the rain was attacking me. A bolt of lightning slammed into the water. Rain burned my eyes. The clouds formed a black barrier canopy so that nothing or no one could escape. The homeless woman had left. Her cardboard sign had fallen to the ground.

Thunder rumbled through the angry sky in the same fashion that my anger roared within my mind. The storm I'd avoided since boyhood had arrived. Amy had abandoned me. God had forsaken me. I stood and shook my fist at the sky.

I yelled loudly into the blaring wind. "Fuck all of you! I don't need anyone!"

I didn't. I'd survived, no, *thrived* very well on my own. I'd fought hard for everything I'd accomplished. I'd been a star athlete. People in the business world respected my intelligence and success. I didn't need to belong to a silly kid's Black Light Club, nor did I need to belong or be the coach of this insufferable dragon boat team.

The wind squalls caused the river's water to white cap. Folding chairs left in the park blew across the festival grounds like the small leaves of an oak tree. Hailstones dropped from the black sky like rocks. But no storm would deter my anger. I had a message to tell, and I'd force the world to listen. I continued my frenzied accusations.

I screamed. "Who in the hell did I need?"

Lightning lit up the entire sky. The grim storm moved fast above my head. The rain intensified and beat relentlessly on the festival tents. The limbs of the oak tree I stood under swayed, appearing to be the arms of a violent monster. A tall pine tree uprooted and fell, destroying the marshaling tent. I held my brick necklace in my right hand and pointed it at the lightning bolt, daring it to attack me.

I screamed, "I am my own man! A man's man!"

The strong wind caused the river's water to crash against its bank, eroding soil with each slamming wave. The downpour of rain blurred my vision. A millisecond flash of blinding light bolted into the river. The ground shook. I ran to my car. Even still, my anger matched the fury of the storm. I cursed God as I held open my car door. My feet slipped in the rain-soaked ground and I fell. My clothes and face became soaked in mud.

I yelled, "I never asked to be the coach of this team! It's not my fault!"

I scrambled into my car and closed the door. I pointed my brick necklace at the angry black sky. My will to live had vanished. I screamed boldly at the storm. "I deserve to die. Why wait for cancer to kill me? Take me now. Lightning strike me dead."

I curled up in my seat like an infant as the storm raged. I had met my appointment with the devil of darkness.

40

Chattanooga

Sunday, July 25, 2010
6:00 a.m.

The steel chatter of a chainsaw cutting through the fallen pine tree woke me. My muscles and joints were sore and stiff. I was scared, confused, and could barely move. I reached for Amy. Where was Amy?

My muddled thoughts began to clear. I painfully recalled Amy's words that I was a barbarian. Had I lost Amy? Had I finally spurned everyone in my life? I pulled the photo Amy had thrown at me from my pants pocket.

I woefully studied the window of my boyhood room, remembering dreaming of having a loving wife, a healthy family, and a successful career, a life where love and grace ruled. I wanted to return to that boy in the window, to a place of hope and forgiveness. Sweat dripped off my chin. I longed for the dream of that young, idealistic, unbroken boy.

As I studied the picture, a frightening ugly sight appeared. I saw a young boy with abnormally weathered skin and dark, colorless eyes. His face looked stone-cold, like a statue. His cheekbones were sharp and obnoxious. The boy's lips were thick and covered with blisters. His forked chin and chiseled mouth spread sadness over his entire body. The sinister image was repulsive.

I closed my eyes and shook my head. Was I hallucinating? Was I dreaming? I rubbed my eyes and opened them. The ugly boy was still standing in the window. What was happening? I held the photo close to my face and noticed he was wearing my brick necklace around his neck. The disgusting-looking boy was me.

Bitterness seemed to shoot from his eyes like lasers. His face covered was with red raw blisters. I could clearly visualize the destructive path ahead of him. How could such a young boy appear to look so old and shrunken? I finally saw what I had never before been able to see. The boy's hatred and bitterness was day by day sucking the spirit of life from his body, causing his body to shrink inward like a withering balloon. I saw my own ugliness.

Rather than a healthy, loving young boy full of hope, I'd turned into a vicious ugly man who destroyed the people he loved—and who loved me. I *was* just like my father. I felt like a hydrogen bomb had been dropped into the chambers of my heart and was about to explode.

I'd never cared about truth and justice. Only my own desires and proving my worth to the world. I'd underestimated the evilness of the demons that dwelled in my soul. These demons were much more toxic than the tumors that lived in my liver. Maybe the etiology of these tumors all along had been the ugly bitterness that resided in the deep recesses of my being, the places I'd refused to visit.

I pulled the brick necklace from beneath my rain-soaked shirt and stared at it. The necklace represented my psychological wall of protection, the barricade of bitterness I'd never allowed anyone to penetrate. The wall had not only served to protect me from the evil attacks of my enemies but also to fortify my internal hostility.

But who were my adversaries? Could the memories of my childhood be wrong? Had my instinct for self-preservation become my nemesis? Had I searched in the wrong places for the enemy that plagued my life? The God I'd cursed had shown mercy and pulled back the veil of my ugliness. My vision was now clear. As Amy had told me, I was the problem. My enemy was me.

I walked to the river as the sun began to rise in the sky. Rays of sunlight penetrated through the gaps of the now-white clouds. They looked like the fingers of God reaching to the earth. A few paddlers were arriving. I stared at the beautifully decorated dragon boats. I thought about the day's race. My heart ached to see Amy and my friends. I prayed Thomas would survive.

To my right, I heard the familiar sound of a squawking bird. I walked in my dried, mud-covered clothes to the river's bank. Along the river's tree-lined shallow water was a colony of ibises. I rubbed my eyes. Were these birds real? What the hell was happening?

But my focus was perfect. The long-billed birds were real

and moving slowly in the wetlands, eating small crustaceans that inhabited the mud. I've read that when searching for food, especially during a drought, small flocks of ibises would travel far outside their usual range. I listened to the birds' sweet sounds. Their loud awkward screeches sounded like a melodious symphony. My symbol of hope. These birds had been sent to be the witnesses of my deliverance.

More enthusiastic paddlers arrived at the race festival site. I looked away from my miracle birds and witnessed their smiles and laughter. The homeless woman had returned to the bench. Sitting aimlessly holding a new sign. A fresh cardboard sign with the word *HOPE* written with a red crayon.

I looked back at the wetlands to see if the ibises had flown away or disappeared, or if they were just my imagination. But the white birds with long purple legs were still feasting in the shallow water.

From the depths of my spirit, the hope of my youth sprang as one of the birds flew away. The anticipations of that young boy staring out his window dreaming of happiness and love, daring to belong. Before the rejection of my peers. Before my dad had given me my brick necklace of hate and bitterness. A young boy filled with confidence and courage, not fear and self-doubt.

I rushed to my team's tent area, found my backpack which had been left under a chair, and dug out my money clip. I pulled out a hundred-dollar bill. With a peace I'd never before experienced I walked to the homeless woman and laid the money in her lap. She stood, smiled as if she knew me, and softly said, "Thank you." She gently handed me her sign and slowly walked away. The fog of bitterness had cleared. The cloud of hatred and humiliation had disappeared like the storm.

I was no longer an ugly, sad little boy. I needed Amy. I needed my team, the Dragon Survivors. I had to find them to beg for forgiveness.

From behind I heard my name called by a soft melodic voice. "Tripp."

I spun around and saw Amy.

I held the sign of hope the homeless woman had given me. My body ached with exhaustion, but my mind was aflame with energy. The clothes I wore were stiff and caked with mud. My face was covered with dirt, and I smelled worse than the Charleston pluff mud at low tide.

Her face was pale as if she'd seen a ghost. I yelled, "Amy!"

She said, "I was awakened with a strong sense I needed to come to the park. You know, my intuition."

I removed the necklace from around my neck and stashed it in my pocket. I no longer needed the symbol of my humiliation. I no longer needed anger to be my motivator. I no longer needed to prove myself or belong to the Blacklight Boys Club. I belonged to Amy. I only needed her.

"Amy, I need to talk."

She stepped back, still angry. "I think you've already said enough."

I held out my hand toward her. "You're wrong; I've not said enough. Please listen, I beg you."

We walked to a bench where the old lady had sat. Amy's face was stern. My angry words had hurt her deeply, and she wasn't about to allow me to repeat that cruel behavior.

"I'm listening," she said, staring me in the eyes.

The palms of my hands were clammy. "My dad taught me

to never apologize. He told me it made me weak. I've just realized the opposite is true."

The tone in her voice communicated anger and hurt. "And how did you suddenly come to this great and wonderful insight?"

"After you left me alone in the park last night, a torrential storm blew across the river."

She nodded. "I heard the thunder."

"I stood in the middle of the park as the thunder boomed, the hard rain washed away part of the bank, and lightning lit up the entire river. I cursed God and begged for him to strike me dead. A vivid forked lightning bolt struck the water. It shook the entire ground. I thought my judgment day had arrived. I ran to my car as hailstones beat against my head." I hesitated, "That's when it happened."

"What happened?"

"As I sat alone in my car and the storm battered the park, I studied the picture you gave me. Maybe I was hallucinating, I don't really know, but instead of seeing me, I saw a young boy with gnarled and wrinkled skin and dark, empty eyes. His face was covered with ugly blisters and a horrible gloom exuded from his entire being. The image made me sick as I realized it was me."

Amy didn't move an inch. "Tripp, you must let go of your hatred and bitterness or everything in your life will be crushed and lost, including me. You've got to walk away from your father's contempt for people."

"I have something else to share with you."

"Oh," she said with a raised eyebrow.

"One sunny bright day when I was about twelve and as I stared out my bedroom window, I had another vision. A vision of the woman I'd marry."

Amy's demeanor changed. She said with a grin, "Did you see how beautiful I was even then?"

Her keen sense of humor made me smile. "I never clearly saw a face; it was more like the sensation of a pleasing presence. But when it happened, a strong impression of peace and confidence overwhelmed me. Last night, when I studied the picture that vision became clear. I did see you. Your face looked perfect. You and me . . . we were meant to be together. And we've only just begun."

She stared at me with compassion but was not yet ready to offer forgiveness.

"Alone, I'm a broken man. My protection was never my idiotic necklace or my hate or bitterness, but all along it was you. I can't imagine life without you. Sean once told me that denial was a wonderful coping skill. And he'd made excuses for the pain in his body for too long. I've also made excuses to explain the pain of my soul for way too long."

Amy closed her eyes as she spoke. "I knew years ago we were meant to be together, that you were the only one for me. But I'm not ready to forgive you. You need to humble yourself and straighten things out with your teammates. Starting with Thomas."

My voice rose an octave: "I must show you an amazing sight."

We walked to the edge of the river's bank. and there we saw the covey of ibises eating in the mud flats. Amy said, "Your symbol of hope."

"I was shocked when I saw them. I'd read about ibises flying inland during times of extended droughts, looking for food, but they were the last thing I expected to see. When I saw them here, of all places, I knew it was a clear message telling me to let go. Let go of my anger and my bitterness. To stop blaming everyone else for my failures. So, I'm trying to let go. I realized neither you nor the team was the problem. No one in my youth was the problem. I understand clearly, I am and always have been—the problem."

"What's the deal with this cardboard sign?" she asked.

"A homeless woman sleeping on a bench in the park gave it to me."

"I think there is hope," Amy said. Her eyes widened. "You're not wearing your necklace."

I clenched my hands above my head. "I'll never wear that necklace again."

Amy finally smiled. "I like that."

41

Chattanooga

Sunday, July 25, 2010
7:00 a.m.

My heart raced as we drove as quickly as possible to the hospital. Not with my usual fear and anxiety but now with hope and promise. I thought of Thomas's great wisdom as he'd jabbed his finger into my chest and told me I'd soon realize I already possessed the grace I needed to change my heart of stone. The memory of Allyson telling me I was a good man with a serious flaw. She was right.

I knocked on Thomas's hospital room door, but there was no answer. I carefully opened the door, but the room was empty. I ran to the nurses' station. "Where is Thomas Huger?" I asked.

"Mr. Huger checked out about an hour ago. He was feeling much better."

I squinted my eyes and looked at Amy. "I must find Pat and Sean."

***

I spotted Sean, Pat, and Brooke sitting in a dragon boat that was tied to the main dock. Pat's face was flushed red. She was still angry. Sean held the team's dragon boat seating chart as he spoke to Pat and Brooke. Brooke wiped sweat from her face. She looked worried.

Amy and I approached the boat. My voice stammered with humility. "Can we talk?" I asked.

Pat snapped, "Haven't we disgraced you enough? You here to build up your precious ego some more? What's there to talk about?"

I peered at my three teammates. "I—I want to apologize. My behavior and my leadership have been dreadful."

Sean said, "Tripp, it's time we part ways. You've made yourself clear that we have embarrassed you and we're not as committed to winning as you. We plan to compete in the final race with eighteen paddlers and do the best we can."

Brooke's voice quivered as she spoke. "I introduced you to this team, and you've simply insulted us."

I bowed my head and nodded with understanding. Amy stood behind me and placed her hand on my shoulder for support. "Yesterday Thomas calmly told me that his cancer had become the grace in his life. At that moment I had no idea what he was talking about. Yesterday he'd jammed his finger into my chest and said with conviction that I had the same grace. I thought he was crazy and had no clue what he was talking about. And more importantly, I had no intentions of changing anything in my life. I refused to see a need to change. After all, it was the other people in my life who had failed *me,* not the other way around. As he pressed that thick index finger of his right hand into my chest, he told me I'd soon understand."

Pat rolled her eyes. "So, all of a sudden you understand?"

I opened my eyes wide. "Call it what you will, but a miracle happened to me last night. I saw myself as never before. The vision repulsed me. I was sick to my stomach. I feel horrible."

Pat asked, "What do you want from us?"

"I'd like the opportunity to talk to the team."

Sean and Brooke shook their heads as to say that will never happen.

Pat looked at Amy. Amy's smile was peaceful. Her eyes looked soft and comforting. Pat studied Amy's face for a moment. Amy nodded at her, offering confirmation of my words.

Pat said, "I'll agree for you to speak to the team but no more bullshit. If you start talking about being humiliated or the team's lack of commitment, I'm out of there."

Sean clenched his fists. His knuckles on both hands were white. "What do you have left to say to the team?" he asked.

I spoke calmly, "Last night for the first time in my life I saw my true ugly self. How anger and bitterness had skewed my every thought and decision. I've been blinded from seeing how my actions and words had hurt people, especially the people I loved. Thomas told me I already possessed the ability to change. He was right. I have changed and sincerely want to apologize to you and the team."

Brooke smiled. "Thank you for saying those words, and I accept your apology."

Sean said, “I can forgive you, but you’re still not a part of this team.”

I stepped over the boat’s gunwale, sat down, and joined my friends. “I’ve come to realize how much I love this sport and this team. It’s so much more than staying healthy and fit. Magic and beauty dwell within this team. During all my years of playing and coaching, I’ve never experienced anything like it. This moment is the time in my life I need to be a part of a team—this team. You’ve given me hope. I belong to this team. I belong with . . . I need . . . my friends.”

“What do you want us to do?” Pat asked with a firm voice.

I opened my arms wide and spoke with candor. “I want redemption. I want you to allow me to coach the Dragon Survivors for our final race.”

Sean twisted his lips in a half, sarcastic smile. “I think we’re past the idea of you coaching this team. I just want to finish this last race and go home.”

I leaned forward and placed my hand on my heart. “I have a plan. I’d like to share it with the team.”

“That is—if the team will listen to you,” Pat said. “You may find yourself tap-dancing in a minefield.”

I made my best effort to smile with my eyes. I wanted Pat to understand my earnest desire. “Pat, I taught you how to visualize the protective light, how to focus on your goal. The only problem was your coach wasn’t a good team player. Last night, a phenomenon happened. I witnessed that light. I saw a light within me that I didn’t know existed. I’d like to share that new light with you and the team.”

Brooke looked directly at me. Her eyes seemed to sparkle. “I’d be privileged to have you coach our team for the final race.”

Sean pinched his nose in reluctance and said hesitantly, "If all members of the team forgive you and vote to allow you to coach, I'll agree to accept you back as the coach."

Sean looked sternly at Pat. "How about you?"

Pat looked at me. "You helped me regain my focus and win a seat on the national women's team. For that I'm grateful. I'm with Sean. If the team agrees, I'll submit myself to you as our coach."

"Thank you," I said.

"What is this new racing strategy?" Sean asked.

I placed my hands on my hips. "Our final 1000-meter race isn't until noon. I'd like to pull the team together at our tent at ten o'clock and share my strategy. Is that acceptable?"

My three teammates said together, "Yes."

I stepped out of the boat and joined Amy on the dock. She smiled. As we walked away, a profound humility overwhelmed me. I realized that in my earlier life, I'd known next to nothing. I had been a much better preacher about living with dignity than a dutiful practitioner.

I prayed my flaw, that hard wall of anger and bitterness that Allyson had so astutely recognized, would now become my strength. I wanted to be the person my teammates would gladly ask to be their coach.

42

Chattanooga

Sunday, July 25, 2010
10:00 a.m.

My life's quest had been to eliminate and prevent my pain, not to face it. I'd hidden my anger and bitterness, and not embraced them. I now needed to share my weakness, my flaw, with the Dragon Survivors. Brooke, Sean, and Pat had gathered the team underneath our tent. I asked everyone to sit before I started speaking. I wanted my teammates to see a real transformation had taken place within my heart. I prayed for the right words.

Everyone sat quietly and stared at me anticipating what I had to say. I spoke softly, "All my life, I've used anger and bitterness to protect myself from criticism, humiliation, and failure.

My dad instructed me to never ask for forgiveness as it showed weakness. But this morning, I disagree with my father. I need to ask you to forgive me."

Amy began to cry.

Allyson spoke, "Everyone has made—"

I held my hand toward her. "Allyson, let me finish, please. For the salvation of my soul and the foundation of my future—I need to do this. I've always blamed others for my failures. I've blamed you for our team's losses. I've manipulated you, my friends that I love, in order to hide my weakness. I couldn't allow you or anyone else to humiliate me. I had to create an image for the outside world so I couldn't be blamed for this team's failures. I now recognize clearly it was my own actions that were humiliating me . . . not yours. My bitterness had blinded me."

I stopped speaking and considered my next words carefully. "But last night, here in this park, the veil that blinded veil was removed. I was shown the answer to my redemption was forgiveness—forgiveness of all who had harmed me and most importantly forgiveness of myself. So, I beg you, please forgive me."

Brooke stood. "I introduced you to this team, and last night I was completely ashamed I'd done that. But I do forgive you, and I'm proud to be your friend and teammate."

A small wedge of the pain within my spirit fled. "Thank you, and I'm prouder to be your friend."

I pointed at each of my teammates. "You're the most courageous people on this earth. Sean wrote in his blog just before he had his big scoop surgery that cancer was better than winning the lottery. He wrote when you get cancer, you learn who your friends are. You begin to understand how to appreciate every day as a gift. At the time I read those words, I thought he was nuts. But now I appreciate his depth of wisdom. I now know who my friends are."

I sighed. A wonderful release of my lifelong shame swept through my mind. "Thomas told me yesterday his cancer had become his grace. He said cancer had taught him to live without fear. You are my friends, and I desire with every fiber in my body to live with you—like Thomas—without fear. Would you grant me your grace and forgiveness and allow me to coach this team for one last race?"

Sean grabbed his paddle and moved to the center of the tent. He held it high above his head. Each team member followed his lead. With eighteen paddles reaching toward the top of the tent, Sean yelled, "It would be our pleasure to have you as the coach of the Dragon Survivors."

Everyone screamed, "Agreed."

As the team lowered their paddles, Pat said in her matter-of-fact voice, "You told us you had a race strategy. Let's hear it."

I straightened my spine and stood tall. "Bonnie has taken Thomas back to Charleston, so we only have nineteen paddlers. In a long race such as a thousand meters, weight in the boat is critical, so it'd be more beneficial to race with eighteen paddlers rather than nineteen. I've prepared a seating chart that balances the weight in the boat from front to back and side to side. We need to eliminate weight, so I'd like to ask our largest teammate to sacrifice this final race for the team."

"Big Daddy, I hate to ask and I know how hard you've worked at practice, but would you be willing to sit out this last race?"

Big Daddy stepped forward with his shoulders back and his

chest out. "It would be my absolute pleasure to yell encouragement from the river's bank, celebrating with an ice-cold beer as you cross the finish line in first place."

I grabbed Big Daddy's hand. He looked me in the eye and tightly squeezed my hand. I gently placed my other hand over his hand as a gesture of my gratitude. "Thank you. You are a good friend."

I hesitantly offered my next suggestion. "Second, I want us to do the fast start. I'm convinced we can do it. We nailed it last night. If we establish a solid lead, we can hold off the Leathernecks."

To my surprise, everyone nodded in agreement—even hard-nosed Pat.

I rubbed the sweat from the nape of my neck. "Currently we have seventeen cumulative points, and the Leathernecks have nineteen. If we win the final race and the Leathernecks finish second, we'll receive five points to their three points. Both teams will be tied with twenty-two points. As the defending national champions, the Leathernecks will again be declared the national champions and win the gold medal. But if we defeat the Leathernecks by a time margin of two and a half seconds, we'll receive one bonus point and will be crowned the national champions and win the gold medal."

"That would be a new national record," Allyson said.

The team sighed in disbelief.

My voice was strong. "That sounds like a huge margin, but if we break it down to an individual's effort, it's doable. Two and half seconds divided by eighteen paddlers is only 0.14 seconds. Me, you, each of us, only need to propel the boat 0.14 seconds faster over the length of one thousand meters to win this race by a two-and-a-half-seconds margin. If we increase our stroke rate by two strokes per minute and maintain that same intensity with each stroke, we can achieve that time."

"We can do it," Pat said. "I'll make sure we maintain a faster stroke rate."

"I'm confident we can do it," Brooke said. "I'll follow Pat's lead so we'll have the same rate on both sides of the boat."

I breathed deeply in relief from Pat's and Brooke's comments. It was my first relaxed breath in days. I pressed my lips together with intensity before I spoke. "Last year, the Leathernecks' one thousand meters winning time was four minutes and fifteen seconds. They'll post a faster time this year. If they record a four-minute, fourteen-second time, then our time must be four minutes, eleven and a half seconds."

"That will be difficult," Sean said, "especially with only eighteen paddlers. We'll need to have the race of our lives."

Skepticism again covered the faces of my teammates.

I looked at Sean. "I want you to call out, loud enough for the entire team to hear, our targeted split times at the two-hundred-fifty-, five-hundred-, and the seven-hundred-fifty-meter race markers. That way we'll know if we're on track for that time."

Sean nodded. "Will do."

"I have a coaches' meeting at ten thirty, and we'll learn the lane assignments. Hopefully, we'll be selected to race in lane four," I said.

I opened my hands and pointed the palms toward my teammates. "We can do this. Just believe."

I closed my eyes. I prayed for strength. A tap on my shoulder startled me. I saw Amy's smile as I opened my eyes and turned toward her. She tightly hugged me. "You are forgiven."

43

Chattanooga

Sunday, July 25, 2010
10:30 a.m.

Approaching the marshaling tent for the coaches' meeting, I felt calm. I was confident the Dragon Survivors had a realistic chance to win the national championship and to represent our great country in China. My poise and optimism had returned.

I saw Bob King, the Leatherneck's coach, laughing with a group of other coaches. I marched to him full of dignity and pride for my team and myself. I extended my hand. He shook my hand firmly as he addressed me.

"My team and I have tremendous admiration for you and your team. What you've accomplished . . . I mean you guys being sick and all, it's amazing. Your team has looked death in the eye and won."

I didn't hesitate in my reply. "Facing death isn't my team's best accomplishment, but learning to live boldly while staring death in the eye—that's our greatest achievement."

He fixed his gaze on me. "Well, your team has shown tremendous spirit and courage."

I pulled my shoulders back not with conceit but with humility. "Thank you, and good luck with the final race. The Leathernecks have been a worthy competitor and an admirable champion."

He squeezed my hand and then released it. "Good luck to you as well. It has been a true honor to compete against your team."

I patted his shoulder. "Thanks for those encouraging words."

The coaches of the other Grand Masters Mixed division teams joined us as we waited for the meeting to begin. A fit, middle-aged woman walked onto the festival's stage and addressed the crowd of coaches. She reviewed several rule changes for the breast cancer division. She communicated there were no rule changes for the premier division. She then looked at Bob, me, and our other division coaches.

She spoke boldly. "There will be four teams in the final championship heat. The Dragon Boat Old Timers from Boston with twelve points will race in lane one. The Windy City Dragons from Chicago with thirteen points and will race in lane two. The Dragon Survivors from Charleston with seventeen points will race in lane three. Finally, the Leathernecks from The Villages, Florida, the Grand Masters Mixed division defending national champions with a cumulative nineteen points, will race in lane four."

I grimaced that my team would not be racing in the faster lane four.

She looked directly at Bob and me. "If the Leathernecks win the thousand-meter race, they will be national champions and represent the United States in the 2011 Hong Kong International races. If the Dragon Survivors win the final race and the Leathernecks finish either third or fourth, the Dragon Survivors will be the national champions. I'll have more to say about Hong Kong in a moment. If the Dragon Survivors win the final race and the Leathernecks finish second, both teams will be tied with twenty-one points, and the Leathernecks, as defending national champions, will remain as national champions."

She paused. "Any questions?"

No one spoke.

She continued sharing race instructions. "We have been notified by the International Dragon Boat Federation regarding a rule change for a team to qualify to represent the United States in Hong Kong next year. The IDBF has declared the team must win their division by a two-point margin."

Bob King blurted out, "So, if the Dragon Survivors win the thousand-meter race and we finish second, then no team in our division will represent the United States next year in Hong Kong?"

She said, "That is correct."

"That's a bunch of crap," Bob King said. "What gives them the right to change the rule at the last minute?"

"It's their organization and their rules," the woman said.

Bob huffed in disgust.

"How about the bonus points for the margin of victory?" I asked.

The race official looked at me and rolled her eyes. "That

would be unprecedented, but if the Dragon Survivors win the thousand-meter race by two and a half seconds, your team would receive one bonus point and would be declared national champions. But to receive two additional points and qualify for Hong Kong you would need to win the race by a three-and-a-quarter-seconds margin. That has never happened."

Bob looked at me with raised eyebrows and a smirk. Another coach standing behind me chuckled. I ignored them.

The race official looked at us coaches with a fake smile. "Any questions?"

There were no questions.

Bob extended his hand. My mind was numb from shock with the news of the rule change. I never felt Bob's hand grabbing mine. "Good luck," he said.

"And to you," I said, still in a quasi-trance.

The coaches walked away, but I stood still and stared at the river. My previous calm had waned. I shook off the sweat from my face. We'd have to win the final race by an unprecedented margin, and the Leathernecks would race in the fastest lane.

How would I break this terrible news to my team?

***

Amy touched my arm and disrupted my trance. "Anything wrong?"

I filled her in on the sudden rule change.

"Will you change your race strategy?"

"No, I'm staying with my approach, but I do have an additional plan."

She smiled. "You always have a plan. Anything I can do to help?"

I nodded with enthusiasm. “Yes, would you please find a store and purchase twenty black Sharpie pens and bring them to our tent before the race.”

She narrowed her eyes and shrugged. “That’s an odd request but I’ll make it happen.”

44

Chattanooga

Sunday, July 25, 2010
11:15 a.m.

My college philosophy professor loved quoting Aristotle. He was my favorite professor, and he'd painted this quote above the door of his office: "One may go wrong in many different ways, but right only in one."

Walking back to our tent, I was desperate to find the appropriate attitude words to speak as a confident coach to my team. I had to make them believe.

I asked the Dragon Survivors to gather in a large grassy area about one hundred yards from our tent. The look in their eyes told me they knew something was wrong.

I tried to keep the tone of my voice calm and encouraging as I explained the rule change a team must win their division by two points to qualify to race in Hong Kong.

"That's bullshit and it sucks," Sean said.

"No, it's impossible," Pat said.

"It's actually not impossible," I said, trying my best to maintain my finest positive countenance. "If we win the thousand-meter race by a margin of three and a quarter seconds, we'll receive two additional bonus points and qualify to race in Hong Kong."

Pat smirked. "What lane did we draw?"

"We're racing in lane three, and the Leathernecks are in lane four."

Several people murmured, "Shit."

"We can do it," I said. "Instead of each paddler pulling the boat 0.14 seconds faster we'll each need to do 0.18 seconds. That's doable."

Pat's lips tightened.

Allyson said, "The odds of setting a national record with eighteen paddlers are extremely low. I vote we just try to win and do our best. Let's remove all of this pressure and have fun."

Several teammates nodded in agreement.

Sean stepped forward. "I'll yell out the split times, and I agree with Tripp; we can do this."

Brooke placed her hand on Sean's shoulder. "I realize how hard we've all worked for more than a year, but we've come to the end of our wonderful journey. It's time to be realistic and face the music. I'm extremely proud of this team's accomplishments."

I fixed my gaze on the team. "A year ago, I'd have said hell no, we're not giving up on our goal of getting to Hong Kong.

But I've changed. My only aspiration now is to paddle this final race with you—my teammates."

"Even if we humiliate you?" Sean winked.

I placed my hands firmly on my hips. "It will be my honor to win or lose with you."

A low but firm voice that I well recognized came from behind me. Thomas stepped forward. "This team is my life. I will never give up. We can win and win in a big way."

I froze and stared with wide-open eyes at Thomas. "I thought you were in Charleston."

"You thought really bad wrong," Thomas said. "I'd never abandon my teammates."

My voice cracked, "But I went to the hospital and the nurse told me you had improved and checked out."

Thomas laughed. "That nurse didn't know squat. The antibiotics finally did their job, and I kicked the infection's butt. The doctor transferred me to another part of the hospital to pump me full of fluid and vitamins. She released me just a while ago."

Brooke hugged him. Sean grabbed his hand and shook it as if he'd pull it from his arm. Allyson started crying. Thomas's body continued to slump, and he looked very weak.

Thomas looked me directly in the eye. "We're going to win, and I'm going to paddle."

His words scared me. I could never allow Thomas to paddle. "No, you're not. I'll not risk your health again just to win a gold medal."

Pat resolutely agreed. "I'll not risk losing my best friend. You cannot paddle."

Thomas muttered, "The hell you say."

Thomas's presence and words gave me a peace that flooded my body from head to toe. "Thomas, you can sit in the boat during the race but I forbid you to paddle. Big Daddy will sit next to you to balance the boat."

"That's dead weight. We'll never win," Thomas said.

I smiled. "I'd rather lose any day with you in the boat than win a thousand gold medals without you."

Thomas smirked and snickered, "What the hell happened to you?"

My wall of bitterness seemed like a lifetime ago. "I finally found your grace. You do understand I cannot allow you to paddle."

He sighed and rolled his eyes. "I understand."

Amy walked into the group and handed me a plastic bag full of black Sharpie pens.

"I have an important request," I said. "I want us to change the name of our team."

"Why? What are you suggesting?" Sean asked loudly.

"I love our team's name," Allyson said.

I walked around my teammates. I rested my hands on my hips. "The most important lesson I've learned from each of you is how to live, not how to survive or how to die. We are more than survivors. We are alive. I suggest we change the team's name from the Dragon Survivors to the Living Dragons. That's who we are. We are alive!"

Sean looked at me and smiled. Brooke nodded in agreement. Allyson wiped a tear from her face.

I threw a pen at everyone. "Guys, take off your shirts, turn them inside out, and write *The Living Dragons* in bold black ink on the front and back of your shirt. Ladies, head to the restroom and do the same."

When the women paddlers returned, we stood proudly in the middle of our tent wearing our new makeshift shirts. Twenty unified teammates simultaneously shot their paddles straight up in the air, pointing to the top of the tent. With one synchronized voice, we yelled, "To the Living Dragons!"

45

Chattanooga

Sunday, July 25, 2010
11:45 a.m.

I sat by the river waiting for the announcer to call our team, the Living Dragons, to the marshaling area. Throughout the weekend, I'd been too focused on winning to take in the beauty of this magnificent site. I wanted to burn this memory into the deepest chambers of my brain.

I hadn't noticed the splendor of the teams' multicolored tents that speckled the grounds like a brilliant kaleidoscope. I'd not noticed the joyous people sitting in small groups talking, laughing, and hugging. The amusing costumes worn by many of the participants had escaped my attention. Some of the breast cancer teams wore bright-pink tutus and white pearl necklaces to celebrate victory against their life-threatening cancer. The festive spirit rejuvenated my tired body. I was ready for one last race.

An official called for all teams to head to the marshaling area and gather around the stage. After everyone had congregated tightly around the wooden platform, a small woman walked to the microphone. She stood beside an easel, holding a sign that was covered with a white sheet.

"My name is Elizabeth Carter, and I'm a breast cancer survivor. I was diagnosed with an aggressive cancer at the age of forty-six . . . the time in my life when I'm supposed to enjoy my family and friends and not to be dealing with surgeries and chemotherapy. I was advised to eat well, decrease stress, and exercise. That's when I found my dragon boat sisters. They gave me a new attitude about life. They sat with me during chemo treatments. They taught me I had too much to accomplish and too many people to love to lose hope. They imparted in me the ability to live one day at a time."

She stopped speaking and took a deep breath. The tone in her voice became more serious. "Out of every one hundred thousand women, approximately one hundred twenty-five will be diagnosed with breast cancer. Of these women, approximately twenty will die. But there has been much progress made as the mortality rate since 1989 has decreased by about forty percent. This festival's fundraising goal to support cancer research was three hundred thousand dollars. I am thrilled to announce we have surpassed that goal. The official funds raised by you wonderful and dedicated people is three hundred twelve thousand and eighty-five dollars."

The crowd erupted in applause and screams as she pulled the sheet off the sign, which had her announced sum written in large, bold red numbers.

As the cheers died down, the festival's speakers roared with the next announcement. "Would the four final teams in the Grand Masters Mixed division please report to the marshaling area."

I crowded my team tight in the marshaling tent. I had one last speech. "Last night I had a realization about forgiveness and grace. I understood that people, like me, who demand the most forgiveness and grace from others, are the ones who are the last to offer to others that same forgiveness and grace. That was clearly me. I've been numb to the world for fifty-five years. I was like the arm that had fallen asleep during the night but had never woken up. I felt nothing and only thought about myself. But like the blood starting to flow in the numb arm I'm now alive. Today I have real hope and real joy. This morning, win or lose, I stand before you—the true national champions."

Allyson moved close to me and placed her arm around my waist. As did Brooke and Pat. My teammates huddled close and hugged each other.

I spoke softly, "In this our final race, let's celebrate our lives and our unity. Let's rejoice in our accomplishments. I suggest we abandon the fast start and race the best we can."

"Hell no!" Thomas's voice, the loudest I'd ever heard it, rang through the entire marshaling area. "I almost died so we could master that start. I demand we do the fast start; stay with your race strategy, and kick some Marine butt."

Sean spoke. "I have my watch and will call out our interval times at the two-fifty, five-hundred, and seven-fifty markers. We can do this."

Pat affirmed Sean's words. "I agree. Let's paddle to win this damn race."

I bit my lip. I knew Thomas's intentions, but I had to try to dissuade him. "I'll agree to the fast start, but Thomas, I forbid you to paddle."

He nodded, grunted, and turned away.

"My friends, let's go win a race," I said.

We raised our paddles and yelled, "To the Living Dragons."

A race official led us to our dragon boat. Allyson walked close and whispered into my ear. "It looks to me like I just witnessed someone completely shave themselves emotionally and expose their vulnerable inner self."

I laughed and hugged her. I looked toward the river's bank and saw the homeless woman who'd given me the cardboard sign. She nodded and smiled at me.

After loading the boat, we gracefully paddled toward the starting line. As we approached the start, I saw twenty paddles in the water—not nineteen. I yelled, "What the hell are you doing Thomas?"

He didn't move or say a word.

I screamed, "Thomas!"

I heard a grunt.

"What did you say?" I yelled.

Big Daddy, who was sitting next to Thomas, and the two paddlers in front of him turned toward me and simultaneously shouted, "He said to go fuck yourself."

The race's starter shouted, "We have alignment."

Oh shit! I thought. Thomas was going to die.

"Ready, Ready."

My teammates extended their arms forward, rotated their

torsos for maximum leverage, and slammed their paddlers into the water like a harpoon stabbing a great whale. The starter's whistle shrieked through the air.

One, two, three. The first three strokes were perfect. I yelled, "Up!"

One, two, three, four, and five. The first set of ups went like clockwork. The second set—flawless. The third set of ups—impeccable. When we settled into our race pace, I looked back. We were more than a boat length ahead of the Leathernecks.

The Leathernecks' coach screamed at his team in a panic: "I need more, I need more!"

As we approached the two-hundred-fifty-meter marker the Leathernecks were gaining on our boat. Sean screamed, "Sixty-two point five seconds."

We were on pace. Thomas paddled like a machine and was in perfect form. What a hell of a man! His nickname as the man who'd never quit was appropriate.

Pat, from her first seat, exaggerated the reach of her paddle toward the canoe's bow as a signal she was increasing our stroke rate. The team followed her lead like ducklings behind a mother duck. We began to increase our lead on the Leathernecks, but they, too, increased their stroke rate.

Approaching the five-hundred-meter marker, the Leathernecks had gained on us, and we were only a half boat in the lead. Sean yelled, "Two minutes, five point seven five seconds."

Both teams were on a national-record–setting pace. I restrained myself from yelling for a power series as we needed to conserve energy for a strong finish. I hoped and prayed the Leathernecks had not prepared for such a fast-stroke pace and would become exhausted. As we approached the seven-hundred-fifty-meter marker, I had an idea. It could propel us to victory if done successfully, or lose the race dramatically if we became overwhelmed with exhaustion.

Sean yelled, "Three minutes and ten seconds."

We were slower than the time we needed to qualify for Hong Kong. I yelled with abandon, "Another series of ups."

The team initially hesitated, but then it seemed like wings, rather than arms, were holding our paddles. The Living Dragons perfectly transitioned into a set of up strokes. *One, two, three, four, five.* Repeated twice more. We surged ahead of the Leathernecks. Their coach frantically screamed, "More power, I need more power!"

Our boat, for the final one hundred meters, floated over the water. My arms were light, and each stroke of my paddle seemed effortless. It was the motion of twenty courageous men and women becoming one. As we crossed the finish line, Sean yelled, "Four minutes and twelve seconds." I felt the Leathernecks finish just behind us.

We'd won the race, but would our margin of victory be enough to win the national championship, and then enough to represent the United States in Hong Kong? Since the official finish line was marked by a laser, we didn't know the accuracy of Sean's watch.

Thomas had paddled like a champion. My teammates—my friends—had left every bit of effort they had out on the water. My heart swelled with pride and love and admiration.

46

Chattanooga

Sunday, July 25, 2010
12:30 p.m.

After the race, each member of the Living Dragons sat quietly underneath our team's tent. No one had the energy to speak. I wanted to say something to my teammates, but there was nothing left to say.

After about ten minutes, Pat stood and spoke. "I have never shared with any of you, except Tripp, the severe panic attack I experienced prior to the national team tryouts. I woke up one morning at two o'clock with my heart racing and my vision obscured. I could barely breathe or swallow as my heart pounded in my throat. I felt like an elephant was sitting on top of my chest."

She closed her eyes and filled her lungs with air. It was difficult for Pat to share her inner thoughts and problems. She typically dealt with her issues in private. She opened her eyes and continued speaking.

"I told Tripp about the incident, and he recommended we meet early one Sunday morning, and he'd lead me through an exercise to learn how to focus. We paddled my OC-2 to Charles Town Landing, and he taught me how to see the light. He told me I needed to create a mental structure in my mind to house my desire. I visualized creating a fortified structure that contained the image of me winning the time trial. He instructed me to then rechannel my fear into that structure and focus only on the race."

Pat looked at me as she brushed a tear from her cheek.

"Tripp told me to imagine I was in my boat, and I was surrounded by a large white light that protected me. He said the light would force all negative thoughts out of my mind, and I'd enter into a spiritual realm—a place of unlimited potential. He told me to imagine that the white light was protecting and guiding each stroke."

The team sat quietly with their gaze fixed upon Pat. "I thought qualifying for the national team was the highlight of my life, but I was wrong. Today—this race, without question—is the best moment I've ever experienced. And we owe it to Tripp." She swallowed hard. "And . . . now he's seen his own light. Now he leads by example. That new light in his life propelled us across that finish line as champions. For that, I will be eternally grateful."

The team stood, raised their paddles above their heads, and shouted, "To Coach Tripp!"

In my mind's eye, I could see Saul's weathered, smiling face as tears streamed from my eyes.

***

The awards ceremony was to be held on the stage near the marshaling tent at one o'clock. We had no idea if we'd bested the Leatherheads sufficiently to be named national champions. I thought I'd be nervous as all the teams assembled around the platform, but I wasn't. I was now a true winner. I was free.

A race official began announcing the winners of the corporate division races. The winners of the club team divisions would be announced last. The Grand Masters Mixed division winner would be revealed next to last followed by the esteemed Breast Cancer division.

As the announcement of each division passed, I started pacing the sidewalk as my anticipation grew. I'd walk about twenty steps and stop. I'd clasp my hands above my head and take a deep breath and start to walk again. My shirt was soaked with sweat. Thomas watched me—laughing.

Finally, the official spoke the long-awaited words: "The winners of the Grand Masters Mixed division."

I stopped pacing and stood still.

The announcer continued: "Third place in the Grand Masters Mixed division with a total of sixteen points, the Windy City Dragons from Chicago, Illinois."

The paddlers and coaches of the Windy City Dragons screamed with excitement and ran onto the stage. Race officials hung bronze medals affixed to red-white-and-blue-striped ribbons around each paddler's and coach's neck. A professional photographer snapped a team picture, and the

Windy City Dragons left the stage.

I prayed to hear the Leathernecks' name called next. My heart raced. My mind was numb as the loud voice over the speaker rang out across the river. "Second place and defending national champions from The Villages of Florida with a total of twenty-two points—the Leathernecks."

Our entire team jumped to our feet and screamed as we realized the Living Dragons were the new Grand Masters Mixed national champions. That meant we'd won the thousand-meter race by a margin of at least two and a half seconds, but had we qualified for Hong Kong?

A hush swept through the crowd as the Leathernecks were nowhere to be found. They didn't walk up on the stage to receive their medals. Where were they? What a bunch of sore losers.

The official again announced, "The silver medal winners of the Grand Masters Mixed division are the Leathernecks."

Still no sign of the Leathernecks team. The race official was silent. The crowd was quiet. The official frowned and flipped her hands into the air. "Well, that's a first."

She grabbed a stack of gold medals. "The winners and new Grand Masters Mixed national champions from Charleston, South Carolina . . . oh, I see we have a name change—are the Living Dragons."

My teammates and I locked arms and walked proudly onto the stage. I stood peering at the spectators and the river. Thomas moved closer to me and wrapped his arm around my waist. Pat pulled me close and also wrapped her arm around my waist. We cried together, staring at the crowd.

Thomas leaned toward me, kissed my cheek, and whispered, "Final victory, my friend, final victory."

The race officials placed gold medals around our necks. Peace transcended my soul as I now wore a new necklace. A necklace of love and not one of bitterness.

From behind the festival's stage, I heard a loud commotion. It sounded like a chant. I listened intently. I made out the sound, "Ooh-rah, ooh-rah."

What the hell?

The chant grew louder and more frequent. "Ooh-rah, ooh-rah, ooh-rah, ooh-rah . . ."

Bob King, the Leathernecks' coach, was leading his team around the side of the stage and in front of my team. They knelt in unison. The coach was holding in both hands as if he was presenting an offering, a three-foot-long black banner with a red edge and with the yellow letters *USMC* embroidered in the middle.

At once in a synchronized motion they stood, clicked their feet together, and saluted. Bob King handed me the banner. He said, "You are the heroes our country honors. We salute you. We are humbled by your bravery. Your team has taught us what living with courage truly means."

The crowd erupted in applause.

Bob took the microphone and addressed the other paddlers. "I'd like to be the first to congratulate you. The race official earlier provided me with the times of the 1000-meter race and with a time of four minutes, eleven and a half seconds, the Living Dragons have established a new American one-thousand-meter record and have qualified to represent the United States next year at the international races to be held in Hong Kong. My teammates, myself, and my country will be honored to cheer you on."

I reached for Bob's hand to shake, but he forcefully grabbed mine and pulled me close and hugged me tight. He said, "You are the true winner. Your team exhibited the best of what we as people are capable of accomplishing."

Little did he know about our profound struggles. Primarily—me taking myself too seriously. Pushing my teammates to the brink of death. I had been a fool. But I wasn't anymore. I'd learned there was an infinite wisdom much larger than me. In the future, I'd treat others with dignity and respect.

I broke free from Bob's hug, ran down the stage's steps, and grabbed Amy's arm. We rushed to the bank of the great Tennessee River. I held my brick necklace so tight it caused the palm of my hand to bleed. I watched the river's swift current flow over the smooth rocks. Its water cascaded up and down, like the wind blowing a thin, sheer curtain inward from an open bedroom window. The ibises had left.

The river gave and took life. My body, my mind, and my soul seemed to flow with the stream's powerful and continuous movement. The murmur of the moving water was soothing music to my spirit.

It was time for the river to take my brick necklace. I dangled the necklace from my fingers as Amy touched my face and smiled. She, too, knew it was the moment for a new beginning. She spoke softly, "We've witnessed several miracles this weekend."

I gently placed my arm around her shoulder and laughed. "As I paddled the last fifty meters of the final race, a voice spoke clearly in my head. As if someone was sitting next to me."

"Yeah, what did the voice say?" She asked.

"The voice was soft, but the words rang loud in my head. *Forgiveness is the foundation of all miracles.*"

She nodded and squeezed me tight against her body.

I threw the brick necklace into the river as far as I could throw it and watched it sink from sight. The water sparkled with glory and redemption. The magical current had taken with it the anger and bitterness that had once ruled my life.

I'd found my home. My new bedroom window. Surrounded by people of great courage and love, not trophies, awards, or money. It'd been a long road. I'd come from a life of bitterness but had found the wonderful light of hope and forgiveness. I found it by the river. But I realized it wasn't the river that gave me life but the souls and spirits of the men and women I'd grown to love. I'd begun to understand the greatest mystery—the mystery of healing that happens when hearts bind together.

I turned toward the festival's stage and screamed, "Ooh-rah!"

47

Charleston

One Year Later

The historic ruins of the Old Sheldon Church, located sixty miles south of Charleston in the tiny town of Yemassee, South Carolina, was ideal for Thomas's memorial service. The mid-eighteenth-century church building was built to imitate a Greek temple. Thomas had been like a Greek god to us, his Living Dragon teammates, and friends.

The red- and golden-brick structure had been burned during the Revolutionary and Civil Wars. Like Thomas, the building's master craftmanship had stood the test of time and the test of living. The building had no roof—only the solid brick walls had survived. The surrounding gothic columns, majestic oaks, and scattered graves created a mystical union with God.

The breeze was calm and cool, and the smell of gardenias was sweet. The sight of magnificent blooming azaleas caused me to be at peace with Thomas's death. During the past year, he'd allowed me to share his inner world. I knew the deepest corners of his soul. His secrets, desires, and fears. We had become closer than brothers. My grief had no boundaries.

Seventeen surviving Living Dragon team members and their families had gathered to honor the life of Thomas Huger. We'd each brought our dragon boat paddles. Brooke offered me a huge hug. Her voice cracked with emotion, "Our third funeral in twelve months, and I don't like it."

"I understand. I was with Thomas when he died. I've eaten and slept very little. I'll miss my dear friend."

Brooke began to cry. "I thought Thomas would be the first of our teammates to die, not Pat."

Pat had passed away from organ failure not long after our national championship victory. She was not able to race in Prague with the US Senior Women's National Team. A large plaque was erected at Brittlebank Park in Charleston, honoring her life and achievements. The Living Dragons agreed to meet annually at her monument and raise our paddles to honor her great spirit, hoping to see her light.

I prayed having the team together again would soothe our grief. Allyson sat crying on the deep, green grass inside the church's ruins. Brooke and I each gently grabbed one of her arms and lifted her. She trembled and breathed heavily. "I miss Pat, Sean, and Thomas so much."

I held Allyson and said, as Amy approached, "Sean was the bravest of us all. He never told any of us about his internal infection from the colostomies. He had to be in great pain. I saw him two days before he died, and he was still talking about paddling in Hong Kong. He instructed me the team should start to practice soon."

Amy said, "Sean was like our sun. We revolved around his bright light and spirit."

"He was a remarkable man," I said.

Brooke gently blotted a tear from Allyson's face. "It's this weekend. This weekend is the international race in Hong Kong. What a trip it would have been."

I said, "No way would I race as the Living Dragons without Sean, Pat, and Thomas. Not even for the world championship."

Brooke nodded. "But . . . we were the champions."

I proudly nodded. "Yes, we were."

The team members and their families gathered around us. I stepped to the middle of our circle. My heart was serene and sad. I said, "The Living Dragons, each of us have become champions—champions of life. We have become exemplars. Showing others by our example how to live their lives with faith and courage. We now live to honor our teammate, Thomas, as we also honor Pat and Sean."

Bonnie, Thomas's wife, entered the middle of our tight circle. Her words were gentle and sincere. "Thomas had that Matthew McConaughey swagger and good looks . . . only shorter. I was never in the same league as him. He was simply irresistible. Your loyalty and that of his Citadel football teammates speaks volumes about his goodness and courage. A few days before he died, he was sitting on the couch in our den holding our grandson. He called my name and then stared at me for several seconds before speaking. He knew he was close to death. He stated his favorite quote, *The road is always better than the inn.* He told me to teach his grandson about this lesson. The favorite road trip of Thomas's highly adventurous life was paddling in the dragon boat with each of you in Chattanooga, Tennessee. He called it his final and best victory."

Bonnie poured a small amount of Thomas's ashes onto the ground.

The seventeen surviving members of the Living Dragons moved closer to the center of our circle. We held our paddles high as we shouted in unison,

"Here's to Thomas, Sean, and Pat. Here's to the Living Dragons."

ACKNOWLEDGMENTS

At the risk of writing a cliché, a cliché I must write. Without my wife Teresa there would be no *The Final Victory*. She was the one who took the initial call I had cancer. She attended every doctor's visit including the sobbing one when my oncologist told us no one could treat me as my tumors were too many and too large. She traveled with me for PRRT therapy to a small East German town where hardly anyone spoke English. She endured the stress of liver transplant evaluations, trips to MD Anderson and the many treatments. She handled depression and fear without my notice. She read so many *The Final Victory* versions it was impossible for her to keep the story line and characters straight. Her love hypnotizes me as it is pure and lovely. Without my soul mate Teresa, there would be no *The Final Victory*.

My agent, Marly Rusoff who agreed to accept me as a client when no agent would or should. She edited and encourage me beyond an agent's responsibility. She transformed my writing by teaching me readers would not remember, "what I told them but how I made them feel." She chastised me when I told her no one wanted to read a word I wrote and I quit writing. She isn't just an agent but a dear friend whose spirit is admirable and noble.

My editor, Anne Brewer who has the patience of Job. Her initial edit caused a complete rewrite. I'd send a section; she'd edit and I'd rewrite. I'd send another section; she'd edit and I'd rewrite. We followed that process for several years. She kept me true and right in crafting *The Final Victory.*

To our dragon boat team's real coach, Pat Barker, who actually wrote the book on Dragon Boating. Seriously, it's called, *Dragon Boats: A Celebration*. Many of *The Final Victory*'s paddling and racing descriptions were inspired by her writing. She made winners out of a group of people who thought we were losers. She told us we could be National Champions and coached us to victory.

To the leaders of Dragon Boat Charleston, Cindy, Sterling, Noreen, and Louise: our moms on the water. Their love carried us when nothing else would and when all in our lives seemed lost. Their spirit and commitment fashioned family. They created a whirlwind, a tornado of caring that followed each of us in the boat and transformed us to wholeness. With them we never felt sick. And to the awesome film director, Liz Oakley who created the amazing documentary *Awaken The Dragon* which has changed thousands of lives.